WIT
THE LABYRINTH

Norman Lewis

R
ROBINSON PUBLISHING
LONDON

Published in 1985 by Robinson Publishing
11 Shepherd House, 5 Shepherd Street,
London W1Y 7LD

ISBN 0 948164 05 0

© Norman Lewis 1950
First published 1950

All rights reserved

Printed in Great Britain by
Richard Clay (The Chaucer Press) Ltd.

O<small>N</small> a fine May morning in 1943 catastrophe came to Malevento. The majority of the prosperous citizens who at that hour were accustomed to take their vermouth in front of the cafés were made into mincemeat or just neatly dismembered. Others, in their houses, their cries silenced by the dust of pulverized marble, instantly assumed those postures of utter submission so familiar to excavators of cities overwhelmed by acts of God. The beggars who formed such an important proportion of the citizenry and who were posted at their habitual pitches were accepted unquestioningly with Lazarus into the bosom of Abraham. At the same instant the blind children of the foundlings' hospital found release in this act of mercy from the empty lesson of their existence. In the city's fountains the turbid water ceased to run and was tinged for a short time as if with a delicate sunset reflection. The bronze doors of the cathedral cast in Byzantium in 1123 curled and crumpled like a discarded wrapping of tinfoil. Beneath the cathedral's collapsing vault the Norman knights, summoned from their tombs in premature resurrection, turned to utter dust. The bells, claimed locally to be the most ancient in Christendom and attributed to St. Paulinus himself, heralded their eternity of silence with a final discord. The colossal image of Christ, until then remote and aloof from mankind on the summit of the dome, now descended, and took the city in its crucified embrace.

In the squares and gardens, the tree-leaves, prematurely yellowed, came floating down, carpeting the ground with fragile, buckled plates of gold. After this the nightingales, common as sparrows in that town, deserted these gardens from which the shade of verdure had been stripped, and in their place came, cautiously, an advance guard of skirmishing cicadas.

Two years and one month later, a British officer stood gazing with some uncertainty at a large-scale wall map of southern Italy. On this map his imagination had superimposed a five-pointed star, the extremities of which he had actually marked with small red flags. The village of Monteleone, in which the Captain's Headquarters were located, was situated precisely at the centre of this star, and the five points marked the outposts of his power. The officer, who was greying, fortyish and well turned out, was practically the last remaining representative of the allied forces in a very large area. He had developed an unconscious habit, when he remembered this — as he frequently did — of throwing his head back slightly and of holding himself rather more erect than usual. He didn't care to remember too clearly that the war was over.

At this moment he was concerned once again with the disposition of these outposts, each one of which was responsible to him for the security of a vaguely defined but extensive territory. He was satisfied with the three northerly points of his star. They had been permanently settled eighteen months previously in fairly civilized and accessible spots. They gave no trouble. The south-westerly outpost was also quite satisfactorily located in a little seaside resort called Torre Bellona, which had not been spoiled by the troops. The Captain rather enjoyed visiting it in the course of his duties. Nothing ever happened at Torre Bellona. Nothing ever happened, but it was another Capri, a landlocked and undiscovered Capri, and therefore a Capri without the loud-speakers and the straw-hatted, drunken soldiers on leave. Too soon he would see this delightful place for the last time. For the last time he would look upon those old, deserted, rust-red villas, the flattened domed cottages of the fishermen and the beached boats with their worn colours and the brown nets, before returning to the remote London suburb, that Giant Despair's castle where there awaited him the grey face of his embittered wife and the ruins of his estate agent's business.

It was his south-easterly detachment that was troubling the Captain once again. This was in the town of Malevento — a

6

town possessing no attraction of any kind and to be reached over an appalling mountain road. A remote and primitive region, in fact, which moreover swarmed with bandits. Men who went down there tended to be beyond the reach of his authority for periods which were far too long. This state of affairs produced all sorts of abuses and even most regrettable incidents — like the one that had recently occurred. The Captain did not enjoy courts of inquiry.

He scrutinized the map, frowning slightly. There was Malevento, lapped by the bare, empty contours. There were crawling blue hairs in this emptiness, signifying rivers, which started out towards the sea, but which after a few miles disappeared again, or ended in the conventional sign for a marsh. Besides that, the emptiness of the map was broken only by a few villages. Some were joined by a dotted line to the roads; the others apparently did not even warrant the dignity of a track.

The Captain took out the Malevento flag and stuck it in the map again at Castelfranco. Castelfranco was a fair-sized town about thirty miles to the south, but above all it was on a good main road. He studied the result, once again frowning, for his star was now quite asymmetrical. Having gone through this manœuvre several times before, the Captain had known in advance that such a readjustment would not suit him. He had a passion for symmetry, for balance. His only remedy, if he was to avoid those detested supervisory visits to Malevento, was to move his south-westerly detachment also — to fix it a similar distance further down the coast. But this would bring it into a coastal swamp where there were only two or three of the tiniest fishing villages; where malaria was so rife and so deadly that it was notoriously unsafe to stay overnight. There was nothing for it, then, but Malevento. He sighed and reinserted the flag in its original position. A slender book of verse lay on the table. He picked it up and slipped it into the drawer. He pushed the bell and a clerk appeared.

'Send Manning in,' the Captain told him.

The F.S.O. was smiling slightly, but without geniality. His manner was pleasant in an impersonal way, but he introduced — for effect, Manning thought — an occasional hint of menace.

'I see you were in Iraq.'

'Yes, sir.'

'How long were you there?'

'Nearly five years, sir.'

He had replied to this question without hesitation, although when it had been put to him a few days previously he had been obliged to think hard for a moment or two. The pattern of these years had been really identical and their seasons compressed into summer and winter. He could not, for the life of him, remember which insignificant circumstances had happened in April and which in September. Only the events of summer and winter were separable. Events which had taken place against a background of iron-hard, white earth and within a horizon of implacable mirage; or other events associated with running water dripping off the cactus and boring little holes in the white mud — these he had lived through as living through an age, a separate existence.

'On what work were you engaged?'

'I was on port work, sir.' The port was non-existent, he wanted to add, but he checked himself cautiously. Half-existent, perhaps, would be fairer. Certainly no port could be said to have a definite existence when no ship had ever called there. A talmudic voice sighed in his ear: 'In Iraq the gold sovereign is worth £5 10s., but on the other side of the river you are buying it for £5. The sovereigns of the King Edward are better because their colour is more fein. Something you must do or you are going crazy. . . .'

The F.S.O. was glancing at a type-written sheet. 'A volunteer, it says here.'

A volunteer. 'Yes, sir.' A volunteer for what? Above all, not that. No, not that. For danger and privations, perhaps; for wounds even. For separations worst of all. For hardships of all kinds. But never for that ultimate frustration, for submission to that internal, nagging voice that never ceased to assure him: You are completely wasted. Yes, voluntarily he had lopped himself off from that shapely illusion of purpose which had been his past life, the raw end of which was like the ungainly stump of a severed limb which although still red and puckered had almost ceased to ache.

'And before Iraq where were you?'

'In Egypt for a short time, sir, and before that in Sierra Leone for a month or two.'

But these could hardly be seen now through the interposed image of that white plain. The white huts in which they lived beneath their asphalted and white-washed roof. 'I stay here,' said the voice again but dejectedly. 'All right — I save up. Perhaps next year I go home. From here in Ashar is good to buy watches for Egypt. You want I should show you what to take?'

'A globe trotter,' said the F.S.O., smiling thinly. 'Meanwhile we have been here in Italy. It's not been a picnic, you may have heard.'

'No, sir.'

The F.S.O. now licked his lips with the tip of his tongue and drew in a sharp, preliminary breath. Manning waited.

'Well, Manning, I'm not supposed to tell you this. In fact, I'm taking quite a lot upon myself in doing so. But I feel it is better for all concerned that you should know. I've received a report about you that isn't a favourable one. You are described as temperamental. I don't know what they mean by that, but whatever it is it won't do.'

'I'm sorry, sir.'

'So am I sorry, Manning. I don't need to tell you now that there's no room in this Section for people with temperaments. Let's get that straight from the start. And don't think because the war is over we can all sit back on our rumps and relax. Quite the contrary. There's plenty of work to be done still. More, if anything.'

9

'I ask for nothing better than the opportunity to work, sir.' A stiff and stilted sentence of the kind one kept for such officers.

'Good,' said the F.S.O., now a grim schoolmaster. 'I'm telling you for your own good. I'm glad I succeeded in making it clear to you. You are being sent to Malevento,' he went on. 'It's been badly knocked about, so you won't find much there in the way of distraction. This is your chance to do a good job of work.'

'What am I to do, sir?'

'Good God, sergeant. Surely you don't expect me to tell you that. How long have you been in the corps? Do your normal job, of course. Submit a weekly report on conditions in general and come into H.Q. once a fortnight.'

'Very well, sir.'

'Don't forget, this is your chance. It may be your last chance.'

The interview with the F.S.O. had re-awakened his bitterness. Beneath it he was unsure of himself and felt the familiar need for self-justification. He wanted to find some sympathetic listener to whom he could confide his malaise; who would be ready to agree with him that no one could have done better in the circumstances. This feeling was strengthened, freed from restraint by the first drink he had had for more than a week.

In the Mess he found another newcomer to the Section. He was easy to pick out as such; a young man with a large blond moustache, who carried with him, in his appearance, in every gesture, in every movement an unmistakable tang of the home country. It would be months before the process of his assimilation into the social unity of the rest of the Section would be complete; before he made free use of their particular brand of soldiers' jargon, mastered their conventional cynicism of outlook, possessed their knowledge of the uses of understatement and of silence. In the meanwhile his sense of social insecurity kept Peto affable and easy of approach.

There were four of the old-timers sitting at the bar a few feet away from them. They were like beachcombers who had rejected redemption. They drank with indifference, almost with distaste, as if in fulfilment of a religious ceremony in the efficacy of which they had ceased to believe. Peto caught Manning's eye and grinned at him secretly, his sense of isolation lessened by this bond – however tenuous – of mutually understood superiority.

Manning was encouraged to speak his mind. 'The cure for all this kind of thing,' he said, 'is a decent job of work.'

The criticism implied in Peto's smile had not intended to go to such lengths. There was no reply. Manning, in defiance of his better sense, took another drink, and his melancholy deepened. He succumbed to the temptation, regularly felt on such occasions, to return to his favourite theme. 'Five years wasted,' he said, speaking his thoughts aloud. Peto understood the reference. 'Might have been in the bag. Don't forget that,' he said, attempting a tone of bluff consolation. 'Could have been worse.'

Just the type of tap-room philosophy you expected from a new boy, Manning thought. Ah, well, perhaps the old sweats knew what they were doing when they kept to themselves. His eye wandered down to Peto's belt. Hasn't had time to wear the blanco out of his equipment, he thought. What do these types know about the bag, or anything else?

Peto's chummy barrack-room voice was heard again. 'Nothing much you can do about it now, old chap. In any case, I suppose you're only marking time like the rest of us.'

'Marking time!' Manning's voice was raised in sudden violence. 'Don't you realize we may be here for years yet? Wouldn't we all be better off if we had some reasonable, constructive work to occupy us?'

Even while recognizing and making allowance for the alcoholic inspiration of this speech, Peto was slightly embarrassed. He found the earnestness of the tone disconcerting – indecent, almost. He looked furtively in the direction of the others, not wishing to lose grace by the encouragement of an obvious eccentric. 'Wonderful bar, this . . .' he said, speaking more loudly than before, for the benefit of the rest.

The bar was indeed magnificent. It had been fitted up in the alcove of a drawing-room. There were some fine pieces of antique furniture standing about and the faces of all present were dappled with small shadows projected from a splendid but dirty chandelier. The daylight stabbed thinly through the closed shutters, as if they were under pressure from the midday sun. Manning had given up the attempt to make Peto see his point of view. He was looking disapprovingly at the row of bottles on the shelf behind the bar. Better to lay off, from now on, he thought. This was the opportunity to make a clean start. To go ahead and do something worth while doing with the rest of his time.

II

THEY descended swiftly from the brown mountainous solitudes; from the mountains which wore their lonely pines like plumes of a catafalque, and where there remained oases of green in the shadows of precipices.

In the plains, summer rode with yellow cohorts across the fields. It was as if a brush dipped in an ochreous wash had been drawn over this landscape, leaving a yellowness composed of many things: of the golden debris of sun-blasted vegetation; of yellow mud-walls and straw-thatched barns; of the yellowness of a river which curled without apparent movement through sun-baked pastures, its banks studded with marigolds; of yellow dust rising as incense before altars of tired convolvulus.

At a distance the town was merely a dirty, formless whiteness, indicated by the roads which radiated from it and by the break in the faded discipline of irrigation ditches and field boundaries. As they came nearer it began to take shape, but was still no more than an agglomeration of slag heaps, low mountains of ashen detritus in the loop of the river.

They stopped on the bridge. On the further side had been high buildings, grouped protectively, their ranks forming an impenetrable wall, and these had simply collapsed, disintegrated into smooth, glacial slopes from which, as they looked, the wind stirred feathers of dust. Where this avalanche met and entered the saffron water below, a milkiness curled into the stream. The motion of the river was revealed only by a sprawling insect on its surface, which gyrated slowly, and by the blueish-white, froth-edged shape of a bloated animal corpse which bobbed its way slowly round a pillar.

On a lip in the further bank, a fissure in the pallid landslides, five black-garbed laundresses kotowed over their work. A gust of wind conjured up a posturing genie which swayed above them.

'The cities of the plain,' commented the driver.

'Is that all that's left?' Manning asked.

'There are a few streets on the other side,' the driver said.

Manning waited for a poetic quotation, but the driver was suddenly occupied with the dust that had blown into his eyes.

They drove up into the town through canyons of what appeared to be ancient rock, through clearings which might have been colonnaded squares, past tumuli of utter destruction, past buildings which although shattered still retained their form. These, penetrated by the skirmishing wind, still flew tattered banners of bed linen.

In the background, like ants undeterred by the demolition of their hill, human forms were still streaming; moving, in fact, with that proneness to canalization remarkable in such insects. There were many women, bareheaded and in black dresses, who carried not shapely pitchers, but ungainly tins, to some inexhaustible fountain. Men, dressed with the designing sobriety of commercial travellers, were treading as delicately as goats and patting with vexation the dust from their dark clothing. And children. Children of wasted beauty. Hollow-faced images of those who rode rapturously on jennets or played in the flowery fields of Quattrocento paintings. These children stalked with patient cunning the rare starving cats to be discovered crouching among the brickwork.

They had reached the less-damaged quarter of the town promised by the driver, stopping before a structure which had been built, without compassion for its surroundings, in ruthlessly modern style. The pompous severity of this edifice, with its portentous staircase leading to the huge doorway flanked by the blunted emblems of domination, had become as desolately shabby as only such a building can. Its façade was pitted all over with shallow craters. The window-openings — gaunt and fiercely rect-angular — were blackened where flames had licked through them. The whole building, in fact, was as parched as if it had been fired in a kiln as a preliminary, perhaps, to the imposition of a glaze.

Little drifts of dust had accumulated in the protected angles of the façade and against the broad stairway. Of the various neglected symbols of empire, a great bronze eagle over the door was most conspicuous, and its protruding head, favoured as a perch by pigeons, had been rendered shapeless by their droppings.

Manning left his kit in the car with the driver and went up to the first floor. He walked along the corridor, in which only one room appeared to be tenanted.

A man was standing with his back to him, rummaging through some papers on a table. He turned round, and Manning saw that he had a youthful face, but a face that looked as if it might have been exposed to some drying process; a process which although insufficient to rob it of its youthfulness had caused the eyes to become unnaturally sunken, the skin a little glazed, the hair in front prematurely thin.

The young man came forward and held out his hand. 'I'm Wilton,' he said. His voice was cheerful. He screwed up his eyes as if staring into strong sunlight. As he walked he gave slightly at the knees stooping like an elderly bibliophile picking over second-hand books. Wilton was wearing a red pyjama top over his K.D. shorts, and there was a brilliant red 'V' stencilled on the dead white skin of his neck, showing where the opening of his shirt usually came.

The room had the look of a scorched eggshell. There were sere-looking proclamations in English and Italian on one wall. They were rent and tattered at the corners where they had torn away from the nails that had originally held them in place. On another wall there was a map in similar condition. The room contained a deal table, two rickety chairs, and a roughly constructed bed consisting of a wooden frame over which canvas had been nailed. A mosquito net hung down above it from a hook in the wall.

'I'm glad you've come,' said Wilton. 'I was beginning to get worried.'

'Anxious to get away?' asked Manning.

'Well,' said Wilton, 'I didn't want this to develop into a permanency. Such things do happen.'

'I can imagine that,' said Manning.

'Mind you,' said Wilton, 'it's not so bad as all that. They try to scare you about it. It's all right for a few days. There's a jolly good cemetery, for one thing.'

'That's good news,' said Manning.

'No,' said Wilton, 'I don't mean that. I suppose you're not interested in inscriptions, though.'

With some difficulty he picked up a large slab of marble which served as a paper weight. There were a few vague lines and notches cut in its surface. 'What do you think of that?' he asked anxiously. 'That's a Latin inscription.'

'Very interesting,' said Manning. He examined the piece of marble again, but was quite unable to identify a single letter.

'There are some Greek ones, too,' said Wilton, 'but they didn't get knocked about so badly. I mean, none of the bits were small enough to take away. I spend most of my time looking for bits and pieces like this. I was hoping to have picked up a Greek inscription before they called me back.'

'What else do you do?' asked Manning.

'Well,' said Wilton, 'luckily enough I'm interested in pre-history, too, so really I'm all right. Otherwise you'd be in a bit of a spot here. What I mean is, all the historical stuff has been knocked pretty flat. Do you approve of Nola vases?'

'What vases?'

'Nola vases. The vases dug up in the Greek tombs at Nola. They make them here. Or, at least, they used to. Wonderful craftsmen. They got the most wonderful imperfections into them.' Wilton was warming to his subject, and the sunken-blue eyes sparkled with enthusiasm.

'You'll be sorry to miss it all,' said Manning.

'Oh, I gave up all hope of picking up a Nola vase long ago,' Wilton said. 'I couldn't afford it. One of the local politicians offered to find me one, but there were strings attached, of course.'

Manning observed his future home in more detail. The walls were spotted with a holocaust of mosquitoes. There was a prodigious crack closed by a thicket of cobwebs running up from a hole in the floor to a hole in the ceiling. Through this hole drooped plaster-clogged wire-mesh. He noticed the bed again.

'Do you sleep here?' he asked.

'Good Heavens, no,' said Wilton, laughing. 'You can't sleep here, with the mosquitoes and the heat. The Sindaco found me a billet outside the town. Most interesting village with Samnite remains. I only use the bunk for the afternoon kip.'

Through an open door Manning noticed a wash basin. A powerful drain smell came from the direction of this room. 'How's the water supply?'

'You can't really say there is any,' said Wilton. 'The tap only runs for a few minutes a day. Best thing is to leave it turned on, and then you collect what there is. Never any chance of the basin running over. Oh, by the way, it's better not to use the lavatory. The cistern takes twenty-four hours to fill.'

'Well,' said Manning, 'that seems to cover the amenities, and I expect you want to be away, so perhaps we'd better be getting down to business. What's the job here?'

'The job?' asked Wilton. He seemed mystified.

'The excuse for drawing rations,' said Manning.

'What do you do? I'm feeling energetic,' he thought fit to explain, 'after two years of doing port duty on a non-existent port.'

Wilton thought for a moment. 'Do you mean the old report business and all that?'

'Yes. How do you fill it out? I mean, what do you put in it?

'Hardly anything,' said Wilton. 'I pick up a rumour occasionally.'

'My God. Don't tell me they still fall for rumours.'

'Nothing has changed,' said Wilton. 'The laws of the Medes and the Persians.'

'I can't believe it,' said Manning. 'Just like the old days back in Africa. What sort of rumours?'

17

'It's a bit awkward these days,' said Wilton. 'If you go over the old stock rumours — the bread-and-butter lines, so to speak — you'll probably remember that some of them were connected in one way or another with the war. You can think of the occasional one that isn't, but the field is very narrowed.'

'Well, anyway, supposing you succeeded in thinking up a rumour,' said Manning. 'What else? You can't possibly make a report only out of a rumour or two.'

'If you feel you have to do better,' said Wilton, 'you can always sabotage a minor communication and report on that. Must say it seems unethical to me, but I've heard of people doing it.'

'A telegraph cable, or something like that?'

'That's the idea. Oh, by the way. I was nearly forgetting. I'm also supposed to check up on hotel registers throughout the area. You know, the transients at hotels.'

'That's something anyway.'

'Yes, but there aren't any. I mean, no hotels, apart from the one here in the town where you eat. Come to think of it, nothing to stop you making up a few hotels. Nobody would ever know any better. After all, not having any transport you can't get to any of the outlying villages. Just as well you can't, because they're full of bandits. Not even the carabinieri go to some of them.'

'I've got a requisition order for a car,' said Manning.

'What's the use of that when there aren't any cars? The only thing to do is to give the carabinieri any of the jobs you get.'

'And what sort of information are you likely to get from them?'

'Not so hot. They make it up as they go along. Everyone you ever have to inquire about is always Okay. Naturally — they collect a bribe for a good report. Might just as well save yourself the trouble and make it up for yourself.'

'I've had years of this kind of thing,' said Manning. 'I thought I was getting away from it at last.'

'I've had five years myself,' said Wilton.

'So you're dependent upon the carabinieri?'

'You're dependent upon everybody,' Wilton said. 'If you play ball with the marshal of the carabinieri he does your work for you. At the hotel they feed you and the food is better than the rations justify. The Sindaco finds you a billet away from the typhus area. You play ball with them and they all look after you. If you don't you probably won't like it here at all.'

'You said something about a typhus area.'

'There's a typhus epidemic in the town,' Wilton explained. 'It's better not to stop here any longer than you have to. Speak Italian, by the way?'

'I was in Florence for three years before the war.'

'Lucky chap. But that kind of Italian won't do you much good outside the town. In this part of the world the people of one village can hardly understand the dialect spoken in another village three miles away. I get on better with Spanish than Italian. Shall I give you a piece of advice? Treat it all as a huge joke. A bad joke, if you like, but a joke for all that. Don't take it seriously. We're all of us helpless. You won't be able to do any more than I have done, which is nothing. So sit back and get what amusement you can out of the spectacle of events you can't influence in any way at all.'

Wilton reached in the drawer and produced a slip of paper, which he handed to Manning. 'This may be of some use to you.'

Manning glanced at what was written on the paper. He read:

Carabiniere: 100 L.
Brigadiere: 200 L.
Maresciallo: Mozzarella cheese.
Sindaco: Spaghetti (tagliatelle preferred), or Mozzarella cheese.
Commissario Pubblica Sicurezza:
                 Bottle Sarti.
Marchesa Manfredoni:
                 Keatings powder — or similar.

'*Douceurs*,' Wilton explained. 'If you happen to want any of the people here to do anything for you, the sum or article mentioned will be considered acceptable.'

'I don't want to start off with that kind of thing if I can help it,' Manning said. 'It gets people into bad habits.'

'Don't think I'm rubbing it in, but if you're going to be here long, you'll need every one of the people on that list. You can't make a move in any direction without calling in one or the other.'

'I don't believe it. No offence, of course,' Manning said. 'I believe it's possible to be self-sufficient, even in a place like this. After all, I'm getting a car to do my own work with. That cuts out this marshal fellow and the police, for a start. Now, what about the Sindaco?'

'He's the one you get your civilian billet from. I told you about him.'

'I can do without one,' said Manning, making a heroic decision. 'I'll sleep here.'

'You can try to, you mean. You might even spend a night or two here, but you won't sleep. The mosquitoes come through the cracks in their thousands, even if you keep the window shut. Besides that, the brickwork of the building seems to absorb the heat. It's actually hotter in the first part of the night than in the daytime. Like being in a hut in the tropics. The stink is terrible, too.'

Manning glanced at the list again. 'Who's the marchesa and why does she have to have louse powder?'

'Oh, the marchesa's a marvellous character. Don't miss seeing her, whatever you do. She lives in a castle known as Looters' Despair because it's centuries since there's been anything left worth taking away. The Americans were the last ones to have a try, and she still exists on the 'C' rations they left behind. She needs Keatings because castles are notoriously lousy.'

'Yes, but what use is she to you as far as the job goes?'

'The job?' Wilton winced slightly. 'I can't tell you for certain, because I've never had to do anything, but the legend is that the Pubblica Sicurezza is used to inform on the Carabinieri, the Sindaco on both and the marchesa on the lot. Only her information is really reliable because her interest in you is a sentimental one. She's far too grand for other motives.'

'What are the feeding arrangements?' Manning asked.

'You turn your rations in at the Hotel Vesuvio, and they give you good wog food in exchange. Wonderful scoff, but you want to remember to lay down the law if they give you spaghetti more than once a day.'

'And where do they come in? Do you pay them anything?'

'Of course not. Look at it this way. You're one of the first three citizens of Malevento now. You, the marshal of the carabinieri, and the Sindaco. It's an advertisement for them. It's good for business to have you there.'

Manning felt doubtful about this arrangement. 'I'd like to take a look at the place. Can we get a drink there? I suppose you do drink?'

Wilton's face lit up. 'Good heavens, yes. Like a fish. I'm unconscious for whole days at a time. In fact, the only reason I'm not plastered now is because I've run out of Sarti. That's why I can't offer you anything. Sorry and all that.'

'They seemed to be putting in some hard drinking up at H.Q.,' Manning said.

'Definitely,' agreed Wilton. 'It's the Section's method of dealing with the problem. You must have realized by now we are all borderline cases. Too much inactivity, blasted hopes and so on. Whenever I feel I'm going to blow my top, I go on a bender. Pass right out for twenty-four hours. After that I'm fine again. Talking about people being crackers, did you see much of the old man? He's the worst case.'

'Seemed sane enough to me,' said Manning. 'A bit acid, perhaps.'

'You wouldn't notice it at first, but it's there all right. He's crazy in a freakish way, like one of the mad Roman emperors. Quite capable of paying divine honours to a horse. It's always best to keep out of his way. Don't let him see too much of you.'

'The driver struck me as being a bit queer,' said Manning.

'Yes, but he's harmless. The F.S.O.'s an expert on Old Norse, and thinks of nothing else. Lives in a kind of saga dream world of his own. You don't notice it straight away. That's where the danger comes in. But all the time he's trying to get you involved in some imaginary epic. Has an urge to expend you recklessly in some hopeless cause, if you know what I mean.'

'Well, as things are now there isn't much he can do about it, is there?'

'No, I suppose not, but he can still make life not worth living for you. You know what happened to our predecessor here?'

'Yes,' said Manning. 'Was it in this building?'

'Absolutely. In the only decent room, too, which makes it worse. That's why I had to put my stuff up here. He didn't snuff it for a few days. Supposed to have been a medical curiosity.'

'What was his trouble?'

'The place got on his nerves and the old man wouldn't do anything about it. Naturally not.'

'Looking at it from his point of view, if that's permissible,' said Manning, 'someone has to be here.'

'Yes,' said Wilton. 'We all know that. But the old man's particular talent lies in finding out whatever it is you most dislike, and then making sure you get it. If he gets to know that anyone — like the last chap, for instance — has a horror of being on his own, he sends him down here. Now just suppose you got to like the place. As soon as he heard about it he'd snatch you away. We had one fellow who hated travelling, and he sent him on endless fruitless errands all over the country. He spent months standing in the corridors of trains and sleeping in transit camps in the depths of winter — you know, the usual damp bedding.'

'It won't be much use his trying anything like that with me,' Manning said. 'If he does I shall just ask for a transfer.'

'The man before me did, but it took too long to come through. By the time it came it was too late.'

'You make it sound depressing,' Manning said.

'It is depressing,' said Wilton robustly. 'As a matter of fact, you can't overstate the case. My advice is to have a good stock of Sarti on hand and keep at it until you come up to H.Q. again. Then you can arrange for the old man to hear that you are enjoying yourself, and he'll take you away and let someone else have a taste of it.'

'I'll remember that.'

'Did they give you any definite work, by the way? I mean, any names?' Wilton asked. He had removed the pyjama top and was now slipping on a rather grubby-looking K.D. shirt.

'They gave me one name.' Manning took out his notebook. 'Mancuso, Luigi, of Santa Maria.'

'Is that all?'

'Yes.'

'Well, I mean, no generalità?'

'No what?'

'Generalità. Family details. Name of father and mother. You know what I mean.'

'None at all,' said Manning. 'That's all they gave me.'

'Good,' said Wilton. 'In that case we can finish off your week's work in about two minutes. That and a rumour or so, if you want to pad the report out a bit.' As he was speaking he wrote rapidly on a slip of paper, which he then passed to Manning.

Manning read:

> Mancuso, Luigi, son of Pietro (deceased) and of Maria Colombo. Born in Lucera dei Pagani, 1914, and until recently resident in S. Maria di Sannio. Without fixed address. Agricultural worker. Unemployed. Mancuso enjoys an excellent reputation in the neighbourhood and was not inscribed in the Partito Nazionale Fascista. No criminal convictions are recorded.

'You make it all up just like that?' said Manning, feeling somewhat shaken.

'Why not? You are given no gen to go on. Italy is full of Mancuso, Luigis. There are five or six villages of Santa Maria within a radius of fifty miles. A bit of guesswork answers their purpose just as well as the actual facts about any one of the large number of Mancusos taken at random.'

'What do they do with the information?'

'It's usually wanted to help them decide whether someone will make a suitable cook in an Army Laundry unit. He gets the job anyway, so why worry?'

'I like Lucera dei Pagani,' said Manning.

'So do I. It was next on my list to be used. After that comes S. Georgio di Sannio. I always chose my place names for their historical associations.'

Wilton had taken him down to the Hotel Vesuvio, and after that he had driven him back and dropped him at the office before leaving.

Manning went back into the office to take stock of his surroundings. He examined the lavatory, with its row of choked pans which had served the whole building, his rising nausea quickly thrust back by long acquired habit. A trickle of yellow, warmish water was coming through the tap in one of the washbowls, so finding a rag he cleaned the worst of the scummy deposit from the porcelain surface and blocked up the waste in the hope of collecting a store of water.

He looked through the other rooms on the floor. There was nothing to choose between them and the one selected by Wilton. The walls were cracked and the cracks stuffed with cobwebs. The floors were littered with the dust and plaster of demolished ceilings. Only fragments of glass remained in the window frames. A few pieces of smashed furniture, evidently considered valueless by looters, littered some of the rooms. Everywhere the smell persisted; there was no escaping it in any part of the building, a dour fragrance in which could be detected strongly the odours of charred wood, of brick dust, and beneath them the undertone of some deep-seated, some furtive and undiscoverable decay.

24

Although it was late, a dying sunlight still invaded the office, bringing with it the stifling heat that Wilton had promised.

He went out into the life-sapped street. Before him there arose a profile of turrets and crenellations, confirmed in their renunciation of the present by the thin screaming of swifts. Into this dignified harmony of ruin, this grimly convincing stage-prop for his mood, the recent devastations, soon to be indistinguishable to the casual eye from those of the preceding millennium, had sought acceptance. Forming, as it were, a backcloth, was a hill bearing upon its crest a vast cicatrice of battlements, and still higher and infinitely remote there stretched the vitreous solitudes of the Apennines.

For perhaps an hour not even a dog was to be seen in the street. Then a black-clad figure came into view, lit by the last scavenging rays of sunlight. This figure clasped, as it seemed, several black, spiky shapes, and suddenly from it there went up a melancholy howl:

'Ombrella-ripar-ao-o-o-'

In spite of his weariness, Manning was fascinated. In this sun-stricken and waterless place, this austere figure, the possessor of this voice of doom, remained then the representative of commerce and enterprise — an umbrella mender!

The old man shuffled by, scuffling up the dust with his broken boots. Once again before he turned the corner the hooting cry went up.

Back in the office he removed his sweat-soaked shirt and hung it on a nail. The basin in the washroom was half-full and he dipped his face in the tepid water in a vain endeavour to cool the prickly heat of his skin. He was too tired to face the prospect that evening of reconnoitring for food. Better, at any rate, he thought, to get an hour or two of rest first.

He made up his bed in a corner, suspending the mosquito net from the hook, taking care to tuck it well in. He noticed one or two small holes in the net, which he would attend to the next day. He glanced up. Already the mosquitoes against the ceiling were floating gauzily through the movements of their sinister cotillion.

25

III

T H E Hotel Vesuvio, originally possessing ten bedrooms and a never-completed Turkish Bath, was now much reduced, a single spacious room serving, according to the hour, as café or restaurant. At midnight this same room assumed the function of hotel by the erection of a couple of Japanese screens behind which four single iron beds, normally standing on end against the wall, could be manœuvred into position. After this hour the rats that moved discreetly about the kitchen during the day came into the usufruct of the whole establishment, which they patrolled in a sporadic fashion throughout the night hours.

The seediness of the Hotel Vesuvio, Manning thought, was not so much a product of the recent calamities as a chronic and progressive decline; something that had developed and matured since the days of the Bourbon satrapy — the glory that had justified those marble pillars and that florid but faded Neapolitan idyll painted on what remained of the ceiling. This same seediness, however, had been concentrated by disaster, and the dust-flavoured decay eked out previously through halls and foyers and antechambers now crowded into the few cubic yards of what was left of the building. Here, then, were gathered together in almost unbearable emphasis all the desolate hatstands, the sere-fronded palms, the dented spittoons, the calendars of a decade before and the insipidly dramatic works of art inspired by the mood of Domenica del Corriere cover-illustrations. In this way, too, the three ancient and sable-dressed citizens had been driven from some remote and now demolished corner and herded, despite their inclinations, to the fringe of that shrunken area now frequented by such casuals as all-night truck drivers and glove sellers from Naples. Here they sat, spittoon flanked, commenting with the benevolent humanity of sated vultures upon the events of the day.

Alberto, the proprietor, leant over Manning, indicating these surroundings with a wide gesture of welcome. 'The centre of the town's social life,' he said proudly. 'Please regard our establishment as your home.' He looked at his watch. 'Would you object to waiting for the marshal for breakfast? He is usually here by now. Of course, if you are hungry. . . .'

Manning agreed to wait.

'Who, by the way, is the marshal?' he asked. Ah, of course, he of the Mozzarella cheese, he remembered.

'A very great man,' said Alberto. 'You might even say that the town revolves around him. He is always out to help such people as yourself. A man of intelligence.' Alberto pressed his forefinger to his temple and twisted it in emphasis.

At that moment there was a commotion in the street. Alberto excused himself and went to the door, and Manning followed him.

A procession was passing, headed by a priest. He was followed by a horse-drawn cart, upon which lay a black coffin. Behind this walked a straggling group of mourners with averted faces. Finally there came a man and a woman. The woman occasionally raised her head to produce a piercing wail, although in the intervals of silence her face appeared to be devoid of any kind of emotion.

The three aged citizens got up and removed their hats. 'Health to us!' said one in a loud and solemn voice. They then resumed their seats.

Alberto turned to them. 'Who would it be, Don Enrico?' he asked, addressing the one who had just spoken.

'The daughter of Luigi Capra di Filippo,' replied Don Enrico with authority. 'She went down with the typhus.'

Manning returned to the table. 'I hear there's a good deal of typhus at the moment.'

'No, sir,' replied Don Enrico, 'no more than one learns to expect. Here there is always typhus. It is a matter of general knowledge that all disease is carried by the wind. We suffer from

27

insalubrious winds, that's all. That's why the town is called Malevento. When the wind blows from a south-easterly quarter the typhus carries them off. When it changes to south-west it's the smallpox.'

'Germs have nothing to do with the wind,' said one of his companions, shaking his head with such finality that his cheeks continued to quiver after his head was still.

Don Enrico turned to him. 'That's the kind of new-fangled rubbish they taught the kids in the Fascist schools. It is an offence against religion to believe that kind of thing. If you talk like that it only means you are a Fascist and should be purged. Fascism has gone, understand that, and with it all it stood for, including the Genial African Sun, public lavatories and germs. We are Christian Democrats now, and when we fall sick, believe me, it's the wind. The rest is all Roman nonsense.'

He cleared his throat and spat indignantly. His companions also spat.

The doorway was suddenly filled by a looming figure which paused on the threshold, like an actor making his entry.

'The marshal's arrived,' Alberto shouted back excitedly to the kitchen, and in response there was an immediate clatter of dishes.

Don Enrico and his entourage rose again and doffed their hats and the marshal advanced with quick steps slapping Alberto condescendingly on the shoulder, disposing of the three old men with a regal wave of the hand, and taking possession simultaneously of Manning's hand and elbow.

'Filippo Altamura,' he announced, 'Marshal of the Carabinieri Reali, attached to the S.I.M. At your service.' Manning's nostrils were momentarily submerged in the blended odours of garlic and brilliantine.

There was something about the marshal that recalled the late dictator. The bold, protuberant eyes that darted uneasily from side to side, these and the rapid alternation of geniality and frowns were exactly in character. It would have been necessary only to take a few inches from the height, to add a few years to the age, and to visualize a bald and polished scalp where those black locks curled, for the resemblance to be remarkable.

A few seconds passed during which, held firmly in the marshal's grip, Manning found himself exposed to an un-wavering smile. Then, quite suddenly, he was free, and there was the marshal in possession of a creaking and protesting chair. But before he was able to enjoy this brief liberty he found him-self, as if by no more than a simple act of volition on the marshal's part, sitting beside him at the table and watching half-fascinated the marshal's arms sprawling octopus-like after plates and cutlery.

'The marshal's ready!' bellowed Alberto, and the kitchen door opened with a crash to a maid carrying a tray.

Manning's eyes were suddenly caught by the glass that had been placed in front of him, and there was the marshal pouring an immense shot of brandy into it. Into his own glass went a little white wine.

'Drink,' cried the marshal. 'You, me — comrades. Col-laborate. You sit here, eat, drink, diversions. Good time. I work for you.' He winked with the assumption, it seemed to Manning, of some mutual and slightly disreputable under-standing. He was employing that syntax-free variety of the lan-guage normally used in conversation with very small children.

'Marshal,' said Manning, 'would you be so good as to address me in normal literate Italian?'

The marshal's smile was in no way dimmed. Two rows of large but faultless teeth were once again laid bare. 'Please forgive me. A silly habit we get into when talking to the Allies. Quite unnecessary, I realize. What I wanted to assure you was of my sincere co-operation in your work. I am here entirely at your disposition. Your colleague will have told you how well we got on together.'

The marshal produced a blue silk handkerchief from his pocket, with which he carefully wiped his hands. Manning observed that they were large and white. On the little finger of the left hand the marshal wore a wide band of gold. Above and below this the unconstrained flesh curved gently, and the backs of the fingers were covered with silky black hairs.

Plates of bacon and eggs appeared before them, and the marshal, using his spoon, immediately dug the yolk out of one of the fried eggs and began to spread it on a rasher of bacon. He was just about to repeat this with the other egg when a thought struck him. Spearing the second rasher with a fork he waved it in front of Manning's nose. 'Your bacon is so delicious in its natural state, direct from the can. Whatever makes you spoil it as you do by frying it? I continually give these silly people orders not to fry my bacon, but I can never make them understand.'

The marshal put down his knife and fork and tested the clearance between his collar stud and throat. He undid the top button of his shirt, and as he leaned forward a religious medal dangled through the opening. 'It's unpleasantly warm already, isn't it?' he said. He took a sip of wine and rinsed it noisily through his teeth.

'But you're not drinking?'

'Thanks, not with my breakfast.'

'Drink up,' said the marshal heartily, and Manning shrank from the half-expected clap on the shoulder. 'All your friends thrived on their morning glass of brandy. It gladdens the heart and knocks out the microbes.' He produced a gold toothpick and placing one hand over his mouth began operations with it.

Manning folded his napkin and made to rise from the table. The marshal hastily stuck the toothpick into a piece of bread and laid a restraining hand on his arm. 'Is there anything I can do for you today? Your friends always told me when we met in the morning for breakfast anything they wanted me to do.'

Manning's hand had closed over the slip of paper in his pocket on which he had written the name given him by the F.S.O. While the marshal had been speaking he had, however, made up his mind. He would go elsewhere for his information. He would use the marshal's services only in the last resort. His distrust of the marshal had been immediate. It was all the more so because he felt sure that this heartiness was nothing more than a studied pose. He wondered what it was intended to conceal.

'The only thing I'm interested in at present is a car,' he said.

The marshal shook his head. 'A car, my dear friend? They just don't exist. They were all snaffled long ago.'

'I saw one in the town this morning.'

'Not privately owned,' said the marshal. 'In any case, why worry about a car? I do all your investigations for you. Amuse yourself — life is short.' Manning found himself holding a sinewy toscana cigar, while flame flickered from the marshal's lighter. 'Yes, life is short. As the great Lorenzo said, "Of the morrow there's no certainty."' The marshal's face relaxed into a brooding, almost melancholy, expression. A fleck of ash settled snowflake-like on the cuff of the neat, pin-stripe suit, and was removed fastidiously.

They looked up.

Alberto was standing by the table, bowing, with his hands clasped together as if in prayer.

'Well, what is it?' said the marshal, his habitually badgering tone replaced by one of sharp irritation.

Manning was suddenly aware of a group of men huddled sheep-like in the rear of the café.

'Body of Bacchus! What are all these people doing here?' cried the marshal. 'What the hell do they want?' A blizzard of ash descended as he stabbed the air viciously with his cigar.

'They are some poor sods who want to ask a favour, marshal,' said Alberto humbly.

'Well, tell them to wait until I finish eating,' fumed the marshal, his good humour now sunk without trace in a raging sea of frowns. He turned to Manning. 'It doesn't look as if there's much sense of refinement about in these days.'

Alberto repulsed the advancing supplicants with gestures of exorcism, and they shrivelled away among the palms and hat-stands, as though by remote control he had released some hidden air valve through which, as events demanded, they were either inflated or deflated.

31

BACK at the office Manning found that the precautions of
the night before had been ineffective against the mosquitoes. He was covered in bites, which he noticed now
for the first time because they were beginning to itch. He was
attending to them when a mild, almost bleating voice outside the
door said: 'Con permesso.'

Manning pulled on his shorts. Before he had them buttoned
up the voice came again. This time louder. More insistent.
'Con permesso.'

Manning went to the door, barefooted, with the cream
smeared over his torso. Before he could reach it a head came
round the corner. 'Con permesso.'

It was a small, weasel-faced man who gave the impression of
having shrunk within his clothes, which were now suspended
from certain osseous projections. This shrunken man stood
there, hat in hand, bowing and smiling nervously.

'I am Vittorio — Vittorio Palumbo. Not that the Palumbo
part matters. I'm generally known by my first name.'

Manning nodded.

'I'm a pal of your friend's. The one who just left. We always
went around together.'

No comment.

'Well . . . I just thought I'd look in and introduce myself. No
harm done, I thought. Wanted to tell you I'd be glad to help you
in any way I can.'

'Thanks,' said Manning. 'That's very kind of you. I very
much appreciate it.'

'Your friend used to come to my home pretty often. Had
lunch with us last Sunday. My wife wondered if you'd care to
come along some time.'

'I'd be pleased to,' said Manning, repenting his ungraciousness.

The little man looked harmless enough. Rather a hospitable gesture, in fact. There was something to be said about living in a country with a few millenia of civilization behind it.

'We'll make it Sunday, then,' said the little man.

'Well,' said Manning doubtfully, 'I'm going to be busy for a day or two settling in here. Could we, perhaps, fix a day a little later?'

'Of course,' said the little man, 'of course. Any time to suit you. Remember the name — Vittorio. The other part doesn't matter. I run the garage in the square. Just ask for Vittorio. Everyone knows me. Don't believe half the things they tell you about me, though.' He cackled shrilly and waved a finger in playful deprecation.

Manning smiled.

The man turned as if to go, then hesitated. He was still grinning.

'Yes?' said Manning.

'There was one thing I wanted to ask you. You won't be offended, will you?'

'I hope not.'

'I feel that we are friends already. It's a funny thing, you don't feel that way with everybody. But I just feel as if I can speak to you. Do you understand me? With some people you don't feel that way.'

'Go ahead.'

'My brother-in-law,' said Vittorio. 'He got into town last night. He came to see me and he's in a bit of a jam. Of course, he has to come to ask me — just as if I can do anything to help him out. I told him. I said, "I've got no influence here. There's no one I've got a fix with. What do you expect me to do for you?" Of course, you must understand he's a rich man, he can afford to pay. But I explained to him. I put it plainly. If I knew anyone who could be persuaded to lend him a helping hand, in fact in this case to see justice done, he wouldn't be the kind to take money. That's how I put it to him, and he understood the situation as well as you or I do. "I understand," he said, "your friends are educated men, *gentiluomini*, but even so it wouldn't show us up too well if we seemed ungrateful. Perhaps a few cases of Sarti wouldn't give offence. . . ." '

'Get out,' said Manning.

The little man came towards him. The slight original diffidence had suddenly evaporated, and now he was smiling a smile of pure friendship. With complete assurance he put a small, monkey-like paw on Manning's arm. 'You are a good man,' he said, 'we talk the same language. You don't like to see an injustice done and I don't like to either. I am asking you to right a wrong. My brother-in-law can get his case attended to for a quarter of a million, and he is ready to pay a hundred thou, no more. All he wants is justice. Nothing more than justice. And if someone could help him out, there's a hundred thou in it for him.'

'Get out,' said Manning again, his tone sharper now.

Vittorio was still smiling, if anything more happily than before. 'All right, then, we will be seeing you Sunday. That's a date.'

'No.'

'Well, you make it any time to suit yourself. You will find us nice, homely people, and I've got a couple of daughters you'd like to meet. Don't forget — Vittorio's the name. Everyone knows me.'

And, still smiling, he bowed his way out of the office. Manning went after him and slammed the door.

It seemed as if the aged functionaries of the Pubblica Sicurezza had all conspired to take refuge in the Archives Department, about which they fluttered with the disconsolate stealth of moths. Manning waited in a creaking silence, drawing into his nostrils with each breath the molecules of decay. Taking advantage of their protective colouring, a pair of old men emerged from behind one of the racks. Manning coughed, and they immediately took flight. After a few moments one of them cautiously re-emerged, peering round the corner, and before he could take cover Manning had caught his eye. 'Hey, you.'

The old man edged over with a crab-like motion. His cadaverous face was set in a bleak and stubborn expression. Approaching Manning warily, he suddenly snatched the paper from his hand. Reading it, his face was purged of its severity and a look of relief took its place. His thin lips moved slowly as he repeated the name over to himself. Then he looked up at Manning, waving the paper up and down, his face slowly distorting in a wolfish but conciliatory smile. He spoke slowly, with the endless patience of a good man, the father of a family, who has to deal with a nice but too insistent child. So that there should be no doubt about them, he formed the words with a great pursing of the lips, much hissing, an exaggerated pressure of the tongue against the teeth. At the same time he contrived to deal the paper a patronizing slap of the fingers.

'Of this name there are five villages in the province. Understand, five?' He held up the empty hand with its knotted, tarsier fingers, bending each one in succession and then straightening it. One — two — three — four — five. Five. Yes, five. Santa Maria is a blessed name, but common. Who knows how many of them there are in southern Italy.' Now the lips pursed in theatrical perplexity. A shrug of the shoulders and the hand held up, palms outwards, in surrender. The old man longed nostalgically for the must-scented solitudes of the filing racks from which he had been enticed.

'Signor Roberto!' he called.

Another official flapped into sight from the bureaucratic jungle. A fat man this time, not grossly fat but with the empty inflation of a dried up puff-ball. He bobbed about momentarily in the background, tearing at his collar which had burst away on one side from its stud.

'Signor Roberto!' pleaded the other again. 'Please come here.' He handed him the paper.

35

The puff-ball glanced at it and emitted a sound like a frightened bird. He turned the paper over, examining the back, and returned it hastily.

The cadaverous one turned to Manning again, the flicker of a pitying smile now showing at the corners of his mouth. 'And, of course, the generalità are essential. Understand, generalità? Name of papa and mamma.'

'Yes, I understand generalità.'

'Ah,' said the old man with immense astonishment. 'You speak Italian. Right then, you understand how it is.' He laid the paper down on the desk, pressing out the creases very carefully and scrutinizing once more both the front and the back, as if to avoid the possibility of overlooking any clue.

'You ask us — ' he placed a padded finger-tip against Manning's chest — 'for a man living in Santa Maria, of which there are five. Of this man all you know is his name and his patronymic. We cannot say so definitely, but there might be ten men having exactly this name living in each village.'

The puff-ball put in his word. 'For all that, Mancuso is not a common name. If, for instance, you had been after Esposito we could have given up. There might be a hundred of them.' He suddenly threw out his hand, releasing the hundred potential Espositos with the gesture of a farmer scattering his grain. 'Instead of which, Mancusos are relatively few.' He symbolized this shrunken fraternity by a fluttering of his half-closed fingers.

'We might be able to do something,' said the cadaverous one. 'It would, of course, mean looking up all the registers, and then naturally we have other sources of information.'

'Of course, it is a long job,' agreed the puff-ball. He rolled his eyes heavenwards. 'But we want to help you. We are here for that. Excuse me — a cigarette, by any chance? ... Ah, thank you, you are too good.'

Manning consulted his notebook. 'By the way, where does the Marchesa di Manfredoni live?'

'Live, the marchesina? In the castle, of course.'

36

'You mean in that ruin on the hill?'

'It's not precisely a ruin,' said the cadaverous one reproachfully. 'A bit cheerless, if you like. A nice little three-roomed flat would be more cosy. But still, when one's a marchesa!'

There was no doubt about it, Manning thought, he must free himself as soon as possible from his dependence upon these incompetent old men. He must put himself in a position to be able to renounce the marshal's doubtful collaboration. The first step towards this end — towards complete independence of action — lay in the acquisition of a car.

His next visit, therefore, was to the Municipio, where he spoke to the head clerk. 'I want to have a word with the man in charge of the car taxation department,' he said.

A dignified carnival figure of papier mâché was duly produced.

'How many private cars are there registered in the town?' Manning asked him.

'There are exactly five,' the old official spoke slowly, but with the pride of an admitted expert called to testify in his particular field.

'And who owns them?'

'One is held by the Carabinieri Reali, two by the Pubblica Sicurezza, one by the Questore himself, and one by the Sindaco.'

'What about the garage owner, Vittorio Palumbo?'

'He has a break-down car and a taxi.'

'Is the taxi in use?'

'No.'

Ten minutes later he had found the Palumbo apartment. It was on the second floor of a scarred and pitted block of flats. He rang the bell. The door opened, and he was confronted by an impressive vision. In the entrance hall stood, one behind the other, the tall figures of three splendid women, two of them indeed girls, and a third, standing in their rear, a matron who was evidently their mother and whose singular beauty they

37

reproduced in less florid form. All three of them possessed the severe eyes of renaissance princesses troubled by thoughts of incest and murder, and although the upper lips of the girls bore the faint down of reluctant innocence, these were visages to poison with suggestion the minds of emperors, to contrive the downfall of principalities, to flaunt to their own undoing their infidelities in the faces of autocratic kings. All three were similarly robed, as if for the celebration of an archaic mystery, in grease-smirched house gowns. A baby crawled on the immense slopes of the maternal bosom. Manning marvelled. How could the wizened manikin Vittorio have sired such a progeny upon those Junoesque loins?

'Excuse me. Signor Vittorio Palumbo?'

A telephone tinkled with spasmodic insistence in the depths of the apartment, and the three heads showed in profile; superimposed medallions of classic beauty, the slightly Mayan compression of the forehead continuing the line of the nose; the everted lips of Nilotic queens.

'One moment.'

The three graces withdrew. An interval of mumbling response to the telephone. A final tinkle of the receiver being hung up, and then the return of the matriarch alone, now inexplicably a Medusa. In his imagination Manning saw the vipers uncoil in her hair.

'Signor Palumbo is not at home.'

'When is he expected back?'

She shook her head, impatient to dismiss him. 'I can't say.'

'Where can I find him?'

Another head shake. Venom splashed from the eyes. 'Perhaps at the garage. Really, I don't know.'

'Would you be so kind as to tell me where the garage is?' A strange and ill-boding reception, he thought.

'Opposite.'

The door had been steadily closing, and now the fine face with its incantatory expression was cut off suddenly.

38

He turned and went slowly down the stairs, stopping at the landing. The window of this squalid platform, this no-man's-land between the flats, gave on to the street. He could see the garage across the road, bomb-shorn of its upper storeys; the cobalt façade of a cabaret, ornamented in the resplendent yellows of Pirelli and Shell advertisements. The interior presented a dim still life of air-lines curled like torpid pythons, tyres piled up as if by some competent player of hoop-la, the well-picked carcass of an ancient car, a mysterious machine, a kind of child's push-cart, in the arms of which squatted a fat cylinder with air-cooling vanes. As he looked, a malignant dwarf shot out of the dark interior, carrying a hook-tipped pole which he engaged with a ring on the shutter, bringing it down with a rumbling crash. There was still a small doorway left in the otherwise blanked-off front of the garage. Through this the dwarf immediately returned, charging with couched pole as if in chivalric encounter with a dragon. The small door shut behind him.

Manning crossed the street and kicked the door in the shutter. There was no sound from within. He retreated to the corner on the same side of the road, and then remembered that he was in full view of the windows of the Palumbo apartment, from between the shutters of which enigmatic eyes now undoubtedly surveyed him. He turned and walked away with purpose, crossing the road again. Then, when no longer visible from the windows, he retraced his steps a short way, and quickly slipped into the shell of a ruined building, from which he could keep comfortable observation on the garage.

The street was deserted but for a passing group of ragged children. They were occupied with a mournful-faced, pregnant bitch which, enticed craftily within range, was received with a shower of kicks on the stomach. The bitch seemed to be quite incapable of profiting from its lesson, and this treatment was repeated several times.

At last the door in the shutter opened. A head poked through, tortoise-like, from a carapace of steel. Finally Vittorio emerged.

He had evidently forgotten something, which he went back to recover, leaving the door wide. Just as he re-appeared at the opening, Manning greeted him.

Vittorio clutched eagerly at Manning's hand, and the lines at the corners of his eyes bunched in trollish geniality.

'Signor Sergente, what a wonderful surprise. I didn't expect you before Sunday.' The arm stiffened noticeably and Manning found himself being manœuvred by it into the street. 'Come and meet my family,' said Vittorio. 'My wife, my beautiful daughters.'

'Let's go into the garage a moment,' Manning said, 'I want to speak to you privately.'

Vittorio stepped back through the opening and held the door for Manning. His face, that smoke-shrunken trophy of a Jivaro Indian, had borne for not more than a half-second the expression of a man who swallows a bitter purgative.

Manning strolled slowly round the garage. Vittorio flitted in the rear, with a smile as of torments bravely supported.

Manning picked up a tyre lying on a bench, a Dunlop cover from the walls of which, however, the trade name, number and size had been partially removed. An electrical instrument reposed on the bench beside the tyre and had evidently been used to perform this operation. 'A civilian tyre,' said the voice of Vittorio in his ear, 'imported before the war. Not a military one.'

Manning turned to look at him and Vittorio shook his head in painful confirmation of this claim.

'Why trouble to take the name off, then?' said Manning. 'What's in all those drums?'

'Oil,' said Vittorio after a period of hesitation.

'Petrol, you mean,' said Manning, sniffing. 'How much do you pay?'

'Believe me, sergente, I keep my nose clean in these things.'

'Where does all the petrol come from, then?'

'The carabinieri store it here.'

Manning picked up another tyre which possessed a Dunlop tread but which was described on its walls as being of Pirelli manufacture. 'The finished product, I see. Where did you get this hybrid from?'

Vittorio's face was twisted in increasing embarrassment. 'I bought it. Everyone does the same.'

'Is that your car?' Manning nodded in the direction of a well polished Fiat, Mille-cento, standing on wood blocks in the corner. He went over and looked round it approvingly. The car seemed in remarkably good condition. 'Do you find a tendency for the doors to develop rattles in these pillarless saloons?' he asked.

Vittorio shook his head in grinning misery.

'How's the steering?' Manning asked, after rocking the steering wheel and trying the wheel bearings. 'It seems all right.'

'Not bad,' Vittorio admitted.

'Transmission?'

'Needs an overhaul.'

'Engine?'

'Terrible. Rebore long overdue. Have to fit new main bearings and regrind the crank-shaft. The oil consumption's phenomenal. It's done a very big mileage. Dynamo doesn't work. Clutch needs renewing.'

'How long would it take?'

'How long?' Vittorio said. 'It can't be done at all in these days. Couldn't get the parts.'

'It must look a lot better than it is,' said Manning.

'Yes,' said Vittorio. 'That's it. It looks a lot better than it is.'

'But to all intents and purposes it is really a wreck?'

'Yes.'

'Never mind,' said Manning. 'It will have to do.'

'I don't understand.'

'Have you ever seen a requisition order before?' asked Manning. 'I've got one here for you. All I need is the details of the car, and I'll hand it over to you.'

41

Vittorio, whose insistent smile had deepened and frozen into a frantic grimace, reeled back as if menaced by raised stilettos. He recovered his balance. 'I'm sorry, sergente. This car can't be requisitioned. Wait a minute.' He pulled out his wallet and extracted a dirty paper.

> This is to certify that Fiat No. 18367L, belonging to PALUMBO, Vittorio, has been voluntarily placed at Allied disposal and is in no circumstances to be requisitioned.

It was signed by the chief A.M.G. officer for the area and dated a year previously.

'Colonel Forster,' said Vittorio, now cheerful once again. 'He was a great friend of the family. He used to have lunch with us on Sundays.'

The telephone rang and Vittorio picked up the receiver. 'Yes, yes, all right. Yes, I know, All right.' He hung up.

'I'm afraid this is no longer valid,' Manning said. 'This office is closed and the officer has left the area.'

'It's my living,' protested Vittorio. 'How am I going to keep my family?'

Manning looked at the licence disc. The car had not been taxed for two years. 'From what you say about its condition,' he said, 'you should be glad to be getting rid of it. You'll get compensation.'

'Sergente,' said Vittorio, suddenly changing tack. 'Couldn't we settle this. You know I told you that there was something else I wanted to see you about — well, we'll make this a separate transaction. I know where to find you another car. If you feel able to overlook this one, it would be worth a good many thou to me.'

'I'm sorry,' said Manning.

Vittorio seemed resigned. He raised the bonnet of the Fiat and showed Manning the engine. The cylinder head had been removed, exposing the pistons. The aluminium alloy gleamed dully in the dark sheen of the cylinder walls.

'It will take a couple of days to get all this put back,' said Vittorio. 'I suppose you can give me that much time?'

'Certainly,' said Manning. 'I'll look round tomorrow and see how you are getting on.'

He jotted down the necessary particulars on the requisition form and handed it to Vittorio, who folded it up and put it in his wallet.

At midday Manning saw the marshal.

'Well,' he said. 'It looks as though I shan't have to avail myself of your kind offer after all.'

'What offer was that?' asked the marshal. 'You mean the car?'

'Yes.'

'You managed to find one? You've been very clever. Wherever did you unearth it?'

'At Vittorio Palumbo's garage.'

'Ah,' said the marshal. 'That one. I see. Well, never mind. Perhaps you'll get it.'

'I'll get it,' said Manning. 'In two days' time, to be exact.'

'Congratulations. So many people have been after that car before and nothing has ever come of it. It's nice to know that someone has been successful at last. I should like to hear about your method some time.'

'Certainly,' said Manning, 'it's quite straightforward.'

'And you are quite sure you are getting it?' asked the marshal.

'Quite.'

'Then, once again, congratulations. I was beginning to be of the opinion that that car couldn't be requisitioned. Palumbo's family must be slipping up.'

'How's that?'

'Well, whenever anyone tried to requisition that car in the past, one of Palumbo's daughters went straight to someone at the top, and that put paid to that. I don't mind telling you that most of us here have had a try at that car at one time or another.'

'Those days are over,' said Manning. 'There's no one left to go to any more.'

'Perhaps she will come to you about it,' said the marshal wistfully. 'In that case it might be worth it.'

'Worth what?'

'Worth letting the car go.'

'No,' said Manning, 'it wouldn't be worth that.'

'Ah,' the marshal said, 'I don't know.'

WHEN Manning left the hotel he found the marshal at his side. 'I hope you've an hour or so to spare,' he said. 'I'd like to show you something of our town. What little of it remains.'

While he was talking they had reached the Corso Emanuele, which the marshal informed him was the main street previously noted for its fine shops and cafés. 'As you see,' he said, 'there's not much of it left.'

'It will be a lifetime before things get back to normal again,' said the marshal. 'Nowadays we just carry on. We are reduced to absolute essentials. People only concern themselves with the bare necessities of life. I ask you — what can you expect?'

They had reached a few gutted walls into which had been built a temporary booth-like construction housing in rudimentary form the business in previous existence on this spot. The enterprise thus resurrected to cope with the population's most basic needs was a confectioner's shop, the window of which was enticingly dressed with a great assortment of tiny, elaborate cakes. For these, sums varying between forty and sixty lire were demanded — approximately thirty to forty times their pre-war cost.

'How on earth do they manage to do it?' Manning asked the marshal. 'I always thought there was a great shortage of flour.'

'Of course,' the marshal agreed, 'there's a chronic shortage. In fact, there is so little to be had at the moment that it is hardly worth while making bread at all, so this is what becomes of most of it.'

In the next booth, vital necessity was represented by the business of a photographer named Filomena, who seemed to be doing a thriving trade and hoped to attract further patronage by displaying a selection of his art. From this window there gazed out upon utter desolation the representative faces of Malevento, upon all of which had been bestowed the air of cretinism which the cameras of such as Filomena so unfailingly discover. This display really amounted to a mass libel, for by vindictive manipulation of his lights, malevolent distortion of perspective, and a savage use of the retouching brush, the photographer had reduced his sitters to the grossest caricatures of themselves. Thus those who were by nature shy and reserved had been made to look sullen, the gay had become imbecile, the serene bovine and the naturally rugged of feature had been shown quite frankly as criminals of the worst type. Could it be, though, he wondered, that the sinister clairvoyance of the camera had in each case uncovered some latent and repulsive characteristic, which it threw into maliciously triumphant relief?

Manning found himself following the marshal into the next shop. Its window, draped in some dark blue material, was empty, and the shop too was empty inside save for a few chairs and a magnificent, silver-mounted coffin standing in a corner.

'Don Ugo Filosa — one of our leading personalities,' said the marshal, introducing the proprietor, who came out of an inner room.

They all sat down and Don Ugo sent a boy for coffee. He was a thin, grey-haired man with a kindly but acute expression. A benevolent ferret.

'Don Ugo likes to meet strangers,' said the marshal. 'He is the most cosmopolitan-minded man in our town.'

'Yes,' admitted Don Ugo, 'I believe in keeping my mind open and receptive to new influences, whether in social or business spheres. Provincialism is the curse of existence in a town like Malevento. One has to wage a relentless struggle against it. I intensely admire the cultural achievements of many countries other than our own. Take the case of the Argentine. Until my brother, who is now in partnership with me, came back from Buenos Aires, I frankly admit that I never realized the measure of progress achieved in the outside world. The standard of living there has reached a degree now when you can be buried in a casket of that new plastic stuff which is as soil-resistant as stone and costs a tenth of the figure. He tells me that some of the colour schemes and choices of finish are a joy to the eye. It goes to show you what mankind is capable of when allowed to develop its resources in peace.'

The marshal admired the coffin standing in the corner.

'Yes,' said Don Ugo with modest enthusiasm. 'It's a wonderful clearance line we managed to pick up. Pre-war stuff at a genuine give-away price. It's the kind of thing that gives us a real satisfaction to sell. The only trouble is it comes in a small size only, and people don't like the limbs to be cramped.' He eyed Manning and the marshal speculatively. 'I'm afraid it wouldn't suit either of you gentlemen.' He sighed. 'We'll never see its quality again.'

'What are you selling these days?' asked the marshal. 'I understand business is as brisk as ever.'

'What do we sell?' Don Ugo wrung his hands. 'Why, plain boxes — that's all you can call them — of the cheapest pinewood. They are so thin they cannot be relied upon to contain for any length of time. It's an offence to the imagination. It hurts me as a craftsman, too.'

As they got up to go, Don Ugo took the marshal aside. He spoke in a low voice, but the shop was so small that Manning could not help overhearing.

'Were you able to do anything in that other matter, marshal?'

'Other matter?'

'Yes, you know, that other matter. About the lead.'

'What about it?'

'Well, can I go ahead and buy it?'

'I'm not stopping you.'

'I want to know where I stand, that's all. You know there's a lot of fiddled lead from the cathedral roof being offered?'

'Yes, I know that.'

'Well, how can I tell what I'm getting if I buy lead? I don't want to get myself in a jam.'

47

'No,' said the marshal cordially, 'better not to do that.'

'Well, what do you suggest I do?'

'I don't know. How should I know? That's your business.'

'But would you take action? That's what I want to know.'

'I might have to. What do you expect me to say? If I thought you were buying hot lead I would have to, wouldn't I? You must be able to convince yourself that you are buying your lead from a legitimate source.'

'Look here, marshal,' urged Filosa, his reserve now gone by the board and making no attempt to lower his voice, 'why not look at the thing from a common-sense point of view? After all, the lead is wasted as it is, lying there buried under all that masonry. If anyone is helping himself — and I don't say anyone is — the sheer labour involved in getting it out must be enormous. Now, suppose that I do happen to get hold of some lead that came from the wrong place — and I don't see how I am to know — don't you agree that it is at least put to a better use in allowing Christians to go to their eternal rest in properly lined coffins than just leaving it to lie there where it is doing no good to anybody?'

'I should say that a theft of that kind is worse than ordinary crime,' said the marshal, 'it's sacrilege. The penalties would be very heavy.'

'Well, the answer is that I can't carry on,' said Filosa. 'You believe in the resurrection of the body, don't you? How do you think all those poor people are going to get on who are being put away, as things are, in coffins that don't contain for more than a few months?'

'You take your religion too literally,' said the marshal with reproof. 'Try to pay more attention to the underlying spirit. Materialism is one of the sins of our age.'

'Well, then, I'd like to know one thing,' Filosa said, trying in desperation another tack. 'How is it that the coppersmiths get all the metal they want? Everyone knows it all comes off the Black. I'll go further than that. I'm ready to point to a man in this town who took delivery of a hundred kilos of stolen

48

telegraph wire the other day. It's in his place now, openly, for anyone to see. Who is protecting him?'

'In my opinion, no one,' said the marshal coolly. 'Perhaps you have been misinformed, or on the other hand perhaps the law is just getting ready to act. It remains to be seen. In any case, I hear this kind of story ten times a day. Usually it doesn't stand up to investigation.'

'You are not even interested in having the name?' asked Filosa with a trace of bitterness.

'I've already told you,' the marshal said. 'If the man's done anything he shouldn't, be sure we know it already.'

Filosa shook his head in exasperation. He showed them to the door, however, with the greatest deference. 'Well, marshal, do your best for me. I know you won't let me down.'

The marshal smiled enigmatically but said nothing.

'Scandalous,' he remarked to Manning as soon as they were outside. 'The kind of suggestions people make these days.'

The last of these booths was occupied by a butcher. Manning followed the marshal over the threshold. There were no signs of activity within. The bench which had been used for the sundering of bleeding joints had been scrubbed until only a few faded stains remained. 'We've had no meat supplies for a month,' the marshal explained. For all that, a cool, sweet smell of stale blood hung upon the air.

The butcher appeared and silently shook hands with them. Placing a cautionary finger on his lips he led them into an inner chamber. In this several ladies were waiting, dressed as if for an informal reception at court. They wore elbow-length gloves and hats from which feathers protruded in various directions. Several shrouded forms were suspended from the ceiling, and the butcher went up to one of them and drew back the covering. This revealed a pig bisected with incredible precision from snout to tail. Several of the more presentable organs had been replaced, although not necessarily in their original order, and were held in place by some mysterious means. Manning was reminded of an

49

elaborate cross-section of a working model in an industrial exhibition.

The ladies were occupied with the other shapes which, when uncovered, proved to be entire lambs, their freshly flayed loins widely separated with that lack of *pudeur* often provoked by death. This area had in each case been decently veiled by the lining of the animal's stomach. The butcher switched on powerful back-lighting, throwing the small cadavers into artistic relief. One of the ladies approached and with gloved fingers delicately drew back a corner of the gauzy membrane to inspect with reverence the tasteful arrangement of entrails thus revealed. No one spoke.

The butcher, however, had been whispering to the marshal, and now, taking one of the lambs in his embrace, he laid it tenderly on a block.

'What is your particular fancy?' the marshal asked Manning. 'The scrag end? A gigot? . . . A shoulder, perhaps?'

Manning shook his head, but the marshal was insistent. 'This is our friend's way of welcoming you to our town. We don't want to offend him, do we?' He made a sign to the butcher, and the cleaver descended with what seemed to Manning quite shocking violence in such surroundings.

When, shortly after this, they left, each was carrying a neatly prepared parcel under his arm.

'We're in the best residential quarter now,' said the marshal as they turned off the Corso into a street that appeared to have suffered relatively little damage.

It was lined on both sides with what are known in the south of Italy as palazzi. These so-called palazzi are in reality blocks of flats, and all, whether on a grander or meaner scale, follow more or less the same plan. There is a large entrance gate known as the portone, through which coaches could formerly be driven into the courtyard, on either side of which a staircase ascends to the flats. Normally there are a number of flats on each floor, and there are four or five floors. Just inside the main gate lives the porter and his family, usually crouching in the semi-obscurity of a single room. There are several more single rooms, bassi, on the ground floor, sometimes tenanted by poor families and sometimes by artisans and small business men like stamp dealers and watch repairers. The porter has an uncanny knowledge of everything that goes on in the palazzo. He and his wife, even if they keep out of sight, usually know which of the tenants are at home at any time and who, if anyone, is with them. In fact, they develop a profound insight into the private lives of the inhabitants of the palazzo, becoming in the end familiar with all their movements, their habits, their various tastes, and are able even to forecast to a surprisingly accurate degree their future activities. In view of this special knowledge, they are regarded as excellent informants by the police, to whom they have learned it best to be subservient and who are continually paying them surprise visits.

'The population is very much concentrated now,' the marshal said. 'One house in five was left standing in the whole city, so enough people hang out in this street to justify its being considered a small town of its own.'

Certainly the street teemed, pulsated with life. The murmur that could be heard coming from it and that invaded the silent, deserted surrounding areas, had swollen into a roar as they entered the street itself. There were the raucous street cries of those hundreds of persons who engaged here at the kerbside in the sale of contraband goods; the ubiquitous squealing and whining of children; the mumbled importunities of a legion of beggars; the scolding of housewives; and the long-distance exchanges of badinage in which whole sentences were outweighed by the immense prolongation of the penultimate vowel. Heard, in fact, at a fair distance, such a conversation resolved itself into an exchange of an occasional isolated, much drawn out vowel or diphthong, one man shrieking with much gesticulation to the other: 'A-a-a-a-a-', and this followed by a pause, a con-

51

siderable silence, while the other's mouth opened and shut rapidly, and then: 'Ai-ai-ai-ai-ai-.'

And apart from the human yellings, there was a legion of shrill birds exposed in cages on the walls and undoubtedly encouraged by the surrounding pandemonium. Their whistles and trillings were eclipsed only by the sudden scream of a parrot or the blaring of a badly tuned radio set left on all day to emit gusty snatches of music alternating with crackling static and the distorted bellowings of political speakers.

Fortunately, too, there were human beings who succeeded in conversing with each other, when the need arose, in complete silence. For instance, it was always possible to observe someone leaning well out from a washing-festooned window on a top floor and carrying on a complicated dialogue with a friend in the street merely by the use of gestures.

In this street were offered for sale the results of that universal petty brigandage that had resulted from the breakdown of public morality in the shadow of defeat. It was as if the country had suddenly seethed with predatory termites; the voracious fauna of a tropical rain forest driven by some irresistible natural force to satiate their mass hunger; darting scorpion-like from crevices, advancing in solid formation like a plague of leaf-cutting ants, dropping like monkeys from lianas, chirping with eagerness, faces distorted with avarice, while fingers clutched, probed, delved and dismantled. Nothing could withstand this onslaught. No more than could the green shoots of sprouting corn withstand the visitation of the locust. Huge, ruined tanks, veritable land battleships, shrank as if their vitals had been attacked by some wasting disease, melted away as if their armour plating had been of ice. Urban buses were seen careering away into the remote fastnesses of the Appenines, there to be reduced in comfort to their component parts. Trams, which had been left where they had come to a standstill when the electricity failed, were spirited away — if such an expression is permissible in connection with trams — in the dead of the night. Even a railway engine, stranded in the open country owing to the looting of rails and sleepers, was driven off, when these same rails and sleepers were quite incredibly relaid, to a place more conveniently located for its demolition. No feat was too outrageous for this new breed of robbers. Small ships mysteriously left the high seas, and portions of their superstructures were subsequently observed miles inland, protruding from the surrounding orchards, as if they had been left high and dry by some stupendous tidal wave. God-fearing fishermen took retaliation on this piracy-in-reverse by scaling hitherto unscalable cliffs to loot isolated castles perched upon them, using thereafter medieval tapestries to repair their sails. Nothing was too large or too small, from telegraph poles to phials of penicillin. In Naples, an orchestra which had been playing to an audience largely clothed in allied hospital blankets, returned from a five-minute interval to find all its instruments missing. On the same day newspapers reported that statues were disappearing from the public squares in Rome. On another occasion most of the tombstones were reported missing from one cemetery and all the resaleable flowers from another. The rare fish from the tropical aquarium of Malevento had vanished in twos and threes over a short period, and soon the aquarium was completely empty. A priceless collection of Roman cameos was abstracted from the museum there and replaced by valueless modern imitations, the thief only learning when he came to dispose of his booty that the originals themselves were counterfeit. At Carlona the new public lavatory disappeared by regular stages and in this order: the seats, pans, cisterns, pipes, doors, and finally the tiles from the walls. The products of such exploits and of innumerable others, some of them even stranger, were disposed of quite openly and often with vainglory in such street markets as this.

The confinement of many families in so restricted a living space had turned women into harridans. Manning and the marshal paused at one portone from which issued an unending stream of abuse. 'I'm telling you for the third and last time,' screamed a voice. This was followed by a furious clatter of cooking pots and the sound of breaking china. Then: 'Slut. Bitch. Whore!' screamed the voice again.

Such conditions affected the men, too. They spent considerable periods gesticulating fiercely at each other, but rarely came to blows.

In this portone lurked a scunizzio. The scunizzi had always existed in Naples, where poverty and misery were taken for granted. They were something new, however, so far as most of the other southern towns were concerned; boys varying between ten and fifteen years of age who had been left to do the best they could for themselves on the streets and had therefore either missed entirely, or been forced to curtail, the normal irresponsibilities of late childhood. The scunizzi, obliged to grow up at a few days' notice, had done this quite successfully from the psychological point of view, although obviously unable to develop their physical proportions in a similar way. They were marvellously adept at petty thieving, and apart from that lived on all manner of black market activities or on finding 'private girls' for soldiers, for peasants up in town on a day's spree or for commercial travellers, who were their real stand-by. The scunizzi wore a kind of uniform of their own, always including a military coat of some kind which was too long for the wearer, thus helping to strengthen the impression that they were really some strange, quite new and stunted race, a species of pygmy, pony-riding Asiatics which had evolved spontaneously in the tundra of stricken towns. These dwarfs were notable for the cheerful efficiency with which they attacked and solved the problems of living. Apart from their gaiety, there was nothing child-like about them. They competed with adults on even terms, and on their own ground they could always win.

This particular scunizzio held a packet of American cigarettes which had been opened — the cigarettes being offered for sale individually.

'How much are your Lustra Scarpe?' asked the marshal.

'That's what they call them,' he told Manning in an aside. 'I mean Loocky Strill, of course.'

'No Lustra Scarpe,' said the boy rather absently.

'What about Bearded Kings?' — 'Raleighs?' the marshal explained.

'No.'

'What have you got, then?'

'Humped Donkeys.'

'Camels,' the marshal interpreted. 'How much, then?'

'Ten apiece.'

'Give me two.'

The boy extended the packet, allowing the marshal to subject several cigarettes to a test which consisted of feeling the central portion of each with evident expertness. The boy watched the procedure tolerantly until the marshal, finally satisfied, made his selection. Then he shook his head. 'I don't go in for that kind of thing. This is my regular pitch. I've got my reputation to think of.'

'They take out the original filling,' said the marshal, 'and then refill the cigarettes with waste tobacco collected from ends. It's done very carefully with a plug of the real thing at each end. How much are your butt ends?' he asked the boy.

'If you are looking for native brands, I don't handle them. I could do you a hundred grammes of best assorted English and American ends for eighty lire.'

'Where do you get them from?'

'Rome, of course. If you are interested in bigger quantities I can quote you, but you'll have to give me a few hours' notice. The demand here is irregular.'

'What else do you specialize in?' asked the marshal.

'Do you want any oriental pills for ladies?' asked the scunizzio, producing a coloured tube. 'Guaranteed infallible. Apart from that I do warranted Naafi and P.X. supplies of all kinds.'

The marshal turned down the oriental pills. He and Manning moved on, branching off into a lane where the houses, small-scale and gloomy replicas of the palazzi on the Corso, although still standing, had been shattered internally. Shutters hung down from glassless windows through which the sky itself could sometimes be seen. In some cases the portoni were permanently closed and secured by chains or by bars of wood bolted across them. Other palazzi had lost their gates entirely and seemed to have been subjected to looters of the kind who have a use or a market for anything they can prise loose and carry away.

There was one such house, however, which appeared to have been quite recently rebuilt, evidently without regard to the cost of the materials used. The façade, after repair, had been refaced with decorative stone. The old-fashioned portone had been abolished and replaced by a street door which although quite ordinary as to size proclaimed the expensiveness of its construction in its highly polished wood, its bright, brass letter-box and the ornate figure in the shape of an angel, also of brass, which formed the knocker. The door also bore a number — five; presumably because this particular number happened to be admired by the door's proprietor, as no other house of the street was numbered and, in any case, this was not the fifth house. This magnificent door had a marble surround, and in spite of the richness of the materials employed the general effect was not without taste, although incongruous — startling, even — in these surroundings. It might have been the residence of a highly successful business man who had come by his wealth late in life and who made no move in such matters without being careful first to take advice.

The marshal pressed the bell, and immediately — as a result, it seemed, of some mechanism connected with the bell push — the door swung open.

Manning was surprised, therefore, to find standing there a uniformed maid who immediately turned and led the way up a plain marble staircase of the type one sees in important Italian banks of recent construction.

They were shown into a room on the mezzanine floor. The

faintly institutional character of the building as a whole was intensified here, perhaps, by the faint odour of incense which hung upon the air. To the subtle atmosphere Manning had previously noted — the blending, perhaps, of surgery and bourse — was now added a third influence, that of the temple; the shrine, however, he was beginning to suspect, of an antiseptic Aphrodite.

On one wall of this room, which was furnished with the expensive modernism that went with the house's façade, hung a large picture before which a candle burned. It was the portrait of an elderly woman whose rather fierce and hieratic expression owed much to the painter's extraordinary technique.

The marshal soon cleared up the mystery. It seemed that they were in the bagnio of the famous Zi' Stefano — Uncle Stephen — well known throughout southern Italy, said the marshal, for its perfect organization, its scrupulous attention to hygienic matters, the standard of propriety demanded of its patrons, the fairness of its tariff.

There was a circumstance connected with Zi' Stefano's acquisition of this house which had become almost legendary. It had previously been owned by the even more celebrated Zi' Margherita, who was the originator of these commendable standards and who, in fact, had raised in this way the tone of her profession throughout Italy and conceivably throughout the civilized world. It seemed, continued the marshal, that in middle age Zi' Margherita had been bereft of her husband. This placed her in a dilemma, as she wished to remain faithful to his memory as far as marriage went but felt at the same time a great need for the help, the protection and the spiritual solace of a man in the successful conduct of her establishment. At that time the present Zi' Stefano, then plain Stefano Trotta, had been in her employ more or less as a manager. Zi' Margherita decided that he would fill the bill nicely as far as she was concerned. There existed, however, a snag in the form of Stefano's wife, to whom he appeared to be reasonably attached and who might therefore object to the conclusion of an arrangement more intimate than the existing one.

Zi' Margherita, being a determined, energetic and above all straightforward woman, decided to lay all her cards on the table. She suggested that Stefano's wife should renounce her marital claims in her favour during the remainder of her, Zi' Margherita's life, in which case she would make the pair her co-heirs.

The proposition was attractive because Zi' Margherita was already in her sixties whereas both Stefano and his wife being only half her age could be expected to survive her by many years. Agreement was reached and both parties kept faithfully to their bargain, living together in the greatest harmony. When, about ten years later, the old woman died, she was sincerely mourned by both husband and wife, who now resumed their interrupted connubial relationship. Even to this day, the marshal assured Manning, neither party ever referred to Zi' Margherita other than by such terms of affection as 'our dear Aunt', or 'that sainted woman'.

The room into which Manning and the marshal had been shown had originally been Zi' Margherita's bedroom and was now kept almost like a chapel to her memory. Only specially favoured guests were ever received there. The portrait of Zi' Margherita had been a post-mortuary one, the Aunt's death having been sudden and unexpected. Owing to the solemnity of the circumstances, the commission was given to a painter who specialized in icons of the Virgin, working faithfully to ancient Byzantine traditions in which other-worldliness, assisted by emphasis on symmetry and the suppression of naturalistic detail, was chiefly aimed at. In this instance the painter was aided only by memory and a photograph taken by Filomena who had been, as ever, unsympathetic in his interpretation. The resultant face that now stared down at them was evidently that of a dark and aged goddess of the underworld, a bejowled Cybele whose dew-laps and double chins interposed a rhythmic counterpoint to the evenly disposed folds of her blouse.

'In such houses,' said the marshal, making casual conversation, 'the real problem is that of the discreet reception of guests. You can divide these into two main categories: those who are arriving and those who are leaving. It's the frame of mind, of course, that's different. In either case nobody wants to be met on the stairs by someone he knows. The waiting-rooms on the mezzanine floor serve as a kind of marshalling yard. The visitor is kept here until the coast is clear for him to go up to the main reception-rooms. In all these kinds of arrangements Zi' Stefano excels. He is a man of great finesse. I don't know whether you noticed the arrangement of the street door. Naturally enough, people are not keen on being seen in the street ringing the bell of this house. So a maid waits in a cubicle just inside the hall, and you haven't time to get your finger off the bell press before the door's opened. At the same time a red light flashes on in the office upstairs, and if anyone is coming down at that moment he is side-tracked into one of the waiting-rooms.'

'And what happens if he is already passed the mezzanine floor?'

'That's where the system breaks down occasionally, but it's a very rare thing.'

The marshal's encomium of Zi' Stefano's organization was curtailed by the entrance of the great organizer himself.

The owner of the house corresponded reasonably well to Manning's preconception of him. He was a quiet man, reserved in manner, grey-haired, of muddy complexion and possessing that facial heaviness, that slightly brooding expression which seemed inclined to accompany worldly success in this country. There was a distinction, which appeared to cut across classes as well as through walks in life. It was not entirely a matter of mere monetary acquisition. Roughly there were two types: the heavy, solemn-faced men who had got where they wanted to be, who regarded themselves, whatever the rest of the world thought of them, as successes; and the sharply featured, nervous and jittery ones who had not. And, of course, there were all sorts of intermediary types who were in the process of getting heavy and solemn or increasingly thin and excitable, and of the former order the marshal struck Manning as being a good example. One day, if he lived long enough, the marshal would be in proud possession of a Zi' Stefano type of face. Manning was sure this was not merely a matter of feeding, because he had already observed certain dismal failures who never failed to cram themselves to bursting point at meal times but whose faces, for all that, were stamped with ever-increasing apprehension of what was to come. Satiation of the spirit, then, rather than of the body. That would be the explanation.

Zi' Stefano sat there answering the marshal's questions briefly and in a voice that was little more than a whisper. He rarely contributed a remark of his own. Manning felt that he was wholly content to continue in this way. He was a man of few words but obviously none the less friendly for this lack of effusiveness.

What would he have taken the man for if he had met him casually — in a bar, for instance? Not a professional man, and not a farmer. No, certainly not a farmer, not even a prosperous one, with that unhealthy pallor of his. No, there was something about him, if you studied him sufficiently with patience and with imagination — something that emerged, a strange factor, subtle and barely discernible but yet apparent in every gesture that stamped him for what he was. And of what was this factor compounded? Above all, of a diffidence, a certain obscure lack of confidence that lived in uneasy condominion with that other and obvious confidence of a man who has arrived.

And it was just this factor which in a vague and certainly unanalysed form gave Zi' Stefano himself considerable trouble. Worse still, he had been obliged to accept the fact that it was a thing felt, discerned by all and sundry. He had noted that never in any circumstances did anyone go out of his way to address him as Don. Any one of those thousand lawyers of straw who had never seen a client, or of the similar number of doctors who had never had the chance to apply a poultice — yes. Or any of those ruined land-owners, men who were becoming almost transparent through starvation, inheritors of a few remote, boulder-strewn acres on the slope of a mountain — yes again. A schoolmaster down on his uppers ... a petty capitalist like Don Enrico ... a successful merchant like Filosa the coffin maker. Yes. Yes. Yes. But he, Stefano Trotta — no. Although nobody, positively nobody had raised an objection to eating a meal at his expense, to borrowing money from him, or even asking him to subscribe to charities — which he did, liberally. But thus he remained, always referred to behind his back as Zi' Stefano or to his face as plain Signor Trotta. Not even Alberto at the Hotel Vesuvio. Not even Alberto, who would bend over him when he took his seat in the restaurant, with the air of the devil producing a select temptation. Not even Alberto would give him Don. And yet, he considered bitterly, he, Zi' Stefano, performed in society in an exemplary way a function which the State recognized as necessary and to which it accorded its protection. He also paid his taxes, owed no man anything, and outside minor unpleasantnesses which were to be expected with competitors in his line of business, had never made an enemy.

Zi' Stefano suddenly cut into the conversation, which until this point had remained on a level of desultory small talk about local conditions and black market prices.

'It was very kind of you to bring your friend along, marshal. I wonder if you'd object if I asked his advice about my place in Naples. You've heard it's been shut?'

The marshal was much surprised. 'Your new place in Naples shut? What on earth for? Surely not for any slip-up in the hygenic regulations?'

'No,' said Zi' Stefano, 'naturally not that. The old-established people there — the ring — knew they couldn't meet our competition by fair means. Couldn't cope with our quality or our prices. So they clubbed together and got some high-up in the military government to have us closed down. No reasons given.'

61

'What were you charging?' asked the marshal.

'We slashed the rate to a hundred lire. That's still a thousand per cent up on pre-war, which is a pretty fair reflection of the rise in the cost of living. But it's a fifth of what the others were charging. And you know our standards. We never cut down on quality.'

The marshal nodded sympathetically.

'We believed we were doing the fair thing,' Zi' Stefano said. 'Not only that, but the smart thing. Disinflation must come sooner or later. We all know that. The sensible thing was to take the bull by the horns, accept the buyers' market as being really in existence, and get back to reasonable price levels again. It's best in the long run, even if it does mean working a bit harder for all concerned. The days of easy money couldn't last for ever.'

'Especially with the Allies clearing out everywhere at the speed they are.'

'Except in Naples, which they tell me is becoming a permanent base,' said Zi' Stefano. 'The only people with money to burn these days are peasants who have been keeping it in boxes under their beds right through the war. Well, without wanting to be considered snobs, you probably realize that's not the kind of trade we cater for.'

'Did you have any concrete proposition in mind?' asked the marshal, caressing the tip of his thumb with his forefinger as if testing the thickness of a bank note.

'Well,' said Zi' Stefano, 'not really a proposition. Too vague for that. Just a few ideas on the subject. What I want to find is someone prepared to put in a word for me in the right place. That's all I really need. If the thing could be properly explained to whoever has the say-so, I'm sure we could get together. I am ready to offer all kinds of inducements, special rates for the troops and so on; or, if the volume of work could be guaranteed, I wouldn't even say no to reserving the place exclusively for allied use. They could carry out all the inspections they like. Run the whole thing themselves if they wanted to.'

'It sounds quite a good plan,' said the marshal. 'You don't by any chance know anyone who could help Zi' Stefano out?' he asked Manning.

'No, I don't know anyone.'

'A pity,' said the marshal.

'Naturally, he wouldn't be expected to take on a job like that for love,' said Zi' Stefano.

'No,' said Manning, 'of course not.'

'He'd be doing two good turns: one to the allies and one to me. I don't forget my friends.'

'I'm sure you don't.'

'Zi' Stefano is too open-handed,' said the marshal. 'That's where he makes a mistake. He always gets taken advantage of. It's an ungrateful world.'

'Ungrateful isn't the word,' said Zi' Stefano. He grimaced mournfully. 'Well, it can't be helped. Perhaps you will turn the idea over in your mind. I am losing a small fortune every day my place is shut. The overheads go on just the same, you know. Have to keep the staff on and pay them, whether they work or not. You can imagine it would be worth a good deal to me to be able to start business again.' Zi' Stefano sighed and relaxed in his chair, evidently relieved at having unburdened himself.

There was a moment of silence before the marshal spoke. 'Zi' Stefano has always been a great admirer of the allies. In the days when we had troops here in Malevento some of the boys used to treat his place just like their own home.'

'They did,' said Zi' Stefano. 'We liked to have them drop in at any time, day or night. I'm not talking about business now. We always had a hot meal and a hearty welcome waiting for them. We tried to give them some of the things they were missing in being away from their own homes.'

'Not like some of the other firms,' said the marshal. 'Tell him that story about the Beacon at Naples.'

'To tell you the truth, I don't much like telling it,' said Zi' Stefano. 'In my opinion it doesn't reflect to the credit of our

63

profession as a whole. Least said soonest mended about that kind of thing, I say.'

'Go on, tell him. It's an old story now and the principal figure went back to his own country long ago. So what does it matter?'

'Well,' said Zi' Stefano, 'the story refers to a well-known Neapolitan industrialist who was very justly given a year by an A.M.G. court for being found in possession of a large quantity of stolen allied goods.'

'The Germans would have put a bullet through him,' said the marshal.

'Yes,' said Zi' Stefano, 'but if they'd wanted to shoot everyone they caught with stolen goods they'd have run out of ammunition. By the time one shipload out of every three of army supplies that came into the port went into the black market, the thing was serious.'

'And those who did get caught considered themselves victimized,' said the marshal.

'Of course. They saw so many getting away with it that in the end it became the normally accepted thing. Everyone was actually trafficking in stolen goods or at least buying them for their own consumption. I don't care who you like to mention: public figures, prominent Churchmen, the aristocracy — they all did it. Even the police.'

'Even the Police?' said the marshal. 'You don't say that.'

'Even the Squadra Nucleo, the specially selected and specially paid body of men whose only job was to fight corruption.'

'The Squadra Nucleo?' said the marshal, raising an eyebrow.

'Yes, even the Squadra Nucleo,' said Zi' Stefano. 'You must know that as well as I do, marshal. The only difference between a Squadra Nucleo man and one from any of the other branches is that his price is higher. While we are on the subject, let me tell you something about the Squadra Nucleo. You've heard that our leading surgeon — no names mentioned — has a stolen car?'

'No,' said the marshal.

Zi' Stefano smiled bitterly. 'The ordinary investigation

64

bureau were put on his track. He made them an offer of fifty thousand lire. They turned it down.'

'Fifty thousand lire is not to be sneezed at,' said the marshal.

'The Squadra Nucleo got to work on him. It cost him a quarter of a million for a new registration book with a lot of faked previous entries. Our leading surgeon. Just think of that.'

'You are too puritanical,' said the marshal. 'What's the fact that he's a surgeon got to do with it? Why mention it, even? Does it make his surgery any the worse?'

'I just say that to give you some idea of the way we are heading,' said Zi' Stefano. 'It's the finger of Nemesis. The writing on the wall. There's no virtue left.'

'I don't expect virtue,' said the marshal. 'Virtue usually goes with gland trouble. All I ask is that people don't stick their necks out too far.'

'From the Questore down to the lowest agent, they have their price, whether it's in millions or hundreds. It's a subject I feel very bitter about,' said Zi' Stefano.

'As Italians, should we wash our dirty linen in public?' asked the marshal.

'I don't care,' said Zi' Stefano. 'Look at all the Questori who have been kicked out or are pushed about from one post to another. Gentlemen of their education. It's shocking. Betraying their trust for pieces of silver.'

'What about the industrialist?' said the marshal.

'I hadn't forgotten,' said Zi' Stefano, 'I was coming to him. Well, as I was saying, this industrialist got a year and, of course, thought himself very badly treated. However, I regret to say that even when you are safely inside an Italian prison it's the same old story. Graft. There's supposed to be a regular tariff for smuggling out secret messages, and the industrialist had no trouble at all in getting a letter to his wife containing the most detailed instructions of what he wanted her to do. He knew a very intelligent girl working in the Beacon at the time, and his wife had to go to see her and arrange for her to visit a high

65

A.M.G. official, passing herself off as the industrialist's wife. The wife was to lend the girl her smartest clothing and jewellery for the occasion. The girl was told to make it fairly obvious to this high official that she would be quite willing in her role of wife to plead for her husband's freedom in a very special way, if by doing this she could be sure of producing results. It all went off as planned, and a couple of days later the husband was released.'

'And everyone was satisfied,' said the marshal. 'The industrialist obviously, the high allied official, who will think of himself as a dashing seducer for the rest of his life. Even more so the girl, who picked up ten thousand lire for a couple of hours' work. She can't be said to have done too badly.'

'No,' said Zi' Stefano, 'especially as I happen to know that her bill of health, which she wasn't entitled to, had been fixed up for the occasion by one of the doctors at the Pace for a bribe of two thousand lire, leaving her a clear profit of eight thousand.'

'I never heard that part,' said the marshal, 'it makes a good finish to the story.'

'Ah,' said Zi' Stefano morosely, 'but the ends of justice were defeated. It shows a terrible lack of ethical sense on the part of the people at the Beacon, allowing themselves to be party to a trick like that. Just imagine if the high official had happened to visit the place afterwards and had found the girl there. They wouldn't have known where to put their faces.'

VI

THAT evening he was invited to the house of the Sindaco, the town's most prominent citizen, corresponding roughly to mayor although perhaps at one and the same time of both greater and lesser importance in the life of the community. Greater — because of the extraordinary times, the dislocation of normal existence, often the near-anarchy in which the Sindaco had the opportunity to wield emergency powers that in other times would have been shared with or delegated to others. Lesser — on account of the semi-breakdown, sometimes complete breakdown, of the mechanism through which such powers might have been wielded.

The man called upon to occupy this post might well have felt his heart quail as he surveyed the prospect that confronted him. Even in some isolated mountain village which had escaped the tidal wave of war, the democratic Sindaco taking up the reins which had slipped many months previously from the fingers of his predecessor, the Podesta, had enough to do to keep his head above water. In large, devastated towns like Malevento, then, the task was plainly Herculean.

These were some of the problems: He would be faced with a partial breakdown in communications, with inadequate food supplies, contaminated water, with diseases assuming epidemic proportions but with no vacant beds in the hospitals, with no nurses, with the medical supplies exhausted. The officials serving him would be grossly underpaid and therefore unavoidably corrupt, the police force would be almost non-existent but bandits so numerous and so bold that they no longer stopped short of invading the towns and fighting pitched battles among themselves in the streets over the division of the spoils. He would find the prisons crammed to double and treble capacity with desperadoes, petty offenders and many innocent victims of frame-ups. The life of his community would be riven by bitter feuds. He would be embarrassed by the existence of over sixty officially constituted political parties, some violent in their methods and each one claiming to possess the sole 'key to the country's salvation'. The public granary would be empty, there being no police available to compel the peasants to deliver their produce for sale at impossibly low fixed prices. Instead the producers would be selling to the black market in Naples and Rome, whence towns in remote rural areas might be obliged to repurchase the produce of their own regions at several times the prices originally paid to the peasants.

These were a few of the tasks. And the man? He would be appointed by the Allied Military Government from a list supplied by the local Committee of Liberation after the said Military Government had made, on its own account, a few preliminary inquiries. Above all, he was supposed to be free from the taint of Fascism. The unearthing of such a candidate was a considerable feat because however little a man might have bothered himself in the past with politics, he found out sooner or later that lip service to the system was essential, unless he was prepared to lead a life of almost complete seclusion. A few there were who remained undaunted by this prospect, perhaps largely on account of the way they were made. They disliked the hurly-burly of life under the average competitive conditions of modern society. They preferred to cultivate their own gardens. Among these were possible candidates.

There were also men who had been Socialists in their youth and before the advent of the Fascist regime. As a result they had lived under a cloud and however much they might have changed their minds since, however much they might have regretted this early allegiance, the Fascists would have none of them. These, too, now emerged from the chrysalis of twenty years as potential reconstructors of the new world.

There were yet others who had been refused admission to the Party because of something discreditable that was known of them from the civil point of view. They had been convicted, perhaps, of a criminal offence in some remote part of the country, and although they had succeeded in hushing it up in their home towns, the facts were recorded — or, at least, had been until recently — in the police archives. Among those to offer themselves as guiders of the people's destiny were many of this class.

There were cranks of all kinds who had also, and on this account, been unacceptable to the preceding regime; picturesquely bearded religious dissenters, men who were frankly employable as circus clowns, obvious eccentrics like the one who, after actually being appointed Sindaco, had a poster stuck up denouncing his whole village for some imagined theft.

There were also a few refugees who had returned with the overthrow of the regime. They had grown to live in a special world of their own, governed by political theories which were sacred and inviolable, but which took no account of the special emergencies of the situation.

Finally, it can be safely said that there were a few genuine Socialists, men of tremendous strength of character who had preserved their ideals untarnished through the bitter and uneven fight. Some of these had been in prison or confino time and again, and had even been bold enough to restate their faith for the benefit of the prison governor whenever they were brought before him for one of the routine questionings. Such men actually existed, but in most cases their best years and their strength had been squandered in the unequal struggle. Even if the warping effect of the long years in prison were to be ruled out, how could these men, most of them in their late middle years, be expected to tackle with success the problems which might well have daunted the most energetic of men standing on the threshold of life?

These categories, however, in the main, made up the reserve upon which it was proposed to draw to assist at the democratic rebirth of the country.

And to whom could the Sindaco turn for aid in the accomplishment of his tremendous labours? To a Council composed inevitably of men regarded as respectable on account of their University studies but in other respects possessing the limitations of the Sindaco himself. He could expect to receive an endless amount of advice — most of which would be interested — but there would be few helping hands. The chief concern of his Council would be, indeed, the settlement of personal vendettas against business, professional or political competitors who in the past had allowed themselves to be carried along by the stream and whose success, the embittered democrats had easily persuaded themselves, could never have been due to any factor but political favour. The emphasis in the deliberations of the Council would fall, not so much upon the rebuilding of the country as upon the successful hounding down and elimination of those who seemed to have brought it to this pass.

The Sindaco indicated the sombre and grossly over-furnished Victorian apartment with a gentle and deprecatory wave of the hand. 'Our ivory tower. Here we lead our quiet and reflective existences, Papa and I, shut away from the turbulences of the world. I rarely go out.' His finger-tips fluttered appreciatively over the lapel of the civilian suit Manning was wearing. 'I tire easily. Perhaps I lack a sense of adventure. Papa and I keep each other company at home.'

He glanced with filial affection at an old man who occupied an armchair on the other side of the room. This ancient sat there, his toothless jaw thrust forward in a habit of aggression, the hairless skull of a newly hatched bird supported on a neck in which every tendon stood out sharply from the profound defiles of skin. Don Arturo Vico's old face was set in an expression of almost painful malice.

The Sindaco continued to look tenderly in the old man's direction. 'Papa's hearing is not so good as it was. You have to speak rather distinctly to make him hear.

'Well, Papa, how's the appetite?' he suddenly bellowed.

70

The old man twisted his rooster's neck eagerly. 'Appetite, curse it!' he shrieked back. 'Why talk to me about appetite when the food's always late these days?'

'His digestion's still good,' said the Sindaco, smiling affectionately. 'Thank the Lord for His mercies to us. And he doesn't need teeth,' the Sindaco giggled, 'he only eats spaghetti.'

'What are you two plotting over there?' Don Arturo suddenly roared, the output from his lungs soughing through the bare gums like a gale in the eaves.

'I was saying you eat only spaghetti, Papa.'

'In the first place, don't mumble like that.'

'I'm not mumbling, Papa,' howled the Sindaco.

'You are mumbling, curse it,' persisted his father. 'Apart from that, don't talk bloody nonsense. God on earth! To hear him talk you'd think I was a hillbilly. I eat tagliatelli, too, don't I? As a matter of fact, I'm partial to it.'

'Well, tagliatelli too,' conceded the Sindaco. 'Spaghetti and tagliatelli. Anyway, there's no difference.'

'No difference?' shrieked Don Arturo. 'No difference between spaghetti and tagliatelli? You're out of your mind. You'll be classing lasagna with spaghetti next.'

'I do,' said the Sindaco with an unexpected flash of defiance. 'I lump them all together. It's just a matter of how the pasta is rolled and cut. There's no discernible difference in the taste.'

'What decadence!' said Don Arturo, averting his head in disgust. 'To stand there like that and brag about one's ignorance in cultural matters, after the education I gave you. What decadence.'

The Sindaco shrugged his shoulders resignedly and turned to Manning again. His thin face, the remnant of his widow's peak now represented by a few sparse but vigorous black hairs, the large, hooked nose, the close, deep-set eyes, his habit of emitting a nervous coughing sound intended as laughter, all contributed to give him the aspect of a gentle and solicitous demon.

'As I was remarking,' he said, 'I rarely go out. I prefer a life of

71

reflection. If anything, I lean temperamentally speaking towards the mysticism of the East. Are you familiar with the Vedanta? Let me show you my life's work.'

He produced from the bookshelf a slender volume. Manning read the title: *Further Considerations on the Problem of Perpetual Motion.*

'I gave ten of my best years to it,' said the Sindaco. 'Naturally, it's a bit above most people's heads. I published it privately for circulation among my friends.'

'I hear you are a barrister,' said Manning. 'Have you never practised?'

The Sindaco shook his head. 'No member of the learned professions who is a genuine native of Malevento ever does so. Sons of good families take their degrees as a matter of course, but the population is too small, in any case, to provide a living for more than a few. To get down to figures, we have about five hundred doctors and lawyers in a population of fifty thousand. This being so, rather than squabble among ourselves we are content to leave what little business there is to outsiders from Naples, fellows who by vulgar enterprise have pushed themselves up from the lower classes and who naturally wouldn't get any clients where they are known.'

'In any case, you find your duties sufficiently strenuous?'

'I should do so if I allowed them to be. As it is, I arrange for the Council to meet here, and we always conduct our business over a good meal. That makes things easier. Incidentally, the Councillors will be arriving in a few minutes' time and we shall all have dinner together.'

Manning's eyes roamed round the walls of the room. There was a large framed notice which said: 'Misery is the Result of Vice and Sloth.' Apart from that, the walls were crowded by closely spaced rows of the works of the Neapolitan impressionists. In one corner, however, this saccharine uniformity was broken by something different which on close examination proved to be a Sienese primitive, representing the nativity. It was in a highly

72

elaborate frame of the period, richly ornamented in blue and gold.

'An authentic Sassetta,' said the Sindaco, who had followed him softly. 'A treasure.'

'Booty of war!' shrilled a macaw-like scream.

Turning, half-startled, Manning saw the old man straining forward eagerly in his chair.

'Loot!' The word whistled through the room. 'Swag taken by the Manfredoni in the Papal wars.' Don Arturo's eyes were burning as if from high fever. 'The Manfredoni were always with the Popes because that made it easier to keep what they got their claws on. All our old families here were Manfredoni retainers and you can be sure we had our share.'

'Don't insist on that aspect of it, Papa,' yelled the Sindaco reproachfully. 'Don't use the word loot either. It isn't loot any more after a few hundred years; it's legitimate property.

'All the same,' he confided to Manning, 'it's a striking thought that a descendant of the original owner might easily get five years hard for trying to steal back what the Manfredoni stole from his ancestors five centuries ago.'

The Councillors were now beginning to arrive, and shortly afterwards they were ushered into an adjoining room where at the invitation of the Sindaco they settled like graceful carrion birds round the dinner table.

The Sindaco assisted his old father into a kind of infant's chair at the head of the table, where he perched, an aged but watchful condor above the glistening wilderness of table linen and plate.

On a side table a curious ceremony was being performed. A maid-servant was forking masses of spaghetti from a huge pot and weighing it on a pair of scales before transferring it to the plates.

The Sindaco winked pleasantly at Manning. 'A little game of ours. A harmless competition we get a lot of fun out of, although the results are a foregone conclusion. It's a contest to see who can eat the most spaghetti. Except on rare occasions when he's bilious, Dr. Serra always wins.'

73

The doctor, a pinkish man with the angry eyes of chronic dyspepsia, shook his head modestly.

The fame of Dr. Serra, the only practising medical man to be present, had already reached Manning's ears. The doctor came of a gifted family of Amalfitano craftsmen who specialized in the fabrication of those ingenious and intricate cabinets of inlaid woods sold chiefly to the tourists of Naples, Sorrento and Capri. The doctor, having inherited all the family's manipulative genius, plus vision in excess of the average, had put this to good use in becoming a surgeon. He specialized in the restoration of virginity by surgical means, openly boasting of having improved upon nature's provisions in this matter by supplying hymens of varying degrees of resistance, according to taste. His fee for this service was 10,000 lire. In this way he had quickly amassed a fortune and acquired a following of regular and highly satisfied clients.

'Papa's the runner up when he competes,' the Sindaco continued, 'although he held his place as champion until only a few years ago. As usual, I'm nowhere in the running. Perhaps competition doesn't accord with my philosophic outlook. Still, I try to be a sportsman and look forward to the day when I may acquit myself with more distinction. It takes the best part of a lifetime to develop a real spaghetti stomach.'

Each Councillor was now confronted with his plate, upon which a mountain of spaghetti rose up, writhing like extruded bowels and ensanguined with tomato sauce.

The Sindaco paused between huge mouthfuls, the tattered remnants of which, hanging tusk-like from his teeth, reminded Manning of an emaciated but amiable boar. 'Look at Papa,' he panted.

The old man, in fact, was cleaning up his plateful with a display of the most impressive technique. Don Arturo's method was to plunge his fork deep into the mound on his plate, and with a few preliminary twists bring up a writhing mass, the load in miniature of a hay-maker. This would be supported by his spoon held beneath until by dint of further skilful twists of the fork the mass

74

impaled on its prongs assumed a compact shape. As this burden neared them, the jaws extended incredibly, obviously to the point of dislocation, in a way indeed which Manning had until now regarded as being the peculiar attribute of certain snakes. The eyes followed the approaching load with an ever-increasing squint. The portals of the mouth reached, Manning heard the faintest hiss, the jaws snapped to, and for a fraction of a second the old man's face was twisted in a grin of passion. Instead, however, of the period of rumination which Manning had expected, a champing of the gums in at least a token of mastication, the cheeks immediately deflated, and this deflation was followed by a sudden boa-constrictor like distention of the neck, a dangerous heightening of the face's colour, a final convulsion — and already Don Arturo's fork was at work again.

'The ornamental style — supposed to have been introduced by the Bourbons,' said the Sindaco. 'Don Fernando IV was said to have demonstrated it for the first time in his box at the Naples opera. Of course, it is one of those old-world graces, a gastronomic gongorism that still survives here and there but to all intents and purposes is as obsolete as lavender spats or a coach and pair. Spectacular, yes — but for competitive purposes lacking in science and speed. It's like trying to win a swimming race with the breast stroke: you just tire yourself out. Now watch Dr. Serra.'

Even to a layman it was obvious that the doctor outclassed all the rest. Above all, his seriousness, his grim concentration, were in evidence. The doctor was conducting a total war. He was demolishing a strong-point, stabbing at his plate viciously and with tremendous speed, ruthlessly severing with the edge of his fork those coils of spaghetti which Don Arturo had tenderly preserved intact. Whereas Don Arturo's expression had been lascivious, Dr. Serra's was indignant. Don Arturo ravished, he slaughtered. This was the victory of hate over love.

'You are not eating,' protested the Sindaco with concern.

Manning had, in fact, come to the end of his tether after the

75

first few mouthfuls. He felt an intolerable distention of the stomach, although there was no apparent decrease in the mound on his plate.

'Take your time,' said the Sindaco, 'take your time. You will be feeling empty again in a few minutes.' He signalled to the maid to weigh out another plateful. 'To you, of course, spaghetti is something new. Perhaps it takes a little time to get used to it, but let me try to explain to you how a practised eater feels – his philosophy, in fact. To us it provides the perfect alliance between the senses of taste and touch. Half the pleasure comes from the act of swallowing. With other victuals this part of the procedure is unavoidably hasty and unimportant, but we spaghetti eaters succeed in protracting it by swallowing mouthfuls which cram the whole of the gorge. By virtue of its blandness, it cannot cause discomfort, and its passage downwards is controlled at will by the real expert – the *illuminé* – by the development of special muscles. All these things, of course, take time.'

A bird-like cackle came from the old man who, breathing gustily, awaited his second plateful. 'If he doesn't like it, what about giving him something else?'

A dish of meat garnished with some kind of vegetable immediately appeared before Manning, which he felt obliged out of politeness to taste. The steam from his fresh helping was by now curling round Don Arturo's nostrils, but his eyes never left Manning's plate. 'Well, how do you like the spinach?' he screeched suddenly.

Manning looked up with poised fork. 'It's excellent, thanks.'

'It should be,' said the ancient voice, breaking into a titter, 'considering we put the blacks sent by the Germans under the spinach bed.' Don Arturo took a medium-sized forkful of spaghetti, guffawed, choked, went purple in the face, while the Sindaco rushed to his aid.

'I'm surprised at you, Papa,' he scolded when the old man had recovered his breath. He turned apologetically to Manning. 'Don't take any notice of him, he's raving. The Abyssinian war

76

went to his head. Papa, I'm ashamed. Blacks under the spinach bed! What will he think of next?'

The old man was busy with his spaghetti again, and although he seemed abashed, his sniggers continued to filter through the mouthfuls.

The next few minutes were given over to silent consumption, and then after unsuccessfully pressing further helpings on the guests the Sindaco rose to announce that Dr. Serra had won the competition with an intake of 1.4 kilogrammes. The doctor acknowledged the cheers and hand clapping, with a weary smile. 'I was hoping to have broken my record today. Probably could have done so with the white kind of pasta. No reflections on you, Sindaco, of course. I realize it is next door to impossible to get. In fact, with this accursed black market going on as it is quite unchecked, who knows when we will ever see the real thing again?'

Cigars were lit and Manning's neighbour to the right turned to him. He was a doctor of philosophy whose head had been averted until now, and Manning had been half-consciously admiring a velvety roll of flesh at the base of the skull. The doctor had pink and vigorous flesh from which surprisingly white hair sprouted. When he nodded his head in emphatic agreement with something that was said, this roll divided into two, remaining thus until the doctor had occasion to shake his head in negation.

'I hear you've been in the north,' the doctor of philosophy said. 'Did you by any chance see any of our partisans in action? I read in the newspaper they are making a film about them.'

Before Manning could reply another voice broke in. 'Why always the northerners?' it growled. 'Couldn't we hear something about the south for a change?'

Among the chink of glasses, the murmur of conversation subdued of necessity by the exigencies of the competition, Manning had noted one voice of extreme richness. Whenever the possessor of it — a commendatore — spoke, Manning felt a chord somewhere in the interior of his chest vibrate in gentle harmony with

77

its resonance. 'The legendary south,' now boomed this voice to the faint jarring of an empty wine glass, 'the south. The magic of the word.' There was a faint belch, followed by a suppressed groan.

'Where the sun always shines,' said a barrister, the pallor of whose skin was that of well-preserved vellum.

'Land of poetry, romance, music, the troubadours.' Dr. Serra, having snatched not more than two minutes of refreshing sleep, now opened one eye and joined in the conversation.

'And of flowers,' contributed the doctor of philosophy, eyeing with distaste the imitation bouquet, a confection of silica and glass beads, in the vase on the centre of the table.

'Throughout history,' said the Sindaco wistfully, 'the south has produced the great fighters, the indomitable guerrilla bands. Under the prodigious Pane di Grano they defeated the flying columns of Napoleon.'

'And crucified the prisoners they took,' screeched Don Arturo. He had been cupping his hands eagerly to his ears and had now caught a sentence. 'I could tell you of another occasion when they roasted them alive and ate selected portions of their bodies.'

'Papa,' said the Sindaco sharply.

'It's all right,' grunted the old man, 'they've finished eating, haven't they? I was referring to Spaccapitta at Acri. It's well known. An historical fact.'

'Well,' said the doctor of philosophy, 'apart from that kind of thing, which is better forgotten, why doesn't some film company give us a record of the glorious Four Days at Naples?'

'Why go so far as Naples?' said the resonant voice of the commendatore. 'What's wrong with a film dealing with the epic of Arzano?'

The suggestion was applauded by all those present.

'It's incredible,' said Dr. Serra. 'No one up in the north ever seems to worry about our existence down here. To them we are all a gang of thieving, guzzling Neapolitans. All the brilliant patriotic exploits that took place in the south seem to have been hushed up. It's a conspiracy of silence.'

'Of course it's a conspiracy. Jealousy on the part of a cold-blooded race of people who envy the graciousness of our way of living.'

'What happened at Arzano?' Manning asked the doctor of philosophy.

'At Arzano? Why, at Arzano we southerners in the heroism of one man gave a demonstration of the stuff we're really made of. We showed the world what we could do. But, of course, it was hushed up . . . An epic which awaits the pen of a Leopardi or the brush of a Salvatore Rosa to do it justice. To put it briefly, a retreating German armoured column halted at Arzano, about ten miles from here, with the intention of making a stand. Arzano is in a narrow valley. They could have made a second Cassino of it. A local man who happened to be there at the time — Lauro was his name — got into one of the armoured cars that had been left unattended for a moment. With this he shot up the rest of the column. One or two of the villagers joined him and between them they kicked the Germans out. The survivors had to run for it.'

'Tell him what the Allied commander said.'

'If it had not been for Lauro, he said, the advance would have been seriously held up. The whole campaign might have been jeopardized . . . What a man! He did it practically single-handed. You should have seen the Germans scooting off. Shows what we can do when we are roused.'

' — when we show our teeth.'

'And after all that, it's hushed up. These northerners find it convenient to say nothing about it.'

'Of course, it wouldn't fit in with their silly legend about the south.'

'And what happened to Lauro?' Manning asked. 'Was he decorated?'

'Ah, what happened to him? Now, that's the extraordinary part. He just disappeared. Vanished into thin air before we had time to organize some proper civic expression of our gratitude. He just vanished.'

The conversation slackened and then veered off to other topics. There was a suggestion of uneasiness in the atmosphere.

When the party broke up, the Sindaco took Manning aside. 'I know you'll forgive me,' he said, 'but I could tell at first glance that you were a man of sensibility. Do you know how? Let me explain. By your appreciation of art. The moment you entered the room. I was watching you, I saw the way your eye went straight to the pictures.'

Manning was slightly embarrassed. 'Of course, I like good pictures. Don't most people?'

'What is it that separates us from the brute creation?' the Sindaco asked. 'A love of beauty.' He hissed the word reverently. A silence languished between them while the Sindaco, eyes raised, caressed the outlines of an invisible classical vase.

'When you go,' the Sindaco breathed. 'When you leave Malevento, I should like you to take with you a souvenir of my country. Something beautiful.'

Manning produced a neutral smile. This was beginning to remind him of the episode in the butcher's shop. 'It's very kind of you, but we soldiers travel light.'

The Sindaco uncovered canine teeth of extraordinary length in a smile of gentle raillery. 'A grand piano? No, my dear friend, I'm not suggesting that. Perhaps a little treasure by one of our supreme masters. A matter of a few ounces. Something to put in your pocket, almost.'

This was a more serious affair than the ridiculous leg of mutton. Manning took a firm stand.

'But don't you understand?' said the Sindaco, flinging wide his arms in astonishment. 'I regard you as an ambassador of your country to my town — the town of which I have the honour of being the leading citizen. In the past, gifts have always been exchanged. A gracious custom. Even if we live in barbarous times, need we be of the times? Can we not enlighten by our example?'

Manning was wondering what the chances were of getting away without having to be downright rude. The Sindaco misread his silence. 'As a concession to your feelings,' the Sindaco said, 'you shall do something for me in return. A regular exchange of gifts. A small service on your part. What am I saying — ? How foolish of me. A large service to me, I should have said, even if not a difficult one for you to perform.'

Manning found himself holding a piece of twisted metal.

'A defective part from the engine of one my tractors. What do you call it? I'm stupidly unfamiliar with these technical terms.'

The anonymous part lay heavily in Manning's palm. He turned it over doubtfully. Its shape held no meaning for him.

'Don't put yourself to a great deal of trouble, of course. I thought perhaps some of your workshop people ... if you have the opportunity of seeing them, naturally.'

'And now,' said the Sindaco, 'let's take one more look at the Sassetta. There are one or two little points you may have missed.'

In the morning Manning found two anonymous letters which had been pushed under the office door during the night.

The first was written in unusually cramped handwriting — perhaps, he thought, with the left hand — and he had some difficulty in reading it. It said:

The writer, who is unable for obvious reasons to give his name, was present at the dinner party last night when Avvocato Arturo Vico made reference to 'blacks' buried in his garden. Although an effort was made to pass this off as a bad joke, it is nothing other than the truth, except, of course, that the 'blacks' were not 'sent by the Germans' but were two of the Moroccan soldiers of your French allies, who were murdered by Avvocato Vico's orders.

A well wisher of your cause

The second writer had not been so careful. His letter had been typed on distinctive paper, and there were a number of easily identifiable irregularities in the characters. Were it a matter of importance, Manning thought, the discovery of the writer would not present much difficulty.

Last night at the house of Avvocato Vico you heard part of the story of the hero Lauro. It was not thought fit to tell you of Lauro's eventual fate. Through the machinations of police Marshal Altamura, with whom Lauro had a long standing feud, this patriot and hero was falsely accused to the Allies and by them interned. Although Marshal Altamura produced various false witnesses, the true facts of the case could easily be established by you through a re-interrogation of these persons. Justice cries aloud that this cowardly wrong should be righted.

A lover of Truth

That morning produced another communication, an official one which he felt inclined to preserve, symbolizing as it did so well the futility of his labours. It was a routine notice relating to a wanted man, intended to supplement the immense list in the Black Book, a copy of which, of course, had never been issued to him. The description of such agents, spies, saboteurs or whatever they were had always struck him by their whimsicality. This was, perhaps, as good a sample as he had ever seen. He was instructed to be on the look-out for a man — Name unknown. Place of birth unknown. Aged 30-5. Height approximately five feet nine inches: Colour of hair medium. Eyes brown. Thought to speak Italian with a slight Venetian accent. Known to possess three teats on his left breast, to have a well-developed sense of humour and a morbid fear of cats.

He read this description and re-read it. Was he, then, to post himself in the highway in pursuit of all men of average height, average colouring, indefinite age; listening carefully for that elusive Venetian burr, watching for the betraying over-readiness to grin, demanding that they lay bare their breasts.

This was his mission epitomized. What lunatic Eurystheus, after six years of war, still dispensed these tasks?

VII

'THE Sindaco!' The marchesina spat with masculine vigour. '... That dirty racketeer. I suppose he's after you for spare parts for his tank?'

'He said something about a damaged tractor,' Manning told her.

'Tractor!' The marchesina threw back her head and guffawed. 'That's a new name for it. Hasn't anyone told you yet that he controls the Vaiano gang? If only they could get that broken down tank to go the Sindaco would be a made man.'

'I thought it didn't look much like a tractor part,' said Manning, making an effort to appear unruffled by this information.

'Swine ... all of them,' said the marchesina, once again spitting copiously. 'What can you expect from so-called Christian Democrats — people with no conception of the principle of authority. It is fortunate you came to me. I am a Manfredoni — of Swabian descent, you understand. Not an Italian pig. Northern blood runs in my veins. You can rely upon me.'

Manning thanked her.

'Do you believe in race?' she asked. 'Do you believe that the characteristics which ennoble a family or a nation are capable of transmission from generation to generation?'

The marchesina asked this question with great earnestness. She had put down her pipe and had reached forward with the faint brassy tinkling of bangles to take Manning's hands in her own.

Pigeons clashed their pinions on the rafters above and a white deposit splashed to the ground close to his foot.

Manning looked up to the marchesina rather nervously. Although the Gothic twilight, which had been deepened by the partial boarding over of the windows, had softened her ageing features, her eyes glowed with a disturbing fire. In increasing embarrassment Manning avoided her gaze, fixing his eyes on a point on the wall just over her head. Here, in a patch of stucco still adhering to the otherwise naked brickwork, a condottiere with his ghostly spearmen passed briefly through the faded fresco from oblivion to oblivion.

The water on the primus boiled and the marchesina emptied into it the remains of a tin of army ration tea with sugar and milk combined. 'I no longer crave for coffee,' she said. 'My forbears campaigned in twenty countries. They had to adapt themselves, and I can do so too.

'Does it seem strange to you,' she asked him, indicating the surroundings with a graceful wave of her beringed fingers, 'to find me living in such conditions? I must tell you, then, that all that counts is the spirit within one. The fact is that the mediocrity of these latter centuries of Italian history has been too much for our family. We stifled under a contemptible order of things.' The marchesina replaced her pipe between her teeth and puffed in furious derision. She still possessed, he thought, what might have been described as a strained beauty. It was the distinguished bones of her skull that seemed to rally it; to impose discipline on the flesh and skin; to preserve them from final and utter rout.

'I want to tell you something,' she said 'something I did not even mention to your friend. I have never been able to bring myself even to consider marrying one of these Italians. With me it had to be one of my own kind — a northerner — you understand, or nothing at all. Can you conceive what it is to possess such pride? Like calls to like.' She squeezed his hand tenderly. 'But why should I unburden myself to you in this way? If it has to be nothing at all,' she tossed her head defiantly, shaking sparks from the pipe, 'well then, with me dies the legitimate illegitimate line of the Great Count.'

Manning seemed bewildered.

'Yes,' said the marchesina, 'the legitimate illegitimate line. We trace our descent back, unbroken in any way, to the Great

Count's union with his accepted mistress. Naturally, it's the noblest line in the south. We are the only branch of the family entitled to difference the arms of the Great Count with the original bordure gobony. In all other cases, bends sinister are of quite recent introduction. You will be amazed to hear that only French was permitted to be spoken in the castle. In fact, the Italians find my accent a distinctly foreign one.'

Manning received another squeeze from the marchesina's muscular fingers.

'Now that I have told you so much,' she said, 'you will have gathered that I have only one regret.'

'Regret?'

'Yes, regret. What is to become of our ancestral possession? This noble monument to the courage and might of my ancestors?'

Manning followed her nostalgic gaze round the great hall — completely empty save for the chaise-longue, and thence up to the rafters once again, where the pigeons jostled one another as they alighted and took off, and higher still where curtains of cobwebs stirred gently as if hinged from above.

'I should imagine you find the upkeep very difficult,' he suggested.

The marchesina nodded gravely. 'We make ends meet by letting out the keep and the bell tower to pig breeders and by supplying pigeons to the local hotel. The soil in the banqueting hall produces first-class vegetables. Needless to say, the towns-people are unhelpful in every way. I have to spend half my time going the rounds of the main enceinte to prevent their being dismantled completely to patch up the peasants' barns. I put it down to the atheism of the times.'

'It must be an immense undertaking,' agreed Manning. 'The fortifications are the most extensive I have ever seen.'

'The largest in southern Italy,' said the marchesina proudly. 'They originally enclosed an area far greater than that of the city itself. They represent an attempt on the part of my ancestors to attain to a noble ideal — imagine the grandeur of the conception! They were determined, cost what it might in treasure and labour, to build themselves a fortress which would be impregnable to emperor and pope alike. They felt themselves to be men of destiny and consequently that their survival was essential to the commonweal. Generations gave their all in an attempt to fulfil this dream. In order to put their plans into action they soon exhausted all the normal expedients of taxation. These measures naturally roused no comment, but the sheer grandiosity of the undertaking called for something more. For instance, we refused permission for a sewer to be built in the town, and then taxed those who applied to dispose of their refuse in the usual way by throwing it into the street. We claimed everything that fell from the heavens. Animals could drink only from our official troughs and were heavily taxed for doing so. We levied special contributions on the sacred feasts, to enable us to keep these properly and to give generously to the poor. Celebrations by the public of births, marriages and deaths in our family became a legal obligation and were, of course, accompanied by gifts. Don't think that anyone protested. Those were the days when people took their religion seriously. The ideal of service was considered a beautiful one. The day in each week they normally worked for their Lord was called the Giornata d'amore. In the interests of our great project we increased the number of such days of love to three or four a week.'

'Your vassals must have led beautiful lives,' said Manning.

The marchesina simpered. 'It's naughty of me to tell you this, but it's really the best part of the story. We even taxed men for sleeping with their wives, and it was no good trying to get out of it by claiming abstention. If salt eating could be made obligatory, so could matrimonial habits. Our ecclesiastical advisers were all in favour of it. "What they have to pay for they will use," was the attitude they took. "It will keep them free from temptation in other directions. Any measure devised to protect the people from temptation is to be commended." So there it was, all

86

correctly put down on paper according to the forms of law and properly notarized. Twenty-one taxable nights a month, with a small allowance for pregnancies. This, of course, all dovetailed nicely with other aspects of our fiscal policy, as we levied taxes on the size of families.'

'What was to prevent their staging a reproductive strike?'

'We would have liked to see them try it!' said the marchesina. 'A strike, indeed. We were not the kind of people to trifle with. My ancestors would have attended to all the repopulation necessary themselves if the need had arisen. Those were ruthless times.'

'But in spite of all these efforts they were never able to complete their building?'

'Yes,' said the marchesina, 'they finally completed it: and herein lies the cruel irony of the story. The castle was to have defied all the efforts of emperor and pope, to have been able to withstand any seige, and to have perpetuated for a thousand years the rule of our family in the south. By the time that the great work was completed, however, the emperor and the warring popes had gone. We had the castle all ready, but it was impossible to find anyone interested in attacking it. In desperation we managed to pick a quarrel with the central power, but all that happened was that some nasty little foreign financial adviser ruined us by such dirty tricks as devaluing the currency and drawing off our labour supply by offering them wages.'

'As a hotel,' went on the marchesina, 'it would be a success. City people like this kind of thing. The peace and the health-giving benefits of the country existence. And in what surroundings! Do you by any chance know any capitalists?'

Manning shook his head with regret. At that moment there was a commotion at the doorway as a hen scuttled into the room, pursued by a lame cock which overbalanced whenever it attempted to follow the sharp turns made by its quarry. These birds engaged his attention because they were practically feather-less. The skin of the cock hung down in bluish folds. The marchesina, annoyed at this interruption, shouted and clapped her hands, and a small, ragged girl came running in and chased the poultry out into the yard again. The marchesina went after her and said something, and the girl went out again and shut the door.

The marchesina came back and sat down beside Manning. She put her pipe aside with finality and laid on his arm a hand, the back of which was draped negligently in loose skin and speckled like a turkey's egg. There was a trace of a smile about her lips. She held her head slightly to one side. 'What is uppermost in your mind?' she asked.

Manning sensed something about this question that made it a difficult one to deal with. He became slightly uneasy and he felt his face stiffening in a self-conscious smile. Before he could think of an adequate reply, the marchesina spoke again. 'You can tell me,' she said, slightly tightening her grip on his arm. 'Don't try to keep it from me. I know.'

'Uppermost in my mind? I don't know,' said Manning. 'I'm most likely thinking of a report I have to write.'

The marchesina shook her head gently but definitely, her earrings emitting a faint discord. 'No, not that. Things like that are never uppermost in one's mind at such a time.' Her hand had stolen down and encountered his, and Manning felt the long, sinuous fingers entwine themselves with his like wrestlers about to overcome the resistance of puny opponents.

'In a moment,' said the marchesina, 'the domestic will go. I have told her to go. You understand?'

He noticed with a faint shiver that in speaking she had changed to the intimate second person singular. The fingers had secured a stranglehold now and were putting on the pressure. A half-hearted endeavour to withdraw his hand was effortlessly overcome.

'We shall be alone,' said the marchesina.

Alone. Manning looked round him as if for a way of escape.

'This is a big room. Do you find it intimate? No, perhaps. Personally, I'm not affected by sheer space. Nevertheless . . .'

Manning's hand was suddenly free and he was holding a handkerchief to his forehead.

'You are hot,' said the marchesina. 'You perspire. Please allow me.' She wrenched the handkerchief from his grasp and began to wipe his face vigorously. Suddenly she stopped, still holding the handkerchief poised motionless in the air. Her gaze was travelling slowly round his head as if in the inspection of an invisible halo. She seemed astonished and delighted at something she saw.

'Our auras are similar,' she said. 'I am irreligious — religion is for the people — but I am a profound believer in the realities of the astral plane. Do you understand me?'

'No,' said Manning. Attempting to gain a few inches of space on the chaise-longue, he found himself implacably restrained by its half-encircling arm.

'Your aura contains much red. Red is the colour of passion. With me, too, red is predominant.'

Manning nodded.

'Now you will tell me what is in your mind.' The marchesina's tone was firmer. His hand was imprisoned again. 'You are free to say what I know you must say. What must come out. I promise not to be offended.'

'I don't want to say anything,' said Manning, noticing that his voice had assumed a singular bleating quality.

'Come, come, you are still shy with me. These are northern notions of chivalry. I respect them. Here we are more expansive. We let our hearts rule our heads. No woman will hate you for telling her what is in your heart.'

'I feel the heat,' said Manning, masking his growing panic with a sickly smile. In fact, as soon as he ceased to mop his forehead the sweat began to trickle down.

'Yes,' said the marchesina. 'You feel the heat. That's it. And this is what we'll do. We shall go to another room where there's a fan. A small room. One where we shall both feel more at our ease.'

89

The marchesina's fingers, sensitive and slender but muscular beneath their loose skin, had taken a firm hold on his sleeve and were tugging at him. She seemed to have gained access to unsuspected resources of strength — spiritual, perhaps, as well as physical. Manning found himself moving under compulsion, half impelled, half manœuvred, as by one of those insects possessing the power to transport with ease objects many times in excess of their own weight. He felt as if at any moment now the marchesina, by means of some purely biological endowment peculiar to herself, would administer him, unresistant, a paralyzing injection preliminarily to enfolding him in those powerful yellow arms and bearing him silently away to the airless, crepuscular intimacy of some low-ceilinged chamber.

In his panic Manning had almost forgotten the main purpose of his visit. Remembering it, he opened a diversionary front in the conversation.

'Ah,' the marchesina sighed, 'politics again. You men are interested in nothing else these days.'

'But do you believe this man Lauro was framed?' Manning insisted.

'Framed?' said the Marchesina. ' — of course he was framed. He's in prison, isn't he? Well, that means he was framed.'

'And who framed him?'

'Marshal Altamura, obviously. The two families fell out in 1811. They were on different sides in the Napoleonic war. Nobody remembers who fought for which. They've been framing each other ever since. When the Lauros are in the police the Altamuras go to prison, and vice-versa. Why bother with them?'

'I wouldn't,' said Manning, 'if they'd be good enough to keep us out of their quarrels. As it is, I see no reason why we should be used as a catspaw in a petty vendetta.'

'Quite right,' said the marchesina. 'Particularly when it must be admitted that Lauro was at least on your side. The marshal never lifted a finger to help anyone but himself.'

He was walking back through the rubbish-strewn area enclosed by the second line of defence walls when he was surprised to find the marshal coming towards him.

The marshal held his silk handkerchief over his nose, withdrawing it occasionally to sniff cautiously. Semi-featherless hens scuffled about and cooled their inflamed rumps in the dust.

'It's the breed,' said the marshal. 'They don't have feathers.'

They skirted a low, broken tower. From its summit suddenly showered down a miscellaneous collection of sticks and twigs, some of which narrowly missed them. A face looked down.

'Hullo there, Orfeo,' said the marshal, waving in good-humoured protest. 'What's going on up there?'

'Clearing out the old storks' nest, marshal.'

'It's unlucky to drive the storks away.'

'Not driving them away, marshal. If they'd been coming back they'd have been here by now.'

'That's the first time they haven't turned up?' the marshal asked.

'Yes,' said Orfeo with solemnity. 'The first time we are without storks. If we'd have known they were going to take it like this we wouldn't have done it.'

'Done what?'

'Well, marshal, the fact is last year we ate the young.'

'I never heard of anyone eating storks,' said the marshal.

'Any young birds are tasty,' said Orfeo. 'Even owls, but they're difficult to get. We were sorry to have to eat the storks, but the gristle on their necks was succulent.' Orfeo's face assumed a reverent transformation at the memory. 'It all started as a bet,' he said. 'Someone ate one for a bet of a hundred lire. We thought it would go against the grain, but it didn't, because as soon as he finished one off he started on the next. Then, of course, we were all in on it.'

'Fishy?' asked the marshal.

'Not at all. A bit fishy down by the parson's nose, perhaps. I mentioned the necks because they were wonderful.'

'Better to have let some of them fly,' said the marshal, 'to serve as an encouragement.'

'Yes,' said Orfeo, 'that's what I said. That's where we have to blame ourselves. We came to an agreement about it just to take one out of every nest, but as soon as we'd tasted them I knew it was all up. We'd have had the old birds, too, if we'd known that they were going to let us down by not coming back this year.'

Just as they were going through the gate, Orfeo joined them. 'I'm going to let you into a secret about birds,' he said. 'I don't mind admitting it was me that had that first stork. I know all about eating birds. There's not one I haven't tried. Vultures are wonderful, remember that. People will tell you otherwise, but it isn't true. If ever you get the chance to pick up a vulture, don't let it go. The flesh may be stringy, but it's sweeter than a spring chicken. But you can't get them round here. Remember, though, if one ever comes your way — '

They passed out through the gate, flanked by a pair of brindled Byzantine lions which raised their time-obliterated heads in roaring ferocity. As they approached, a mongrel which had been sniffing one of the lions speculatively, lifted its leg.

'I was able to get your information rather more quickly than usual,' said the marshal.

'What information?' asked Manning, attempting to speak casually but realizing with a flash of resentment what had happened.

'The name you are interested in. Mancuso. Your friend used to hand such requests directly to me at breakfast to save time. Those silly people in the Pubblica Sicurezza are really very helpless. They become unnecessarily worried if the details they are given are not quite complete.'

'How did you know where to find me?' Manning asked.

The marshal lifted his shoe and examined with distaste the fowls' droppings stuck in the cavity between the heel and sole. 'There are so very few places to go to in this town,' he said. 'All the possibilities can be covered in a half-hour. One's existence here is so public. It's quite like living in a glass house.'

'So it seems.'

'By the way, talking about living conditions, why don't you take over your friend's old billet in the hills? It's peaceful up there. One can relax. One does not get that unpleasant feeling that somebody is looking over one's shoulder all the time.'

Back in the office again he made a start on his report. It would kill half an hour, he thought. Perhaps he could even stretch it out in some way so as to suck up an hour of this unending flood of time. He lifted a paper off the desk, uncovering a sharp-edged oblong in the layer of white dust that had settled since morning.

The sun was shining fully on the opposite wall now, and the heat sizzled through the brickwork and rose in trembling waves over the torn proclamations.

He put down his pen and went through into the washroom, where one of the basins had half-filled with water that had thrown down a reddish precipitate. He dipped a mug into the basin, crushed a tablet of Halazone, dropped it in and drank the warm fluid. The released chlorine scraped faintly at the back of his throat.

He wrote:

> Routine contacts were made with leading personalities of the town, including the Sindaco, the Commissario of the Pubblica Sicurezza, the Marchesa di Manfredoni, and CC.RR. Marshal Filippo Altamura.

A space, then:

> MANCUSO, Luigi, son of Arturo (deceased) and of Laura Vernicelli (deceased), born in Foggia 1912. Originally living at Vico Trinità degli Spagnuoli 8, Santa Maria di Stabio. Mancuso was released from army service for reasons of health in 1942. He re-enlisted, however, in 1943 and

93

became a member of the well-known Sabotage Unit, 10th Flotilla MAS. He has been since then in the north of Italy, but is reported to have been seen recently in his home village. Macuso was inscribed in the PNF in 1932. There are no criminal convictions. (Information supplied by CC.RR.)

Manning put down his pen and then picked it up again:

CC.RR. Marshal Filippo Altamura, attached to S.I.M. and posted to this town, states that he was originally sent here during the campaign and placed at the disposal of F.S. and C.I.C. personnel in the area. As he still draws allied rations and appears no longer to serve any useful function it is suggested that the Italian Authorities be requested to withdraw him.

'Would you describe me as a survival of the fittest?' asked the marshal, gently pressing with his thumb the mosquito that had settled on the back of his hand. The mosquito's slender, splayed-out corpse exuded a speck of blood. The marshal flicked it away and looked up. 'I don't get malaria, I don't get typhus, I don't get smallpox. Half the kids in my village kicked the bucket in various epidemics and those that survived always seemed to me to be weakly. But I'm still here in the flesh.' He pinched his cheek in emphasis. 'What brought this subject up, by the way? Why am I rambling on like this?'

'I was asking you where I could find the captain.'

'Ah, yes, of course — the captain. We were talking about the captain. That's where my train of thought started. Well now, it would be difficult to see the captain. After all, we don't even know which place he went to. Ha, ha.'

'Which place?'

'I was joking,' said the marshal cheerfully. 'He's no more. Snuffed out.' He closed his eyelids expressively with his fingers. 'Two captains in two years and both gone the way of all flesh. Both promising, brilliant almost. Perhaps lacking in stamina.

94

Naturally, with the manpower situation the way it is, they can't afford to keep sending down replacements.'

'What did they die of?'

'The first one was carried off by the typhus,' said the marshal. 'His end was a pitiful sight. The fact is, the Romans come and go. They don't take root down here. Don't seem to thrive on this soil. The place will be getting a bad reputation in Rome. It means I have had to do the best I can on my own for some time now. Pity, when you come to think of it, always to send Romans. They can't get used to these conditions. They take pills all the time and cover themselves with all sorts of powder, but they go out like candles. Overnight, almost. In a way, perhaps it's more merciful.' The marshal withdrew the faded lily-like blossom he wore in his buttonhole, sniffed at it disappointedly, crushed it between finger and thumb and let it fall to the ground.

'And the second captain?'

'His end was enshrouded in mystery,' said the marshal, savouring the phrase. 'He was with us only a few days. So full of enthusiasm. One night he went out by himself and never came back. After six months he was presumed dead. Naturally a lot of ghoulish old wives' tales went round about it, but the real facts of the case are probably quite simple, if only we knew. He most likely missed his way in the dark and fell into the river.'

'Will they promote you eventually?'

'I'm not educated,' said the marshal. 'I don't show up too well beside these Roman gentlemen. To be a captain you have to know a bit of Latin, play tennis and drink tea. Even in the Party I never distinguished myself. Fortunate, in a way, when you come to think of it, because as things turn out I'm not eligible for defascistization. On the whole,' said the marshal with philosophy, 'I can't grumble. I survived the war, I don't get purged and my blood's too strong for mosquitoes, fleas or lice.'

There was a moment of silence.

'Excuse my dropping in on you like this,' the marshal went on, 'when I see you are busy on some important job. It just occurred to me that you might be at a loose end tonight. You'd never think it to look at the place, but we do have a bit of fun occasionally.' His mouth drooped in the suggestion of a leer.

'I'm busy now,' said Manning shortly.

'Well, later,' said the marshal. 'See how you feel. We'll be seeing you for dinner, in any case.'

VIII

WHENEVER he raised his eyes they encountered this solemn signoria of ancient men. By virtue of his enormous solemnity and sheer patrician girth Don Enrico occupied the central position in the group. Whenever he spoke it was with the authority of an augur. About Don Enrico's face there was an owlishness produced, perhaps, by the red-rimmed sagging of the lower eyelids which exposed an abnormally large area of the whites of the eyes. Below the eyes depended deltas of skin, the folds of which were as rhythmically disposed as the rippled surface of mud flats in a tidal estuary. Encroaching fat had laid hold on Don Enrico's organism, not even sparing his tongue. Swollen enormously in his mouth, it impeded the free passage of the sounds produced by his vocal chords, so that his words finally emerged thickened and hissing. Don Enrico's sensitiveness on this point caused him to refrain from speech except on occasions when a pronouncement of weight was called for. Normally he sat, fitted comfortably into the mould of his chair, looking into space, his fine hands clasped over the escarpment of his belly — apparently looking into space, for Manning had already come to realize that this Gautama-like detachment of Don Enrico's was affected by a curious phenomenon soon after money had been rung up in the till. A minute or two would elapse and then Don Enrico would arise, pat at the creases in his trousers, look round him and make some inaudible remark to his entourage before starting off in the direction either of the urinal or of the street door. Whatever Don Enrico's destination, he would pause on his way back and linger in the vicinity of the till, waiting for Alberto to come up and open the drawer. Don Enrico would then take out the latest increment and subject it to a close scrutiny before handing it back to Alberto, who returned it to the till. Don Enrico handled notes with great tenderness, exploring their surfaces with the wooing fingers of a lover.

When Manning remarked on this to Alberto, he laughed. 'He's the capitalist. He owns the biggest share in the place.'

This evening the till had remained closed for some time, and Don Enrico had sat there immobile. On his flanks and in the rear sat the other old men.

'Saturday night,' said Alberto, 'it's the high-spot of the week for him.'

On the faces of these men was stamped a profound melancholy. The oval eyes of youthful innocence had shrunken into gems which glittered implacably in a wasteland of encompassing wrinkles. Unlike Don Enrico, they were thin men, and the folds of skin which in grosser faces would have enclosed second chins sagged down over their sharp collars. Their expressions held a bitter and permanent scepticism and the deep lines at the corners of their mouths could be twisted only into ironic smiles or depressed in melancholy and fanatical determination.

'Who are these men?' asked Manning, appealing despite himself to the marshal.

'The original anti-Fascists of our town. Some of them were sent to confino for their opinions. The rest just kept clear of politics and were persecuted and half starved as a result. People who refused to have any dealings with the Party didn't do too well in any enterprise.'

'They don't look particularly cheerful now that things have changed.'

'No, they used themselves up protesting. Finally it became a question of habit to kick against everything. When the new regime came into being they were, of course, passed over in favour of penitent sinners in the distribution of jobs. Now the only pleasure left to them in life is to write each other anonymous letters and to start actions for defamation. Funnily enough,' said the marshal, 'of all the known anti-Fascists in these parts none has prospered by the downfall of the regime. Really, it almost makes me wonder if there isn't something fundamentally wrong with these people who want to go against the stream.'

Two more lean shapes entered the café; the first tall, straight and military of bearing in a rather fragile way; the second bent over, shuffling at his heels, dog-like, subservient. Both walked in the faltering manner of blind men, groping their way towards a table in the furthest corner of the room. The leader of this pair turned his head stiffly and exchanged a signal of recognition with Don Enrico, ignoring the rest. The other gazed at the floor. They sat down, facing each other in silence across the table.

'Our Fascists,' said the marshal, 'the rabid Fascists of Malevento. The tall one is Capolongo, hero of the Spanish war. Heroes of the Spanish war were always picked out for highly paid sinecures in the Confederazione Fascista dei Lavaratori dell'Industria, but it often took a long time for confirmation to come through. It was a splendid job when you eventually got it, because all you had to do was to make a fighting speech at the Annual Convention. The speech was written out for you, and you learned it off by heart.'

'From the look of him he didn't put any of his money away for a rainy day.'

'He didn't have the chance to. They kept him hanging about for nearly three years until he got the job. But before he had the chance to collect his first month's salary the Confederazione was dissolved.'

'Who is the other?'

'Calunnia. He used to be the editor of our local paper. Before the March on Rome he was just starting to make his name as a Socialist. Afterwards he used to contribute articles to the Fascist press under *noms de plume*. He was particularly strong on Imperialism. In 1939 he finally came out into the open and applied as an ex-combatant for Party membership. Application turned down. He made a re-application and heard nothing more about it. Then, just a fortnight before the armistice — and much to his dismay, of course — he got notice of his acceptance as a Party member.'

No, there was no possible renaissance here. No rewakening with joyous wings from the nightmare. The mountains had been in labour and had brought forth a spate of cold ashes. This race of condemned men had started out at birth on a journey across a plain set with desperate obstacles. Some of them had succeeded in keeping their integrity, but even then age and despair had yearly hung a fresh chain round their necks, and now finally the prize-winners, the indomitable survivors, had come to take their reward — this. Happy indeed those that the typhus had caressed with its yellow fingers and laid in their graves.

Something akin to panic fluttered over Manning's entrails as he thought of the wilderness of days to be endured in this place. Each day like the one he had just struggled through; days of sweat, brickdust, empty sunshine, blistered walls, yellow waters, parched hillsides. And these days followed by nights doled out hour by hour by the cicada. A scabrous breakdown in the ordinary reasoned flow of existence from nothing to nothing. A point where the needle had become entrapped in a worn-out groove in the record, so that he must live through a flat and wailing repetition until the arm of the gramophone was jolted forward by some outside agency. He was to be kept here. He knew it through something more powerful, more convincing than reason. The military machine would keep going under its own momentum. Occasionally some fatuous task would be flung to him to keep him quiet, but the years would go by and he would still be immured in this place; isolated as utterly as a man marooned on a lonely Pacific island.

'But you are not drinking,' said the marshal sympathetically.

He raised his glass, his eyes fastening over the rim on that row of bloodless, witch-hunting faces. The brandy poured like erupting lava down his throat, leaving a thick-lipped yellow rim on the glass through which the faces grimaced in menacing despair.

In a sudden inescapable vision he saw himself as he was. He

accepted the bitter fact that the frustration of the past five years had broken his fibre beyond repair. He was like a piece of cardboard which has been crumpled and then straightened out but which under the slightest pressure would collapse along the line of its old weakness.

The marshal's voice sounded in his ear as rich and unctuous as that of a priest reading the responses. 'You have to make your own pleasures in a place like this.'

Ah, pleasure! That prickly satisfaction always paid for at a usurer's rate of interest. Not pleasure. Just some method, some inspired clue to a way of living through this end-obscured hitch-up in time; the demonstration of some magic sleight of hand by which this penance might be cancelled out, or if not cancelled out then dreamed away.

The glass was miraculously full. He drank again, and this time it seemed as though the fire had died out in the gushing lava. Immediately, however, there started in his ear a faint but insistent ringing like that of a distant telephone. The marshal, leaning crony-like towards him, sipped with the judiciousness of a cabaret tart.

A suppliant voice floated down to him from somewhere in the rear — a hasty mendicant patter of whining syllables. He wheeled round stiffly in his chair, his neck and spinal column having suddenly solidified. Behind him had ranged themselves a row of figures, heads slightly inclined and hands clasped together, like Hindu dancers acknowledging the applause of their performance. What was familiar about these morose petitioners? Of course; they were none other than those who had pestered the marshal on the previous morning.

'If it could perhaps be arranged . . .'

'Could we possibly . . . ?'

'Is there any hope . . . ?'

Hope?

Christ, then — these suppliants had detached themselves, had released their squid-like suckers from the marshal and were attaching themselves to him. He looked round in panic at the shadowy forms in the background — those who prayed mutely like Gothic saints and those others who gestured with cupped fingers, grinning in insolent allusion. A leering goblin — undoubtedly Vittorio — brushed past. ' — two hundred thou — ' Filosa was there, wishing to corner him, to question him on an aspect of his religious faith: 'Do you believe in the resurrection of the body?' Zi' Stefano had also appeared in this succession of apparitions holding with melancholy insistence before Manning's eyes a wrist upon which an extraordinary watch was buckled. It showed the days of the week, of the month, and the names of the months themselves, and performed as well the usual functions of a watch. 'See,' breathed Zi' Stefano softly, 'today is Saturday the 16th and tomorrow is the third Sunday after Trinity.' He unbuckled the watch and tried to strap it on Manning's wrist, only being prevented from doing so by the malefic materialization of Orfeo, carrying a small sack which Manning knew from its significant bulkiness to contain the offer of a dead vulture.

He averted his head in disgust, and there, without any possibility of disbelief, was the marchesina, an enshrouded female form which gesticulated discreetly in his direction; and sure enough, waiting upon the threshold, he observed the Sindaco, his gentle smile strangely demoniacal in the gloom. *But the Sindaco rarely goes out. He lacks a sense of adventure. What inauspicious occasion . . . ?*

'Saturday night,' said the marshal, obviously reading his thoughts. 'Don't take any notice of these people. They're badly bred.'

Above the insistent ringing of the telephone in his ear there proclaimed itself the more urgent clamour of the bell on the till. Don Enrico pushed himself out of his chair, his belly reeling forward and sagging tautly in the restraint of his trousers. Walking as if at the head of an invisible procession, he made for the uncloseable door of the urinal. The flush thundered and he re-emerged, buttoning himself with grave abstraction. The till bell rang again, and Don Enrico turned sideways with a note in his hand, as if in private and decorous consummation of his recent visit.

Outside the window avalanches of shadow slid from the silent towers and choked the streets. The town recoiled on the verge of night. A zigzagging point of light shot up and was extinguished in the building's inky silhouette. As he turned to observe this phenomenon, the trace of an indulgent smile worked its brief transfiguration in Don Enrico's face. 'Poor things,' he sighed.

Another frantic rocket shed its trail of sparks.

'What a beautiful thing childhood is,' hissed Don Enrico gently. 'The days when we were all angels! These poor kids never knew what it was to have toys but nothing can quench their spirits.'

'They catch bats,' explained the marshal, 'tie rags soaked in petrol to them, set them alight and let them go.'

'Those kids are wonderful,' said another voice. 'They could teach us a lesson in philosophy. Even the Romans have noticed it. They say they are making a film about them.'

'And where does the petrol come from?' came the carping voice of one of the embittered anti-Fascists. 'Do you ever think about that side of the question? Robbed out of someone's tank, of course.'

'Yes,' admitted Don Enrico sadly, 'that's wrong, of course. They shouldn't do that.' He relapsed into a gentle silence, and as his voice faded away his face wavered back into the cotton-wool of the background.

Manning surveyed his surroundings again. He blinked very hard, forcing his eyelids together with a strong muscular effort. When he opened his eyes again the walls, which had previously tended to close in on him, had now receded to their normal distance. Perhaps even slightly in excess of normal, for the café seemed to him at this moment to harbour an unusual diverseness of activity.

103

Coincident with this instability in the café's dimensions he had noticed with some interest a useful decrease in his own dependence upon space. It was as if the relative laws had been to some extent relaxed in his favour. Fragments of conversations being conducted in voices hardly above a whisper in the furthermost corners of the café floated to him as if travelling on a beam.

These various goings on he began to place under scrupulous review, not failing first to note, however, that his glass, from which he had not removed his eye since last drinking, was now, obviously through legerdemain, quite full again.

Don Ubaldo the schoolmaster and Dr. Serra, for instance. He could hear them as plainly as if he were sitting at their table. They were talking about food.

And there were the anti-Fascists, as ever. A bench of destitute inquisitors — or even inquisitors' victims, arraigned as a formality at some preliminary tribunal before donning their fatal Sanbenitos. Starting up frequently from their midst, as if in a vain attempt to present a petition but in reality charmed by the bell on the till, was Don Enrico.

On Manning's other side, over there vaguely on the right, were the ex-Fascists from whose lips the heady cup of power had been so ruthlessly dashed. The hero of the Spanish war held himself as erect as ever in his chair — a sedentary Quixote, a parody of a parody who had changed his lance for a toothpick, with which in apparent illustration of some martial exploit he stabbed the air furiously. Manning's newly acquired beam faculty came into action, and he heard Capolongo say: 'I stood up to him. I let him have it straight from the shoulder. I told him, "Look here, Doctor," I said, "you know what you can do with your pills. The best thing in the world for flatulence is sleeping on your left side, and don't try to argue the toss with me about it," I said, "I've suffered from it all my life." '

He turned his head slightly and the rest of this conversation was immediately cut off. Now he was listening to Don Ubaldo and Dr. Serra. The schoolmaster seemed to be making out a case for vegetarianism.

'Nonsense,' Dr. Serra said. 'In my time I've eaten my way through entire herds. I've consumed hundreds of sheep and bullocks, and quite a few goats. You could stock a State farm with all the animals I've eaten, and I'm none the worse for it.' He blew out his cheeks indignantly.

'But think of the cysts, the tumours, the tubercles and the carcinomas you've eaten. I hardly like to mention some of these things, not knowing the Latin names for them, but as a medical man you'll understand. What I mean is that you don't imagine that with meat at a thousand lire they're going to throw away anything.'

'I know,' said Dr. Serra, 'don't tell me. I know. But I don't care. I'm no worse for it.'

The suppliants had retreated into a corner and seemed to be recapitulating for their own benefit the story of their recent rebuff. Or perhaps they were creating of this a mime, as they appeared to be praying, mourning silently, laughing mirthlessly, going through the motions of warding off evil, of winnowing corn, of sowing seed and of climbing invisible ladders.

Hovering on the fringe of this group were Vittorio and Orfeo, grinning gnomes, both intent, it seemed, on cutting off stragglers, in isolating a man from the rest of the company — Vittorio to whisper saturnine suggestions in his ear and Orfeo to show him in secret the contents of his sack.

Now Manning saw into the kitchen with a kind of magnified vision, observing as with a powerful telescope the kitchen's infinite variety of detail, its pots and pans, its instruments adapted for frying, roasting, disembowelling and boiling alive; its unrecognizable fragments of cadavers, its rows of bottles containing in reality pickled fungus but recalling sinister surgical specimens in brine or alcohol; the ceiling festooned with the black, serpentine shapes of sausages swaying from gentle contact with the heads of those who passed beneath. Hither had the Sindaco translated himself, supervising Alberto's activities over a giant saucepan. Occasionally the Sindaco, a brooding and critical mentor, leant over Alberto's shoulder to introduce his powerful nose directly into the odorous upstream, assuming thereafter an expression of pleasure that was coloured with suffering, the mien of an anchorite involved in mystic communion with the unknowable. The kitchen was full of smoke, which now increased in density and now partially cleared, with the result that the Sindaco's body was sometimes invisible, his head floating unsupported in surroundings to which it seemed peculiarly well suited.

Light flickered in the corner of Manning's field of vision, and turning his head he saw another comet soar up from the darkness outside and come flashing towards him, trailing its sparks. This time it was coming straight at the window. Miraculously at the last instant — by the guidance of an instinct that would survive while consciousness lasted — the crash was averted and the tiny rocket zoomed up to clear the building.

And now Manning felt once again the glass rim between his lips, but the liquid had become strangely tame and flat. The marshal's arm lolled chummily round his shoulder, and the marshal was making a suggestion of some kind which involved, to his satisfaction, fleeing from this place, from this insupportable congregation of those who prayed and those who despaired, now united as they were in a whirling ectoplasm. It involved going forth instead into the night which hid in its veil endless dark and disturbing potentialities. Adventure! The cry seemed to come soundlessly through the marshal's lips.

The night was fanned by moths' wings and into the frankincense of the town's corruption had seeped a hill fragrance of aromatic shrubs. Borne forward as if upon wings, the marshal whirled him on. Intrepidly they plunged into reeking canyons of stone where fissures of light and the twanging of guitar strings betrayed the unsuspected persistence of human life. There were figures immobile as sentries or as those who watched over biers, their faces lit by a cigarette's glow. Candles burned dimly in shrines, illuminating a myriad curling snapshots of the dead for whom benefits were craved. There were open doors through which glowed phosphorescent interiors, the purpose of which inevitably was to house an immense and shadowy bed. In these streets, which in day time echoed with cries and expostulations, a night mood had fallen, one of whispers and of stealth of movement.

They entered now a street of utter darkness, treading lightly over the rich carpet of refuse. Suddenly, as if by some canine instinct, the marshal stopped and rapped gently on an unseen door. There was a widening chink of light, and Manning saw the marshal's arm stretched out, pushing the door discreetly open until the gap was wide enough for him to squeeze through. In a moment he looked out again, his face back-lit by a greenish effluence. He beckoned.

Manning found himself in a single-room basso, the typical dwelling-place of an entire southern family. Here the acts and rites of existence would be performed before a domestic audience. It contained a few bare sticks of furniture. Two bunk-like structures, built against opposite walls, apparently harboured silent, motionless forms. On the floor a stirring of the shadows caught his eye, and only then he realized that a third blanket-covered human shape lay there on a mattress. The lighting of the room depended upon an electric bulb of infinitesimal candle power, its filament glowing coldly below a conventional sacred picture of a Virgin, darkly orientalized, her immense and sorrow-ful eyes peering into the gloom. In her arms a melancholy child bore upon its head a many-tiered crown. The artist might have taken his model from any of those surrounding, disease-stricken villages, in the faces of whose children he could read the pre-monition of a hopeless life.

The marshal bent over and lifted back a corner of the blanket, and Manning glimpsed the pallor of naked thighs. The form thus revealed twisted as if in a vain attempt to avoid the searing of their gaze. The face of a young girl was turned up to them in tight-lipped question and then buried in the mattress beneath its black curls.

There was a creaking in one of the bunks, and Manning was just in time to catch sight of a raised head and a staring eye before the figure lying there drew up the blanket and turned over to face the wall.

'The father,' the marshal whispered reassuringly. 'Would you like me to wait for you outside? You can take your time. It's a decent family. Clean. Respectable.'

Manning, his eyes still centred on the form on the mattress, was groping behind him for the door handle. He was embarrassed above all by what seemed to him the incivility of discussing the situation, even in whispers.

The marshal had raised his voice slightly, perhaps with a complimentary intention. 'When a decent family in straitened circumstances agrees to receive you, it's considered a compliment. Means you're one of us. Outsiders have to go to Zi' Stefano's. I mentioned earlier in the day that we might be calling. Said you were a special friend of mine.'

Manning didn't reply.

'Well,' said the marshal, 'as gentlemen we don't want to hurt anybody's feelings, do we?'

From the father's bunk there came a sound closely approaching a snore. 'He's trying to make us feel at home,' the marshal whispered. 'You don't have to say a word. Just leave a trifle — anything you like — when you go. Comes a little strange at first but you soon get used to the system.'

'I'll wait for you,' said Manning.

The marshal was disappointed. 'I thought you would have appreciated the simple domestic atmosphere. Wasn't thinking about it myself. Still, as a matter of common politeness — ' He followed Manning into the street. 'Just five minutes, then, and I'll be with you. Always come back later if you change your mind. Never tell which way the cat's going to jump.'

He went into the basso again and the crack of light narrowed and was extinguished.

Back at the office Manning found that his head had suddenly cleared. The marshal's last words still sounded in his ears. 'It's a question of delicacy, of finesse, with us,' he had pointed out. 'There are certain physical necessities which have to be admitted. The climate doesn't help. But anything crude repels us down here in the south.'

The south. From this word some virtue had departed. The flowering arcadia had shrivelled in a wind laden with corruption. He longed to shut out from his brain this antiphony of cicadas.

On the desk lay the report, where he had left it. Cautiously he found himself reading what he had written about the marshal.

> As he draws allied rations and appears no longer to serve any useful purpose, it is suggested that the Italian authorities be requested to withdraw him.

Withdraw him. Yes. Get him away. The sooner the better. The marshal. The stale sunshine. The perfume of decay. The vanquished faces of the old men at Alberto's. Make it stronger, then. He took up his pen and altered the sentence to read: 'appears to serve no function whatever'. If only he had had any positive grounds for doing so, he would have made it stronger still.

By the morning his mood of the previous day had veered round with a suddenness and violence which in itself should have been a warning. His sense of shame at his performance in the Vesuvio seemed to have bred a new and invulnerable resolution. Come what might, he would make the best of it; stick it out. There was still a chance to make good — in his own eyes at least. And that was what counted. He would make a start by unravelling the Lauro case. Good thing it had turned up. Keep his mind occupied. Nothing much to it, but all the same he would do it for the satisfaction to be got from doing a job well.

And then there was the question of the drink to consider. The drink. Perhaps he could cut it out altogether. Well, why not? After all, he had stood up to the first three years pretty well without the help of that. Surely he was not too far gone? No, he thought not. Yes, it would be better to cut it out. As Wilton had put it, these Italians soon found out your weaknesses and used them to get the better of you. He was right about that. No doubt about it.

In this frame of mind he went into the office, prepared to start work.

He had shifted the office equipment into the room next to the one in which he slept, and the first thing he noticed was that someone had been there during the night. Either that or there had been a sufficient breeze to shift the report slightly from the position in which he had left it. Because there in the night's deposit of dust was a faintly darker square marking the paper's original position.

He remembered that somewhere in the depths of the building there lived a caretaker. This man had never been formally dismissed, so he clung to his post in the hope that the municipal authorities would eventually feel obliged to pay him. He was remarkable in that underneath the dispatch rider's mackintosh which he always wore he went naked, a fact that Manning had chanced to discover from noticing that a rent in the back left a portion of his buttocks revealed.

After much shouting down the stairs, this anchorite now came slowly into view, dragging himself along on his thin, puttee-wrapped legs.

'Was there anyone in the building last night?'

'Yes.'

'Who?'

'Me.'

'Of course, I know that, but who else?'

The caretaker shrugged his shoulders. 'Who knows?'

'Well, don't you know when there's anyone on the premises.'

'No.'

'Why not?'

'If anyone wants to come in here without permission he is not likely to present himself to me. Now, is he?'

'No, but can anyone get in?'

'I suppose so. There are enough holes in the cellar. I'm always chasing kids out of them.'

'And can't you hear if anyone gets into the building at night?'

'No.'

'You are quite sure of that?'

'Yes. I stick something in my ears before I turn in. Can't sleep otherwise.'

'So it's quite likely someone did get in last night?'

'No.'

'What do you mean, no? If you were asleep with your ears stuffed up you wouldn't know anything about it, would you?'

'No.'

'Well then?'

'Why should they get in. There's nothing to come for.'

His face was that of a somnambulist. The effort to talk, to climb the stairs, seemed to have been too much. His atom of energy was spent.

'Where are you off to now?'

'To have a snooze.'

'With your ears plugged up?'

'Yes.'

'Is it true that the more you sleep the less you need to eat?'

'No, it's not true.' Wakefulness disturbed the man's face at the tantalus of food. Manning gave him a tin of rations and he slowly hobbled away, clasping at the flapping front of his coat.

THE marshal exuded geniality. 'A surprise,' he said. 'I have arranged to give you a demonstration of the forces of law and order in action. You will see how we work. These scoundrels who trouble the countryside — it suits us to let them think we are asleep, and then suddenly when they're least expecting it we swoop, and there you are.' He crossed his wrists in the conventional gesture understood as portraying the wearing of manacles.

Manning noticed he was dressed for action in a clean flannel suit with a silk scarf knotted at the throat. There was a vaguely festive atmosphere.

At that moment there came the falsetto screech of tyres on the roadway. The door burst open and a strange group of figures entered the room as if conjured up by the marshal by some necromantic process. 'We are operationally handicapped by the manpower shortage,' he explained. 'I had to arrange for some friends to help us out.'

It was obvious, in fact, from the eccentric jauntiness of their clothing, from their straw hats and bow ties, indeed from the impression they gave of playing the part of extras in an old silent film, that these men were detectives. The face of every one of them was stamped with a vast and furtive criminality. They represented in the flesh the triumph of cunning, and it was clear that this only separated them from the common run of felons.

The man who was evidently chief among them, carrying as badge of rank a black umbrella, mopped the sweat from his face and pressed with affection his week's growth of stubble against the marshal's cheek. The marshal motioned him to a chair, where he sat cracking his finger joints, his boater tipped forward over his eyes and his lower lip thrust out in a malignant parody of Maurice Chevalier.

In the background the supporting members of the cast of this burlesque had ranged themselves, chatting with crow-like amiability, grimacing, picking their teeth and playfully slapping each other's cheeks with their finger tips.

The marshal looked at his wrist watch and got up suddenly. The false Chevalier, giving his fingers one final and reluctant crack, followed him, and the whole party made for the door.

Outside, the detectives piled into the mechanical museum-piece which had brought them, while Manning and the marshal followed them in the marshal's car.

The river held the town in its flaccid embrace and from its yellow surface the morning sun now enticed white wraiths of mist. The day was still clear, although the heat was slowly spreading its canopy in the southern sky. Their road curled across scorched farmlands; through neglected vineyards where flowers still glimmered in the leaf-darkness of the vines; through groves of ancient olives, across whose roots melon plants trailed their yellowing ropes. Among the trees, huts of branches and straw could occasionally be glimpsed. These were used by the peasants to sleep in at seasons of exceptional activity in the fields.

And now, the marshal explained, they had received a report of bandits having appropriated some of them. 'They are getting grossly stupid,' said the marshal. 'The old timers would never have been so careless as to sleep in the same place more than one night.'

The car stopped and the detectives poured out. In response to some common telepathic impulse, they reached in their armpits and withdrew shining Beretta pistols. There was a snapping of bullets into breaches. Cigarettes which by skilful timing had now burned down almost to the stubble-fringed lips were spat out, and straw hats and the single umbrella were deposited on the car seat from which the dust was first carefully wiped.

The marshal nodded to the false Chevalier, who, with one hand on his tie and pouting with malice, waved his men into action. They plunged off over the moribund vegetables and were soon lost to sight amongst the trees.

About fifteen minutes passed before Manning saw them returning. They were accompanied now by their quarry — four men who walked in single file between them with the solemn and deliberate tread of mourners and who wore about their necks the yoke of an unbearable dread. The faces of these men were covered by uniform death-masks, eyelids half closed, lips bloodless.

A detective seized one of them by the arm and hustled him along. 'Don't hit me,' said the man in a colourless, matter-of-fact tone, 'I'm an epileptic.'

The false Chevalier roared with sinister mirth. 'An epileptic — eh? Well, I'm half crazy, too. You'll soon see for yourself.'

A short length of chain was produced from the car and each man attached to it by the wrist. The detectives manipulated the arms of these lifeless creatures in the manner of boisterous tailors fitting customers for a suit. Then the bandits were jostled into the car. The man who was squeezed into the front seat between the driver and another detective had to be wedged in sideways with his arms stretched tightly over the high-backed seat. The others, huddled together like trussed chickens in the rear, had been forced into a position which ensured their heads knocking together as soon as the car started off over the rough ground.

The detectives now replaced their straw hats, straightened their bows, and took up position, two of them riding on the running board of the old Bianchi, while the remainder crowded in with Manning and the marshal.

On the return journey the marshal seemed preoccupied. He spoke several times to the detectives in a tone that was sharply critical but in dialect — his remarks, it seemed, not being intended for Manning's ear. Manning noticed that they were returning by a different route, and soon the car stopped on the outskirts of a village. The marshal asked Manning to drop them there and to oblige him by taking the car back to the town. 'We have a few inquiries to make which may take up a little time,' he said.

On the way back Manning called at Vittorio's garage. Although it was not yet midday, he found it closed. Something about this circumstance awoke in him an uneasiness which deepened when at the Palumbo apartment, too, he found no signs of life. After repeatedly ringing the bell he was told by a neighbour from the adjoining flat that the whole family had gone off to Naples on the previous day.

It was quite by chance that when Manning closed the office he went to the restaurant for lunch by a different route from the usual one. Although a longer way round, this had the advantage of permitting him to walk in the shade for practically the whole distance. It took him past the Carabinieri barracks, and just as he approached the grey-painted near-ruin he saw the detectives leading five manacled men into the building.

That night he questioned the marshal about it.

'You took four prisoners this morning, didn't you?'

The marshal's good humour had returned. For a moment he seemed not to have heard. Manning repeated his question: 'There were four bandits, weren't there?'

'Four bandits?' said the marshal. 'Four bandits? No, there weren't four bandits, because four is impossible. Has to be five or more to qualify as bandits.'

'Without quibbling over technicalities,' said Manning, 'where did the fifth man come from?'

'From Certona, where we stopped. Remember it? Filthy place.'

'Was he a member of the same gang?'

'Not originally. Too small. We promoted him.'

'Why?'

'Why? Because we had to, of course. We only got four — right? Well, four's no good at all. Might as well let them go. Can't charge four men with unlawful association to commit crime — that's banditry. It has to be five. So,' the marshal smiled gently, 'five it was.'

'Couldn't you have charged them with something else?'

'No good. A lawyer would have been along by tomorrow and bailed them out. The village where they come from would have passed round the hat. Raised a million, if necessary. Village people are like that. Romanticism. Once out on bail we would never have seen them again. This way we have got them where we want them. Five to thirty years. No bail allowed.'

'But surely the fifth man will be able to prove he's innocent?'

'Of course not,' said the marshal with finality. 'A whole list of previous convictions. No one would listen to him with his record. You don't think we would have picked up an unsuitable subject, do you? I have to do my job the best way I can with the material at my disposal. It's better that one man should get more than he deserves than that four should get less.'

'I don't see it that way,' said Manning.

'You would if you were in my position,' said the marshal. 'And, by the way, what's the news of the car?'

'None.'

'But you were getting it today. It was today, wasn't it?'

'I found the garage shut up. No one about at all.'

'Don't say that.'

'The whole family's supposed to have gone off to Naples.'

'I expect they'll be back tomorrow,' the marshal said. 'We shan't know you, driving about in that smart car.'

'They'll be back sooner or later. Vittorio knows he has to give the car up. It's only a question, at the most, of putting it off a few days.'

'Of course,' the marshal said. 'And let me advise you to be firm with him. Don't stand any nonsense.'

'I won't.'

'In the meanwhile, don't forget that my car's always at your disposal.'

Five minutes after he had left the Vesuvio and was walking down the Corso, a feminine voice just behind him called, 'Signore!' The Corso, swept clean – devastated almost – by the sun, became a desert between the early morning and the evening hours. He had heard no approaching footsteps over the surface of pounded rubble. 'Signore!' He turned with surprise. Holding out her hand towards him, panting from the effort to overtake him, was Vittorio's younger daughter. She held a paper. 'A message for you, Signore.'

Before reading it he knew what was coming. He could have quoted word for word, almost, what was written there.

> The order made by A.M.G. Malevento, 1.5.44. is hereby confirmed. Fiat No. 18367L, belonging to PALUMBO, Vittorio, will in no circumstances be requisitioned.

This paper bore the stamp of the highest allied authority in Naples. Before returning it to her he carefully noted down the name of the officer who had signed it. 'Do you know this officer, Signorina?' he asked.

'Of course I know him,' she said. 'He's a friend of our family.' Her manner was very haughty.

'All right,' he said, 'we'll see about it.'

That evening he sent off a report.

> To F.S.O. 100A F.S.S.
>
> Sir, With further reference to report No. 1 of this detachment, dated 8.6.45, in which it was suggested that the Italian authorities be requested to withdraw Marshal Filippo Altamura, details are enclosed herewith of a grave irregularity committed by Marshal Altamura.
>
> Although it is appreciated that Italian civil affairs are no concern of this detachment, it is emphasized that the marshal is surplus to his establishment here. He states that his sole purpose is to liaise with the allies, but this appears to be used to cloak acts of injustice and oppression.
>
> Marshal Altamura is also accused of having victimized LAURO, Ugo di Domenico, stated to have been engaged in

partisan activities in the area and to have been interned by us in 1943. Details of case and names of witnesses are requested.

No. 3 Detachment 100A F.S.S. Malevento
9.6.45

And two days later the reply arrived:

To No. 3 Detachment 100A F.S.S. Malevento. 11.6.45
Your requested information.
LAURO, Ugo di Domenico, interned betrayal to Germans escaped allied P.W.s. Statements by CONSOMATO, Anna, PASCARELLA, Carmine, TIOBBE, Cesaro. All living Malevento.

In the envelope there was a second enclosure:

To No. 3 Detachment 100A F.S.S. Malevento 11.6.45
MANCUSO, Luigi, fu Filippo e fu VERNICELLI, Laura, of Santa Maria de Stabio.
Co-operation of Italian Authorities to be secured immediate arrest this man. Suspected war crimes.

X

'So you didn't get your car after all,' the marshal said. 'What a pity. After you'd set your heart on it, too. Never mind. We shall make do with my old one. It's not much to look at. You don't mind that, I hope?'

'I didn't want to put you to the trouble,' Manning said.

'Trouble? . . . nonsense. Quite the reverse. Never any trouble to me to co-operate with friends. I've always found it pays. We help each other, pull together — things go smoothly. We do things the wrong way, fall out perhaps — no one gets anywhere. Too bad about that car, though.'

'I haven't given up yet.'

'Good,' said the marshal. 'I'm sure you'll be successful in the long run. I look at it this way: it affects the prestige of all of us to let these people get away with it.'

Manning made no reply. Bloody nerve of the man, he thought. Hardly stop himself from laughing in my face.

'In the meanwhile my car — my person, everything — is at your disposal. Don't think of yourself as being under any obligation.'

'Thanks.'

' — At all times. Remember that. At all times. Nothing is too much trouble.'

'When shall we get to Santa Maria?' Manning asked. With the almost incredible prospect of action his spirits had quickly recovered. It meant putting up with the marshal for a few hours longer, but this couldn't be helped. As soon as they got back he'd find some way of getting a car. After that he'd be a free agent. Wash his hands of the lot of them.

'We'll take it easy,' the marshal replied. 'We don't want to get there before nightfall. A hilltop village is approached and entered by night. You don't want anyone to see you. The arrest is made at dawn. People like this with something on their consciences usually leave their sleeping place soon after daybreak.'

In the back of the Bianchi was a middle-aged carabiniere, sweating slightly in his thick uniform. By his side, as if the carabiniere had deposited a bundle on the seat, sat Don Ubaldo, the schoolmaster, a small, dried-up man with a face of yellow parchment. At their approach he removed his hat, revealing the shining undulations of his skull, to which a few white hairs adhered.

'Don Ubaldo asks for a lift on his way to Barletta, where his old father lives,' the marshal said. 'It's his only chance of getting there. He has had a pass for some time, but can't afford the fare.'

'My father's sixty-five years of age, and lives all alone,' explained Don Ubaldo.

Manning looked at him again. He would have taken Don Ubaldo himself to be sixty-five. The marshal intercepted the look. 'Don Ubaldo is not so old,' he said. 'I doubt if he could give me ten years. He doesn't live very well. Schoolmasters are badly paid.'

The car moved off slowly and Don Ubaldo leaned forward.

'I have reduced the study of how to avoid death by starvation to an exact science,' he said in a rasping whisper. 'I avoid all forms of effort, I get up for only a few hours each day. After that it really depends upon what you eat and drink.'

'I gathered as much,' said Manning.

'I'm not trying to be funny,' said the schoolmaster. 'It is not a simple matter. My salary is twelve hundred lire a month. You couldn't keep alive on it by ordinary methods over a long weekend. The essential part of my system is to discover something that takes your appetite away, and stick to it. What is important is to avoid real meals. I mean, you may have a sudden windfall, but never mind, you have to stick to the regime. It gives your stomach a chance to shrink properly.'

'They call him the Just Man,' said the marshal. 'He's the only man in Italy who doesn't patronize the black market.'

'What nonsense!' said Don Ubaldo. 'I drink coffee, don't I? How do you think I get it? If Our Lord Jesus Christ had been sent among us now He would have had to go on the Black himself in order to fulfil His mission.'

'If you don't mind, Don Ubaldo,' said the marshal, 'we draw the line at blasphemy.'

'I'm sorry — as I was saying, it is all a question of scientific stomach shrinkage. I set to work years ago when I first saw the way things were working out. Mind you, you never reach a point where hunger doesn't trouble you at all.'

The marshal was interested. 'I sometimes get peckish myself without the immediate possibility of doing anything about it. How would you deal with that?'

'Do you know Gianturco's Café? You probably don't. Actually, only an old inhabitant like myself would know where to find it now. It's just a hole in the wall. You have to mountaineer to get to it. That's the worst part — the energy it uses up.'

'Of course I know it,' said the marshal. 'Old Gianturco used to be famous for his continuous spaghetti. Nobody else ever made it like him. You could go on winding it up and never come to the end. Get the whole plateful wrapped round your fork in one unbroken cord. It's a shame to think of the way the arts are dying out.'

'Nowadays,' said Don Ubaldo, 'his widow sells a coffee substitute. It's horrible, almost undrinkable. You get a small cup for five lire, and on an empty stomach it makes you feel sick. Cumulatively it has some sort of effect on the liver. It tends to put you off food. That being so, I go there several times a day. Apart from that, I never eat anything else but bread. Sometimes I manage to get hold of a few drops of olive oil to soak the bread in.'

The marshal pointed towards a neglected field of tomato plants. The plants had shrivelled and the small, elongated fruit lay scattered about like rubies on the earth's withered bosom.

'There's an answer to your problem,' he said. 'What's wrong with a good feed of tomatoes? We could stop now. The crop is probably derelict. You could collect a sack full in half an hour.'

'Tomatoes!' cried Don Ubaldo in horror. 'Impossible. In my condition you never think of eating anything that might provoke a looseness of the bowels. Don't you understand? You have to retain such food as you eat. The most I allow myself is a weekly action. In fact, I do everything possible to discourage peristalsis.'

They were passing now between hills, insubstantial in the heat and seen rather as a reflection in dark water. Above these hills the Apennines hung in suspension the remote filament of their outline.

'Dust,' said the marshal.

Dust.

The car hissed as smoothly as a sleigh over the blanketed road, and dust curled through their tyres and billowed into the sky behind them. The marshal closed the windows, driving with his handkerchief held over his mouth. But dust poured in like smoke. Soon it covered them completely. At first the sweat on hands and face oozed through, but fresh layers of dust absorbed it. The dust tasted sweet in the throat.

Don Ubaldo looked about him with approval. 'Our homeland,' he said, smiling gently. 'These trees, these buildings, these fields. They are all part of our heart.'

Biting the end off a cigar, the marshal clenched it savagely between his teeth. 'Part of your heart, if you like. Not part of my heart.'

They travelled through a ghostly landscape, a landscape which dust had transmuted to one of bleached coral. Even the occasional farmhouses wore veils of gossamer, only blemished or frayed by the flicking tails of asses. Hens flustered, stiff-winged, from their path, propelled as if by a series of explosions. The peasants on their donkeys went divorced from the earth, each enveloped in his swirling shroud. Turning to gesticulate as the car passed, their white masks suddenly cracked and through them showed the lines of mirth, of avarice or of weariness. Their daughters, bearing bundles upon their heads, had become caryatids from the alabaster of whose features, however, there shone black eyes.

After this calcareous belt came others of coloured earths, and the peasants who worked in them were accordingly ruddy or ochreous. It was, indeed, possible to deduce from their colour where they had been to their fields, and when they met and mingled on the road they looked like groups of tired mummers returning from a pageant.

Now the road began to climb, the hills closed in on them and divided into steep and arid cones, each bearing upon its summit a crystalline aerie of human habitation, up to which spiralled a ribbon of road. Poised on a pinnacle rising sheer out of a wilderness of prickly pear, a cactus-impaled village, still chapleted with dissolving mist, drew Manning's attention.

'Rocca degli Angeli,' said Don Ubaldo excitedly.

The marshal stopped the car to give them the opportunity of a better view.

'The result of a really large-scale miracle on the part of San Gennaro,' explained Don Ubaldo. 'Imagine that — a whole village built overnight. Nothing shoddy or jerrybuilt about it, either. The saint used only the best procurable materials.'

'How does the story go?' asked the marshal.

'It happened in the days when the people of these parts were continually troubled by Saracens,' said Don Ubaldo. 'Things got so bad that the mere sight of two or three unusually sun-burned strangers was enough to make them take to the hills. In fact, local ruffians only had to stain their faces and wrap towels round their heads in order to be able to loot the villages at their ease.

'After putting up with this state of affairs for a number of

123

years, the villagers decided to appeal to San Gennaro as their patron saint. The saint appeared and suggested resistance. It seems that although saints are very peaceable men during their lifetime they sometimes acquire after death a taste for bloodthirsty enterprises. In fact, San Gennaro offered to lead them in battle, just as Saint Iago frequently appeared in person to lead the Spaniards when people of non-European origin were being attacked.

'The villagers finally allowed themselves to be persuaded — although not without misgivings — and from that time on, led by the saint waving a large sword which because of his unsuitable clothing he managed with considerable difficulty, they succeeded in repelling several attacks.

'Unfortunately, they soon noticed that San Gennaro was to be seen only when the enemy was grossly outnumbered. In fact, it seemed that although a Roman when originally on earth, he had slowly degenerated into something like a Neapolitan in the relaxing climate of the better world. The crisis was reached when a Saracen band which the villagers outnumbered by only about ten to one put in an appearance. San Gennaro was the first to throw his sword away and clear off to the hills. Of course, the villagers were very disillusioned about this, and while the Saracens were burning down their houses and carrying off their livestock they spoke sharply to the saint.

'San Gennaro, however, was far too much of a Neapolitan not to have something up his sleeve. Why, he suggested, go back at all? Why not stay where they were on the top of a mountain and settle themselves out of the Saracens' reach? As an inducement and some sort of recompense for the trouble he had put them to, he agreed to build a suitable village overnight.

'Of course, there's another story which denies the miraculous building of the village and says that what actually happened was that San Gennaro really persuaded them to drive out the inhabitants of a village already existing on this spot. These original inhabitants were of doubtful orthodoxy in their religious views, so naturally San Gennaro detested them even more than the Saracens themselves.'

They approached a sprawling town whose buildings toppled in a confusion of cubes through its ruptured ramparts.

'Busento,' announced the marshal. 'We can stop here for an early lunch. Further on the villages are so poverty-stricken we won't get any food.'

'The ancient Busentum,' echoed Don Ubaldo. 'Once a town of great wealth. Immensely fertile soil, but situated on a geological fault. Unfortunately Providence thought fit to curb any tendency towards pride by visiting it with an endless succession of earthquakes. There have been at least a hundred major shocks in this century, and this has been going on from the beginning of time.'

Indeed, the shape of Busento had suffered obvious modification by this act of divine correction which by shaking them in its dice box had levelled the towers of ten successive kingdoms. Now only mean streets remained, but in their crouching habitations the builder had had the choice of the most grandiose materials. Into the façades of the saddlers' shops, the wheelwrights, the rope makers, the bakers, and into Busento's rows of dark and cavernous homes had gone noble blocks of masonry. On these, mutilated eagles, lions and bulls battled eternally for liberation from their base confinement.

Ancient women squatted at the entrance to their hovels. Here, under the half-obliterated standards of Anjou and Aragon, they awaited death in the black-hooded abandonment of old age. For their distraction at this moment a mad girl in mourning leaped and gesticulated along the street in frantic parody of a dancer in a Greek tragedy.

'God's blessings are not always obvious,' said the peasant who sat next to them at the table of the locanda. 'Thank God we escaped the horrors of the war and we aren't troubled much by such things as changes of government. Here we live by our own hands.'

The locanda was as long and narrow as a passage, its further end being obscured in gloom in which the shapes of immense wine barrels could be discerned. A single long table ran down the centre. Seated at it were the older and more prosperous of the peasants who could afford to take their relaxation here at midday.

'Eating?' asked the restaurant keeper. He shuffled over to them, laying down plates and then picking them up and rubbing their surfaces with a grey rag he kept in his pocket.

Manning commented on the old man's extreme swarthiness. 'It's dirt,' said the marshal without emotion. His face, indeed, was as withered and blackened as if it had been exposed to the same smoke as that in which his hams had been cured. He climbed on to the table, unhooking one of the hams which hung among the sooty beams. He grasped it firmly, his encrusted thumbs sinking deeply into the greenish surface of the meat.

'Couldn't he wash his hands?' asked Manning.

The marshal called to him. 'Don't you ever wash?'

The old man looked up, wiping his hands half-apologetically on his trousers. The marshal persisted. 'Why don't you wash your hands before you mess our food about?' The man's face assumed a stubborn expression. He nodded towards a pitcher which stood in the corner. 'No water to waste. We need that for drinking.'

'It's not to be wondered at, at all,' the marshal confided when the old man had gone off to draw wine. 'It's part of their general attitude. They just don't notice the existence of dirt.' He motioned to the carabiniere. 'How often do you wash, Giuseppe?'

'I wash my hands and face once a day,' said Giuseppe with simplicity.

'I'm referring to your carcass,' said the marshal, 'what about that?'

Giuseppe grinned in slight embarrassment. 'I have an all-over on Easter day. I know you think it funny, marshal, but where I come from it's considered the proper thing to do. We look at it from the health point of view. The more you wash under your clothes, the more risk you run from infection.'

The wine was ink-coloured and had a harsh, coppery taste. Passing his tongue over his teeth after he had drunk, Manning found they were roughened and furred by its asperity. The schoolmaster smacked his lips in appreciation. 'This stuff's just right. No chance of it affecting the bowels.' He had refused the ham and was making a meal of bread and oil. He astounded the others by belching grandiosely on this fare.

The peasant who had spoken when he first came in addressed them again. 'My father kept count of the earthquakes for years. After he passed the fifty mark he gave up and went to Rome. He only stayed there a year.'

'The instinct which draws one back to one's home is amazing,' said Don Ubaldo.

'It wasn't that the old chap was sentimental about the place. He just felt like an outsider anywhere else.'

'He was right. All the men in Rome smell like women and the women don't smell at all,' said the carabiniere with contempt.

'According to the Romans they shouldn't,' pointed out Don Ubaldo gravely. 'Don't you know their proverb, mulier bene olet quae non olet?'

'If that means a woman smells well that doesn't,' said the marshal, 'it's a funny thing, because we have a proverb down here that says more or less the opposite.'

' — On the whole,' went on the old peasant, who had taken no interest in this disgression, 'we're not so badly off here with our earthquakes. Things are terrible in these parts. I can assure you that in one way or other most of the villages are worse off than us.'

'Don't talk like that,' said a second peasant. 'Worse off? Look at Cavano, for instance. They've got everything. The top joint of the middle finger of St. Stephen, a centimetre and a half of the rod of Aaron and a jar of the fat of St. Laurence.'

'And the malaria,' said the first grimly.

127

'All right then, take Santa Maria della Croce: a bottle of the authentic blood of St. John which never fails to liquefy on his feast day, an image of St. Michael exuding an inexhaustible supply of manna which is still sold at practically pre-war prices. Even you can't deny that it's a certain cure for the sciatica. Why! Pope Pius II himself visited the shrine. Not only that but —'

' — the malaria. Even the manna's no good against the malaria. Half the population's slowly dying from it.'

'Well then, at Rocca d'Aspide: a footstep of St. Paul imprinted in the rock, the crucifix that spoke to St. Thomas Aquinas, a picture painted by St. Andrew.'

' — and the malaria.'

'You are a materialist,' said the second old peasant in bitter disappointment. 'These glorious possessions which are the envy of the whole world seem to mean nothing to you. I am sorry, I can't enter into an argument. We see the world through different eyes.' He appealed to them. 'For God's sake don't take any notice of this old fellow. He is so engrossed in his bodily needs he never pays any attention to the things of the spirit. He will be telling us they have malaria at Cardito next. It's the village next to us. It's famous for its wonderful churches.'

'No,' said the first, 'not malaria: only bandits. And for just that reason. The place is so healthy that the only way they can keep the population down is by killing one another. They have a cemetery where they say no one has ever been buried who died a natural death. They're proud of it. When Musso talked about abolishing malaria he was out of his mind. How could we afford to abolish malaria? It's a prime necessity. That's unless you prefer bandits. Just as silly as all this talk about abolishing war.'

'I'm with you there,' said the other. 'But do you realize that half our troubles have arisen because there's not been a real war for centuries? Now look at the last war. Do you call that a war? They just don't understand the meaning of the word war now.'

'You're right. It was a complete waste of time. Might as well not have had one.'

'Of course I'm right. What did they do, after all? The soldiers just came here, put half the girls in the family way, knocked down all the bridges, and went away again, leaving us worse off than ever and with just as many mouths to feed. What we needed was a real, old-fashioned war. When the Spaniards and the French came here they killed us off like flies and put the survivors to profitable work. Having reduced the population to reasonable limits they stayed with us and organized the place. They didn't selfishly take one sniff at the air and run off again. They kicked our backsides and made us work hard. It's a little painful while it's going on, but you must admit that in the long run it's better for everyone concerned.'

As they passed out from the locanda's dankness of wine and of sweat-impregnated serge, high noon cast its winding-sheet over them. The peasants escaping with them from the dark interior bent their heads and wrapped their cloaks around themselves as if in protection from dagger strokes. Those whom they had seen waiting outside the harness makers and the wheelwrights had now collapsed under their carts in the attitudes of sudden death. The crones in the doorways hid their faces behind the bony lattice of their fingers. The sun hurled spears of shadow at them from the eaves. A rank silence had descended upon the town.

They drove out into a glowing landscape, a place of scuttling rodents, its surface gilded with the refuse of the spring's brief verdure. Over it flocks of white goats tripped with fairy-like delicacy. And beyond — in a phantom desert, a wilderness of white boulders and of quartz rocks — were vast tumuli, mountains composed simply of heaped up boulders which shimmered in a soft but savage light.

And still through this wilderness the peasants trudged whitened like clowns and raising their dust-tranquilized faces towards them as if to escape drowning in the tide of dust that swirled about them.

A white-washed carabiniere stood in the road, hand out-stretched. 'Could you manage a lift to Cardito?'

He squeezed into the back seat. 'Are you thinking of stopping there by any chance?' he asked.

'No,' said the marshal.

'Just as well. I only mention it because the Cuccurullo gang's up to its old tricks again. Yesterday they stormed the Municipio and took the arms off the Urban Guard.

'Blunderbusses?' asked the marshal.

'No, they got five carbines and three pistols. Two passers-by who poked their noses into it got knocked off and one of our chaps caught a packet. I'm the replacement.'

'I always heard that the Vaiano outfit controlled this area. Don't they have a tank?'

'They had one but it packed up after a few days. Now Cuccurullo's back again.'

The road now entered another of those typical villages — villages whose fetor was enclosed in an emanation of languid blossoms, whose arrogant towers — now stabling asses — lifted their crenellations from the quilted armour of mean roofs.

In the outskirts of the village there were no signs of life. As always when bloody acts are in preparation, a hush had fallen. Only a flight of the silent jackdaws of the south deserted the roofs at their approach.

Before them the road was constricted between rows of bassi, single-room dwellings the large double doors of which formed almost the whole of one wall; and now, with all these doors closed, the street was blind, withdrawn. Each lintel was surmounted by a pair of cow's horns.

Suddenly the marshal slowed down. He pulled the car over to the side of the road, stopping close to a basso on the door of which had been chalked a blue St. Andrew's cross. He kicked at the door, clicking his teeth in vexation, and an old man appeared. The marshal pointed to the cross. 'Who's responsible for this? Get it rubbed off immediately.' 'It's done by an enemy,' he explained to the others.

'Ex-Fascists?' asked Manning.

'Fascists? They never heard of them. These things go back to the Carbonari, or earlier. They've forgotten long ago what started it all.'

They got back into the car and started off again.

At the end of this blind-eyed street, softened with haze, was a pink-walled church with a dome like a Tartar helmet. Against the pink wall moved a group of black figures.

Through the telescope of Manning's imagination formed a vision of the sad-faced men at the end of the street who awaited them, daggers muffled in sleeves, with the reluctance of executioners.

The marshal was driving very slowly. He nodded in the direction of Manning's tommy-gun. 'What is the accurate range of this machine?'

'About thirty metres.'

'Loaded?'

'Yes.'

They drove on, the marshal holding the wheel with his left hand, his right being thrust into his jacket pocket. Turning, for a second perhaps, to glance at the houses, Manning glimpsed the white face of a woman at the only unbarred window he had seen. It was immediately withdrawn. Giuseppe and the other carabiniere sat, holding their short-barrelled rifles which looked as insubstantial as children's toys. Don Ubaldo had disappeared from sight.

At the road junction by the church they turned to the right, passing within a few yards of the mute and motionless gathering there. Except to turn their heads, none of the group moved, content to watch them with the introspection of caged tigers. Close quarters had revealed, however, a reality less spectacular than Manning's phantasy had prepared, and in place of savage-faced assassins he observed that Cuccurulo's bad men had been recruited from hungry-looking ex-soldiers who wore threadbare remnants of their uniforms and were attended by moronic hangers on.

131

Don Ubaldo now bobbed up again, making some remark in praise of the old days when successful drives employing whole carabinieri battalions, and taking thousands at a time in the net, had been organized against such evildoers.

'If you're choosing a roundabout way of saying something in favour of the late dictator,' said the marshal, 'I don't want to listen to it. At least have the decency to keep your mouth shut for another few years.'

By late evening they came into view of the hilltop town of Santa Maria di Stabio.

The marshal insisted upon waiting until dark before climbing the road which wound through a score of hairpin bends up to the town.

They passed between hedges of dimly seen cactus, the road lit only by the glimmer of their sidelights and by the sparks struck from flints by the peasants' horses. As they passed the group of peasants, there floated to them snatches of wailing African songs, chanted to the rhythm of grinding cart wheels.

'The fame of Santa Maria di Stabio was perpetuated by Horace,' said Don Ubaldo. 'The divine poet complained that its inn was the worst in Italy, and it's certain not to have changed.'

'Is there much malaria?' asked the marshal.

'What do you imagine, in the middle of that swamp?'

'The evildoers of this town,' said the marshal, 'have always had a taste for politics. Before Mussolini's time it produced anarchists. After that it was castor-oil dosing squadristi. Just the place where I would expect to look for a war criminal. How do you account for that, Don Ubaldo?'

'Poverty,' said Don Ubaldo. 'I always plump for poverty. Although why poverty in one area should produce homicides, in another kidnappers and in another fanatics, don't ask me to explain. The trouble here, of course, is what I should call legal exhaustion. It all goes back to the fact that the tenure of the only cultivatible land in the neighbourhood has been in constant

132

dispute for eight hundred years. Did Duke Ruggiero intend his grant as a gift outright, or merely in emphyteusis? The document was too loosely worded, and so you see the town has only a doubtful justification for its existence at all. At all events, this problem has provided a living for a swarm of lawyers, and they are the only ones that have really got anything worth speaking of out of the land.'

'Under what right was it held by the Duke himself?' asked Manning.

'Ah, my dear sir,' said Don Ubaldo, 'the Duke's right? What a question. Why, the only basic right, of course. The right upon which all other rights are founded. That of conquest. After all, we must begin somewhere. Where on earth would we be if we called such a fundamental right into question.'

The old woman admitted them into a low-ceilinged room lit by an electric lamp, its rays, enfeebled by the dense spottings of flies upon its surface, hardly penetrated to the corners. Narrow iron bedsteads were placed at regular intervals, as if in the ward of an overcrowded lazarette, and beside each bedstead stood a chamber pot in the shape of an amphora.

The marshal had suggested that it was best to go straight to the inn rather then to risk being too conspicuous in any of the taverns of the town.

Don Ubaldo was delighted. 'Undoubtedly this is the very inn of which Horace wrote.'

The room was untenanted, and choosing adjacent beds as near as possible to the source of light they undressed, laid their clothes across the foot of the bed and stretched themselves on the mattresses, which sagged in obedience to the contours of an infinite nightly succession of human forms.

Mosquitoes traced menacing arabesques of sound above them, and Manning drew the dun coloured sheet protectively up to his eyes. From it came the faint odour of the skin of ageing functionaries which infrequent and soapless washings had failed to expunge. When he pulled down the sheet, preferring the assaults of the mosquitoes, he smelt the cat-like pungency of Giuseppe's unwashed body.

Presently a dim, black-hooded form entered the room, treading tip-toe and carrying its boots. At the foot of the beds it half turned and bowed before entering the penumbra, from which immediately there leapt up menacing fakirs of shadow as the figure divested itself of its clothing. The shadows sank down in a salaam and immediately the silence was molested by a briefly ascending scale as water entered the amphora. Then silence again.

Another cloaked and hooded figure entered. Another and yet another. Slowly the room became a forum of vague, wavering shadows, a bowed and grief-stricken procession returned from following a catafalque, each mysterious form carrying boots, each stopping to incline its head in their direction, and then the inevitable prolonged chirp of the pot being filled.

Who, then, were these conspirators? Had they blundered unawares into a convention of those anarchists of old which this town had spawned? Could these be the mute officers of a veritable secret society?

'Commercial travellers,' whispered the marshal. 'This is a half-way house between Naples and the south.'

XI

WHILE Don Ubaldo slept on, they arose and dressed in the paling darkness.

Leaving the inn they joined the torpid procession of peasants drawn from their beds by the magnet of their distant grey fields. The peasants streamed, silent zombies, from the courtyards of the great ranchhouse-like dwellings where they continued at night the semi-communal existence of their labours. Groping their way down from the rows of living-rooms on the balconied upper storey, they got out their animals from the stables beneath and hitched them to the rows of carts in those courtyards which, later, would be invaded by the womenfolk, who washed the linen, cooked and mended there in a raucous domestic communism. But at this hour the men and the young girls who worked in the fields, feeling none of the tired gaiety of relief brought by the day's ending, trudged sullenly towards their tasks, their stomachs awash with unsweetened coffee and polenta, jabbing with irritation as they went at the known sore places in their animals' anatomies.

The address they sought was just such another of these communal dwellings, half ranch and half oriental khan. Here, owing to the fact that two or three members of the reduced professional classes had come to live in the house, there was a porter occupying a single room among the stables. The marshal tapped on the glass top-half of the door, and as soon as the porter had removed the chain he pushed the door open and went in, signalling the others to follow. The porter, divining the nature of their visit from the sixth sense possessed by the clan of informers to which porters naturally belonged, brought them chairs and waited with resignation.

'Where's Mancuso?' asked the marshal.

'Uh,' grunted the porter cautiously, accompanying this sound with a slight backward jerk of the head.

'Well,' said the marshal, 'come on, speak up. Is he here or isn't he here? They must have taught you when you did your military service how to give a straight answer to a straight question.'

'He's not here,' said the porter, surprised that this had not been understood from his previous grunt.

'How long since he was here?'

'A few days. Maybe three or four.'

'Where is he now?'

'Uh.' Another jerk of the head.

'You don't know?' said the marshal. 'Come on, now, don't be foolish. Don't waste our time.'

'I don't want to mislead you,' said the porter. 'I know how to keep my nose clean.' Although there was no possibility of being overheard he lowered his voice. 'He's probably gone over to La Vipera.'

'What's La Vipera?'

'It's the masseria up by the monastery. The ones that are on their last legs usually finish up there. The monks give them a drop of soup every day.'

'What's the matter with Mancuso?'

'T.B. He only just about made the journey to get back here. When he found his mother had gone and he'd made the trip for nothing, he cleared out again; but in his state he couldn't get far.'

'He's still a Fascist, isn't he?'

'Of course he's a Fascist. He's one of those born stupids who don't realize that when they are beaten the time has come to forget all this nonsense and do the same as everyone else does. We've had a bellyful of them. Look at Salvatore.'

'Salvatore?'

'The famous one, the parachutist. He was in all the papers a few years ago. You must remember him. Decorated three times for heroism —' the porter smiled nervously in Manning's direction — 'I'm sorry. I mean what they used to call heroism until the armistice was signed. You know, taking machine-gun nests single-handed and risking one's life for one's pals, and all that kind of nonsense. Of course, I realize now that such people were no better than dirty dogs – correct me if I'm wrong.' The porter gave Manning another nervous glance. 'I'm not trying to be funny and I don't want to get into trouble. It's just that I get a bit confused.'

'You're quite right,' the marshal reassured him.

'Well,' said the porter, 'all these men who used to be heroes until they refused to take any notice of the armistice – I mean these people who were heroes until it was officially explained otherwise – they keep drifting back. Salvatore, for instance. He turns up not so long ago after being missing for God knows how long. "Mother," he says, "I've come back." He was never able to say how he got here. You might even say that war had turned him into a baby again, because his mother picks up what's left of him like a feather and puts him to bed. Presently the doctor turns up. He shakes his head. "I can't do anything for him. He's torn his tubes right out. He'll have to go back to the military hospital." His mother asks him: "Do you want to go back, son?" And he shakes his head. I was there and I saw it. After all, if St. Christopher had performed the miracle of bringing him back to his own people to die, what could you expect? As there was a hole right through him he couldn't eat. His mother lit cigarettes for two days and put them in his mouth. After that he could still hold the cigarettes between his lips but couldn't draw any more. And there have been plenty more like him. When they are incurable from T.B. they release them from the Prisoner of War hospitals if they want to go home. Of course, some of them, like Salvatore who haven't got T.B. and are just dying of wounds, escape, or perhaps, as they say, one of the Saints comes for them and takes them away. How else could you explain it? They turn up here, rags on their feet, starving, dripping blood and pus, coughing their lungs up. Can't give an account of how they got here. Only their own mothers who bore them could ever recognize them. I am speaking, of course, of bloody

137

Fascist hot-heads, ne'er-do-wells. We used to consider them heroes when we didn't know any better.'

'And yet the Saints seem to be prepared to do something for them,' said Giuseppe with perplexity.

'People say so,' said the porter. 'Not that I believe it personally. But if there's anything in it, all I can say is that the Saints probably don't see things in the same light. They can't have much idea of politics by the time they don't care which side a man was on.'

The marshal, whom Manning had just heard mutter under his breath the words 'bravi figliuoli', now came to earth. 'The question,' he said, 'is whether or not we can lay a trap for our man. Whether we can find some way of persuading him to come here. Has he any relations?' he asked the porter. 'Did anyone ever come to see him?'

'He's got a sister up in the north.'

Giuseppe caught on. 'Of course, we could send a message up to La Vipera to say his sister is here. She could be in some kind of trouble. That would fetch him back.'

The marshal pondered over the idea and then reluctantly rejected it. 'We can't afford to take the risk. He might know that his sister couldn't possibly have arrived. We had better go ourselves. How far away is it?'

'About four kilometres. The monastery's on the hillside at the end of the valley and the masseria's just underneath it.'

'There's no way of getting up to the masseria without being seen?'

'You can cut through the marsh and the old oak forest instead of going round by the road. That is, if you don't object to stinks. That way you're in view only for the last few hundred metres.'

Following the direction indicated by the porter they descended a narrow street, its walls torn and blunted by the axles of passing carts, which brought them to the outskirts of Santa Maria. Here the houses were stripped of their balconies, their arches, their turrets; in fact, of all their fanciful ornaments and projections.

The sloping, tiled roofs had become flat or, in oriental fashion, showed the rudimentary suggestion of a dome. Finally, as they passed out of the town through the continuous row of houses whose façades joined to form a rampart, they came upon a few of those hovels in the shape of bee-hives or of clustering cones which reflected here the ancient building style of the great plain of the Capitanata — a memory perpetuated in stone of the straw shelters of neolithic nomads. Their way carried them down through patches of derelict cultivation showing up like worn-out hairbrushes in the bland desolation of the hillside. At their crackling approach grasshoppers whirled into the rays of the newly risen sun. On barren fields, stones which had been strewn with a prodigal hand gleamed like bleached bones in the rush of yellow light. Where the earth retained any of its virtue long, rank thistles grew, and among them white butterflies threaded their way in endless maypole revel. Half walking and half running they stumbled down the slope, ducking beneath the solitary olives, stubborn survivors of ancient groves, their boughs propped up with rocks and mantled with the transparent shells of snails.

They reached the valley. Threads of water glinted at their feet and their boots broke through a web of coarse grass into black slime.

A diurnal owl flapped on moth's wings above the sedges. On the edge of this swamp survived a colony of withering asphodels, each flower having suckled in its bosom throughout the night a slug which now withdrew itself in preparation for the eventide renewal of its embrace. Here, too, were many yellow, daisy-like flowers; bright planets, each encircled by its satellites of winged insects.

Soon, having crossed the swamps, they saw above them the white walls of the monastery, and below it on a level space where the hill flattened out, the derelict farm buildings of the masseria La Vipera.

They had approached the hill by its steepest side, and as they toiled up the slope they saw that a man was sitting in the arched gateway. Soon he got up and went in out of sight. A few minutes later, while they were still clambering over the broken walls where terraced cultivation had once been carried out, and still perhaps two hundred yards from their objective, they saw another figure come into sight behind and above the masseria, making its way slowly up a steep path among the rocks. Seeing this, the marshal ordered Giuseppe to skirt round the masseria and go after this man, while he and Manning, climbing down into the road, made for the gateway.

Those who, in farming this land, had joined battle against impossible odds had long since laid down their arms. Hence the absence of the smoke of fires, of the heartening shriek of cart axles, of the creaking of well ropes, and of the familiar and pleasing sound of animals in their byres. The stairway of access to the balcony having broken away, the swallows had now entered into undisputed possession of the upper rooms. The walls, once painted a bold and defiant red, had faded to one of those tranquil tones by which, in sunlit climes, decrepitude is ennobled.

In the shadow of broken wheels, of the dry well, haloed with discarded scythes, reclined figures which had escaped, so it seemed to Manning, bearing their unscathed profiles from Etruscan funerary vases. The rare and authentic urn faces of spearmen, models which the painters of antiquity had chosen, unanimously rejecting the portrayal of shopkeepers, of lawyers, of peasants, policemen or politicians; those countenances engraved with the common taint of over-valuation of life. These serene gladiators, on the contrary, swordless before death which awaited them with its net and trident, proclaimed themselves voicelessly as ravens among crows, potential founders of world-shattering dynasties missed by an incredible oversight of nature in the accomplishment of its purpose. Here, then, they lay in their togas of rags, the wasted flesh displaying the dignity of their skeletons, and by their sides, their guitars and the trifling impedimenta of soldiers; a negligent and sardonic corrective to the conqueror's pride.

A gaunt shape in the tatters of a parachutist's uniform lifted itself from the ground and prowled towards them. Coming face to face with Manning and significantly ignoring the marshal, he stopped, heels together, bowing slightly, and asked in a calm and pleasant tone: 'You are looking for someone?'

At the marshal's preparatory intake of breath the parachutist transfixed him with a hawk-like stare; and the marshal, who in some magic manner seemed to have shrunk within the tawdry spruceness of his clothes, had become the prey of a humility so abject that Manning almost pitied him. *But the survival of the fittest — you don't believe in it yourself, marshal!*

The marshal discarded, abandoned like a hopeless recruit on parade, the flashing glance reverted to Manning's face. 'You are looking for someone?'

Vain now to await the marshal's authoritative intervention. 'We have come for Mancuso,' Manning said.

'You won't find him here,' said the parachutist, composed but swaying slightly.

'Mancuso's the one who tore off his bandages and died yesterday,' said a voice.

'No, that was Gargiullo. Mancuso had a haemorrhage and passed out the day before.'

'In any case,' said the one who had first approached him, 'I can assure you he is not here. Nobody stays with us for long, you know.'

There was nothing more to be said. Manning observed at that moment that the carabiniere had returned and was hovering in the background, trying to attract the marshal's attention.

'It was him, all right,' said Giuseppe. 'He went up to the monastery. Just beat me to it. There was I, shouting to him to stop, and he was looking round quietly, watching me come up and then tapping on the gate, looking as if he was not in any particular hurry. They opened the gate just as I got there. I could almost have put out my hand and touched him.'

'And you didn't go in after him?' asked Manning.

Giuseppe looked surprised. 'A monk came out and told me to go away.'

'And, of course, you went away. Come on,' said Manning. He led the way up out of the courtyard, noticing that as soon as he could no longer see the faces of the wounded there, it was as if a hypnotic spell had been broken.

He walked forward with brisk resolution, the marshal and Giuseppe following on his heels. There came to him at this moment an uneasy revelation, the knowledge that in reality he was keenly anticipating the manhunt that Mancuso's flight would provide. The manhunt with its end almost as certain as that of the bull when it enters the bull ring. Quickly he sought for some means of justifying this barbarous impulse. Well then, was it not his duty to bring Mancuso back? Failure to do so would involve him in disgrace; to say nothing about his personal distaste for this breed of fascists. In any case, no blame could be laid at his door for the devising of a Nemesis which persecuted soldiers to their graves but let the politicians off scot free. No, it was not that he proposed to carry out his orders as efficiently as he could that gave him cause for alarm, but the fact that the icy spirit of detachment which he had always admired was so notably lacking. Far, indeed, from remaining a military automaton, an instrument of justice (or injustice, if you preferred it that way — but at all events an instrument), he recognized the presence of an exultant satisfaction which strove hard but completely without success to clothe its repellent nakedness in a respectable motive. Of what ingredients, then, were compounded that quickening of the pulse, that excitement which showed itself in the accelerated intake and expulsion of his breath? The conclusion, however much he might indulge in mental squirming, was not to be avoided. He enjoyed hunting down a fellow man, even one he might respect. He who had always successfully evaded the necessary slaughter of domestic animals, who had never hidden his disapproval of blood sports, who had been a squeamish and reluctant fisherman, derived the keenest satisfaction from the hounding of one of his own kind . . . even a man at death's door.

He sensed a flagging in the marshal's spirit, and noticed also that Giuseppe appeared to consider the matter of their mission concluded, as he had quickly unloaded his rifle, subsequently re-slinging it on his shoulder with an air of finality.

'We've got him cornered, marshal,' said Manning, assailed by an unheralded gust of good fellowship.

The marshal did not reply.

'I wonder if we shall have to search the place?'

'We can't do that,' said the marshal.

'I'm not going back without Mancuso.'

'Then let's hope he turns himself in.'

'Seems a pity to have to take him,' said Manning, 'but he must be a bad case before they go to so much trouble over him.'

The marshal remained silent.

As they followed the path winding up the hill through the waste of trivial flowers, the walls which from afar had encircled the monastery like a chaplet now soared up, cutting off from their view the square, primitive strength of the buildings themselves.

Manning, who felt himself virtually unsupported by the others, pulled the bell-cord that hung down outside the great gate.

Somewhere in the obscure depths of the interior there sounded in response an insignificant jingling. He could also hear a remote clatter of churns, the leisurely slapping of sandals across court-yards — but always receding — the swish of a birch broom on wet stones — the setting, made audible, of the monastery's placid routine.

He pulled the bell-cord again and tapped sharply on the gate with his boot.

In the meanwhile the marshal and Giuseppe scrutinized with interest the details of opposite horizons.

Once again he was about to wrench at the bell when a diminishing trail of footsteps suddenly hovered, reversed their direction and were amplified in shuffling approach. The wicket gate opened, and Manning saw at a glance that this high wall served a function like that of a fortress's outer ward, and that they were still separated from the closely grouped monastery buildings by a narrow belt of land strewn with large rocks, around which gardens had been planted.

In the gateway stood a young monk with bloodless lips and a cadaverous, light-shunning face.

'... The soldier who has just come in?'

The monk shook his head. The mouth was expressionless, but the sunken eyes behind the spectacle lenses were hostile.

Standing inside the gate, the monk having given way with reluctance, Manning noticed that Giuseppe had removed his hat and was standing outside like a new boy in the presence of a schoolmaster. The marshal was still absorbed in the horizon, and returning to the young monk Manning was in time to intercept a glance that went past him down towards the angle of the wall where in turning the flank of a building it took in a steep, rocky bank, a natural feature which the original builders had evidently regarded as ineradicable. In this bank he noticed with awakening intuition a cleft, the narrow entrance to what looked like a cave.

Walking off purposefully in this direction and calling to the marshal — from whom, however, came no response — he suddenly and surprisingly found the monk at his side. The monk was tugging at his sleeve, and when Manning shook himself free and began to run the monk ran too, with a speed that seemed in no way reduced by his emaciation. Being obliged once again to break free of his grip, and this time with some violence, Manning noticed that the weight of the body which he repelled with a thrust of the left arm was no greater than that of a child of ten.

He stopped to orient himself in the vast, dim interior of the cave, which funnelled out from the narrow entrance through which two bodies could hardly have passed together. Towering above him and forming a semi-circle of half-obliterated forms was a Byzantine fresco in which a beardless Christ, a young man of terrible countenance grasping the hilt of a vanished sword sat in judgment in the company of faceless archangels.

Beneath the vaguely delineated but majestic fragments of this tableau and barring his entrance to a further passageway the monk had placed himself with outstretched arms. His spectacles had gone in the struggle and the thinly diffused light flashed in concentration from his eyes. For the first and last time he spoke. 'Do not disturb the bones of the dead.'

Again Manning was past him, brushing him aside almost unnoticed as he plunged into the gloomy chamber beyond. Drawing his torch he shone it round the walls of this vault, which breathed on him the still, sour breath of undisturbed centuries. In the walls tiers of niches had been cut, shallow hollows where the feeble rays picked out curved segments of ribs — a thigh bone, a forearm, perhaps a portion of a skull, all pitiably diminished, blackened and powdered. If all these bones, he thought, could be, gathered, made miraculously to come together, there would not be enough upon which the flesh of one man might be moulded.

Standing guard over these loosely garnered sheaves, the dancing afreet of his torch revealed a broken rank of saints, their fingers raised according to the conscience of the beholder in blessing or in commination. Throughout the neighing of horses and the thundering of hooves that had filled the dark ages with their sound, these stern observers had kept their night watch over the remains of their followers. The cringing humility of fishermen of meagre catches was rightly translated here to the portentous stance of those who had died for their faith by the edge of the sword. The eyes of once mild disciples were levelled at him in enormous challenge.

As he advanced the torch rays flickered successively in the hollows and recesses below the hems of apostolic robes. Suddenly there arose, flinging itself from a niche, a ghastly figure, shaking off as it did the thin covering of bones which ineffectively it had piled upon itself. The desperately scrambling shape reached a wall fissure hitherto unperceived, through which it tried frantically to squeeze itself, succeeding in the fraction of a second that it took Manning to reach the spot. The face showed momentarily in swooning profile, a disappearing hand clutched the air and was gone. Manning half pushed himself through the gap and shone down his torch into the night-choked abyss below. The light diluted feebly into a powdering mist and lost itself in wavering inefficacy in that immense emptiness. A fragment of rock crumbled under his weight and dropped away into black sheep's wool.

'Mancuso!' he shouted. 'Mancuso!'

The vault flung back to him the last two syllables in rumbling accusation.

Behind him in the charnel house had gathered a murmuring assemblage of monks, austere sheep over which some werewolf spell of defiance had been cast.

The marshal and Giuseppe were waiting for him outside the monastery gates, glum silhouettes against the muscled lion-skin of the distant hills.

Joining them, Manning looked down. Immediately below he saw the farm, the rafters showing in places through the decayed roof like the ribs of a vulture-despoiled carcass. The tiny, toy-like figures of the wounded soldiers were still clustered motion-less in the yard, a group of idlers nonchalantly awaiting a public beheading.

The marshal continued his sombre contemplation of the scene. 'Where's your man?' he asked.

'Back there,' said Manning.

'Got away?'

'No. He's finished. Fell down a chasm.' Saying this he felt the first prickings of an uneasiness. The excitement was over, had stilled, died away and left him with a flatness representing the swing in the other direction of the pendulum of his spirits. But this was a positive, almost aggressive flatness. There was a kind of growing hollow sensation, too, and he suspected that any moment now something behind his diaphragm would turn

146

gently. On reflection, the consummation of this chase had been curiously revolting. Against the fair, exuberant light of day he thought of that dark labyrinth from which he had emerged and from which Mancuso had not. He was shaken by a fit of shuddering, which he hoped the marshal had not observed.

The marshal, however, was not looking in his direction, and Manning sensed his disapproval.

'If you had been there we should have got him,' Manning said.

'Some things are done and some things are not,' said the marshal. 'This is one of the things that are not done.'

'I thought this business about sanctuary was a thing of the past.'

'Not here.'

'A matter of five or six hundred years ago. Since then times have changed.'

'Yes,' said the marshal, 'they have. But not with us. At least, not this kind of thing. Other things, perhaps. We don't say much about it, but we respect it for all that. You will find that those who don't aren't well thought of here.'

'Are you shocked?' asked Manning.

'No. I'm surprised. We hear so much about the humanity of you people, this has been a surprise to me.'

XII

T H E change in the atmosphere of Malevento was unmistakable. Within a few hours of their return from Santa
Maria Manning had first noticed it. Since then the general
coolness had increased with every day that passed. He suspected
the marshal of being at the heart and root of all this, and yet the
marshal was the only one whose attitude seemed to have under-
gone no variation. The good humour of the marshal seemed,
if anything, to have increased.

There was something disquieting in this. A few days
previously Manning had seen the marshal as nothing more
remarkable than a Latin petty official with standard musical-
comedy characteristics; a flashy, gross and even ridiculous figure.
But beneath this it was as though the outlines of a powerful and
sinister personality were now forming. The marshal was good
humoured because he had no need to be otherwise. His good
humour was the product of unassailable self-confidence. Manning knew that by his pursuit of Mancuso, culminating in his
invasion of the monastery, he had put the whole of Malevento
against him. But whereas the rest of the citizens were open in
their hostility, the marshal had showed a single flash of resentment and had immediately recovered himself. Manning saw
something in his face, too, that had not been there before. It was
the face of a lesser Medici who, sated with minor triumphs of
commerce and speculation, now demanded a keener satisfaction:
that of the manipulation of men.

A marked silence descended upon the other habitués of the
Hotel Vesuvio whenever Manning entered. The routine suppliants too had been affected, having it seemed quietly relin-
quished their aspirations as far as he was concerned and re-attached
themselves to the marshal. He overheard two of them mention
the matter. 'No use troubling yourself with the Englishman,

he's a hard one.' The speaker who pronounced this verdict rocked his head from side to side, his mouth expressively depressed at the corners. The gnome-like Orfeo had suddenly ceased his haunting. The Sindaco's gently saturnine smile was not to be seen. The almost daily invitations to visit the marchesina no longer arrived.

On the contrary, a new and more sinister type of individual appeared on the scene. For example, a priest called D'Alessio presented himself, a black-clothed cleric with the face of a Judas and an overwhelming breath, the full force of which he bestowed upon Manning as he leaned towards him in baleful confidence.

D'Alessio wanted permission to carry a pistol. '. . . my political activities — you understand?' Then he added: ' — if only you and I could work together!'

That other such dubious allies hovered in the background was made evident by a spate of anonymous correspondence in which denouncers — describing themselves as lovers of truth or lovers of justice — charged the leading personalities of Malevento with the most horrid crimes. All these admirers of virtue stressed their anxiety to co-operate with him for the utter ruin of the person cited.

This phenomenon assumed another and more positive aspect; a development which seemed almost the result of a commonly accepted policy among the citizens of Malevento. It seemed that they desired at all costs to avoid meeting him in the streets. There were the various functionaries of the Pubblica Sicurezza and of the Municipio, most of them small, drab men with whose faces he had been becoming vaguely familiar and who had previously gone to great lengths to greet him obsequiously. Now they demonstrated abnormal powers of vision by recognizing him at a great distance and suddenly turning into an alleyway or some quite unlikely business premises such as those of the coffin-maker.

These manoeuvres were always carried out at such a distance that it would have been impossible to charge the persons concerned with deliberate offensiveness.

Then again, the night after the return from Santa Maria he was sitting out of sight behind an old, torn Japanese screen in the Hotel Vesuvio when he heard Don Enrico discussing with the old guard of the anti-Fascists some person unreferred to by name who seemed to be regarded as possessing the evil eye. 'Jettatore or not,' Don Enrico laid down – using the common term for such ill-starred persons – 'you obviously can't tuck your thumb under your forefinger and point it at him unless his back's turned, when it's no use. The best thing is just to spit in his direction whenever you can. Speaking for myself, I've arranged the spittoons so that there's one by every chair-leg.'

Alberto came up at that moment bearing a bottle of brandy for him, and when Manning spoke to him there was a significant silence from the other side of the screen.

He was getting through his bottles of brandy quite quickly now. There was a sovereign virtue in this fierce liquor with its flat taste and the strange, underlying flavour as if it had been kept in some rank skin. This virtue lay in its immense efficacy as a destroyer of time. In those depths of surprisingly clear amber the hours frayed away and dissolved like shreds of metal in a potent acid. Painlessly they passed as he lay on the bed in the office, naked but for a towel over his loins, the beads of sweat glistening on his skin and edgeless thoughts floating through his brain.

Gradually the siesta habit, to which he had taken quite effortlessly, extended itself at both ends and was eating into the working day. He paid for this indulgence, of course, in the hours when he forced himself into activity.

He was obliged, for instance, to attribute to this taste for brandy a rather disturbing experience.

He had woken up and found an empty brandy bottle at his side, but with only the vaguest impressions of what had taken place on the preceding afternoon. The recollection of these events could, in fact, only be recaptured piecemeal, returning in broken episodes.

First he remembered Alberto producing what had now come

to be regarded as his daily ration of brandy — a ration which had recently been somewhat increased. This had been at possibly 3 p.m. A little later, while feeling almost preternaturally clear in the head, being in fact in a reasoning and analytical frame of mind, he had noticed the inception of a queer semi-paralysis in the legs. This had nothing to do with a drunkard's normal unsteadiness of gait, but involved something approaching a loss of control over the joints, in particular the ankles and the knees, which he seemed unable to flex without a deliberate mental effort. Concerned, then, with this alarming problem, he made his way, attracting from passers-by curious glances which were by no means lost on him, in the direction — as he supposed — of the office.

It seemed, though, that after a while and following a short but startling period when this alcoholic paralysis threatened to spread to his arms, constraining him to hold them out sideways like a tight-rope walker or even, as one being held up at the point of a pistol, stiffly above his head, he found himself at the riverside. Here it occurred to him that a possible remedy for his trouble would be to paddle in the shallows. No sooner had he recorded this reasonable notion than, carefully removing the bottle from his pocket and laying it on the bank, he waded in — the briefly considered desirability of undressing having been dismissed as a trifling concession to custom not consistent with his present mood.

A second later his mouth was full of warm, root-soaked, stagnant water and his ears were closed with a muffled roaring. Coming up he tried to strike out, but found he had lost all control of his limbs. Momentarily he saw a hand that might have belonged to someone else's body — something which he accepted without surprise as being quite detached from him — floating on the surface of the water just before him. Then his head went under again, and just as suddenly a weak, half-possession of his nerves returned, sufficiently at any rate to bring him to the bank, from which he had never drifted more than a yard or two.

Here he found himself able to hang on to a tuft of overhanging grass, but instantly realized the complete impossibility of raising himself up by it and climbing out. He was considering quite calmly how this was to be done when he saw immediately above him, staring down, the face of the marshal, which at this moment and from this angle possessed something of the predatory beauty of a stooping falcon. Manning's first impression was that the marshal had been a detached observer of this scene, that his manner was speculative rather than urgent, and somehow in his brain there flashed a spark of panic as the marshal now knelt down and reached out his hand.

That which had been in the marshal's face, however, was quickly replaced by an expression of elaborate concern. His arm was taken in a firm grip, and a moment later he was lying on the bank with the marshal bending over him solicitously.

'I followed you,' said the marshal. 'I felt sure you were not feeling well. How fortunate that I happened to be there.'

This, then, had been the story of the previous afternoon's adventures; and now, his faculties perfectly restored but with perhaps the slightest possible dizziness rocking him as he walked, he was going towards the hotel when he noticed a peasant who was coming in his direction pull out a handkerchief and hold it over his face. In itself, of course, nothing — and he only half-registered the occurrence. However, turning a corner a hundred yards further on, precisely the same thing happened. Well, he thought, they've every right to. After the country this place must stink pretty badly. He sniffed the air. The acrid corruption that had never left his nostrils for the first few days seemed to have vanished. But, of course, he had become acclimatized.

He glanced across the road just in time to see yet another peasant press a handkerchief to his face.

Something almost definable as an inner voice said, Of course, they're hiding their faces from you. To which his reason replied, *But these are strangers to the town. They don't know me.* Quite obviously, he said to himself, these peasants have really carried out the action I have noticed. That is to say, it is no figment of the imagination. But the fact that I attach any significance to it, or indeed notice it at all, is merely indicative of a hangover of unsuspected proportions. A stage further and one might reasonably start worrying about hallucinations. In the meanwhile, however, dismiss it.

And he was just dismissing it when a peasant couple came in sight. They were quite a distance away, and suddenly he decided to put the matter to test. The peasants were walking towards him rapidly and self-consciously, as peasants seem to walk in the town. The man was slightly ahead of the woman. He was dressed in black and held an eccentrically shaped stick. The woman carried a heavily loaded basket heaped up with some produce or other. They would both be on the way to the local market, where the woman would squat down behind her contraband butter and eggs, leaving the man to go off to the tavern. Manning watched them like a hawk, waiting for one or the other to produce a handkerchief. Closer and closer they came. Despite himself he felt relieved now that they were only a few paces away. Suddenly the woman put her hand on the man's arm and stopped him. Manning slowed down while the pair turned away and the man bent towards her. By the time he reached them the woman had removed the cloth from the top of the basket and was wiping her face with it. The man had raised his hand, as if in sudden weariness, to his eyes.

Manning grabbed the man by the arm and swung him round. 'Why are you covering your face?'

The woman screeched, and picking up her basket in both hands ran off a few steps with it. The man dropped his stick and raised his hands in protest. 'He's crazy,' said the woman, who had stopped a few yards away. 'Leave him alone, Ercole. Don't have anything to do with him.' She put down her basket and appealed with scrawny gestures to more peasants who had appeared on the scene.

XIII

SHE sat there, her legs crossed, wearing, in spite of the heat, a short fur coat of some cheap, flattish skins, and a necklace of pink pearls. When she shifted her weight the office chair, which had legs of uneven length, rocked slightly.

Manning sat down facing her across the table. His forearms were resting on the table and between them was a sheet of paper. He looked her straight in the eyes, She smiled slightly in a puzzled way. Manning did not smile.

'You are Anna Consomato?'

She nodded.

He wrote 'Anna Consomato' at the top of the sheet of paper and drew two lines under it. After that he lifted the paper and glanced at the particulars, such as the date and place of birth, given in the police report which lay underneath. Below 'Anna Consomato' he wrote:

> Father Antonio (dead). Mother Teresa Landolfi. Born Caivano 23.6.20.

He looked at the girl again. She had a good-natured face with a clear skin and large, bright eyes of an indefinite colour. She had used her lipstick to produce a fuller curve than that of the lips, which was a pity, but she had atoned for this in some measure by leaving her eyebrows alone.

Manning held out a packet of cigarettes. She took one and examined it closely. 'I don't much care for the English kind.'

'Have a Camel, then.'

He lit the cigarette for her and she puffed at it rather avidly for a few moments before removing it from her lips. She smiled at him again. She had two distinct expressions, he had already noticed. In one there was nervousness. She was almost harassed. And then, when this combat with her nerves had reached a certain point, she seemed to make a special effort to take herself in hand. The result was a sudden change-over to excessive self-confidence. Now she was confident. She tapped at the end of her cigarette with a finger the nail of which, deep crimson and slightly rugous, looked like an artificial attachment, possibly of celluloid.

'Signorina, how do you live?'

The smile was suddenly frozen.

'Why do you ask?' She had a most attractive voice which took full advantage of the typical southern drawl.

'Perhaps you'd better answer. It gives a good impression if you answer quickly and to the point.'

'I work.'

'Where?'

'At Fontana's.'

'Who is that?'

'The hairdresser.'

'Where?'

A slight hesitation, perhaps. 'In the Via Scarlatti.'

'I thought the Via Scarlatti no longer existed?'

'Well, you see, they moved from there.'

'Where to?'

'To the Largo Caterina. On the corner. What's the name of the street?' The harassed expression had returned.

'But you don't work there?'

'No.'

'You worked in the Via Scarlatti?'

'Yes.'

'Until 1943, then?'

'Yes.'

'Good. Now we're getting somewhere. And since then?'

'Since then at various places. Why are you asking me all these questions?'

'Not with Fontana?'

'I did some typing.'

'Who for?'

She wrinkled her forehead and moistened her lips by pressing them together. This operation removed a portion of the over-painting, leaving her mouth slightly asymmetrical. 'I don't know. I can't remember. The Avvocato Ciecco, for one.'

'When did you work for the Avvocato Ciecco? Was it this year?' She shook her head. 'I don't think so.'

Manning went to the office window and looked out. Two scunizzi, tattered leprechauns, wandered down the street below him, which looked as though it were carpeted by dirty snow except that there were no footprints. Further down he could just see the crossing, where a few pedestrians passed and where a hooded photographer, like a familiar of the inquisition, stalked potential victims. Looking up again he noticed a pigeon attempt without success to alight on the minute hand of a clock which for the last two years had registered twenty-four minutes to twelve. The pigeon slid down the hand, stabbing out with its wings in an attempt to regain its balance, then righting itself awkwardly with a clashing of pinions. Beyond this Manning saw the mountains, shadowless at noon, and lumped over them, sagging slightly between the peaks, the clouds.

'Signorina, how do you live?'

'I told you. I already told you. Why do you ask me all these questions?' She was rattled, forcing herself as if with difficulty to be indignant. 'I live at home.'

'Yes,' said Manning, 'but you eat, you drink, you buy clothes, the rent is paid. Where does the money come from?'

'My mother helps me.'

'What does she do?'

'She washes clothes.'

'Then I'm surprised you don't help her. I mean, with money.'

She bit her lip, the colouration now completely blurred. 'I have an uncle who sometimes sends me a little.'

'Would you have any objection to giving me his name and address?'

'I can give you his name, but I don't know where he lives now. He moved last year. I'll give you the old address if that will do.'

Manning shook his head.

'Where are you living at present?' He looked under the paper. 'Still the Parco Salerno No. 8?'

'Yes.'

'The best address in town,' said Manning. 'Very luxurious, I'm told. And how many rooms have you?'

'Five.'

'But your mother washes for a living? I'm disappointed.'

'It's of her own choosing,' the girl said. 'She could have lived with me.'

'An honest working woman,' said Manning, 'she'd probably feel uncomfortable in those surroundings.'

'What do you think I am?' Here was the outburst he had expected. It was as if she had lost control of her hands, the fingers of which were trying to detach themselves, to flutter away as she waved her arms. 'Why don't you leave me alone? What have I done to you?'

'How do you live, signorina?' he repeated the question gently, studying with interest a crevice in the wall just behind her head, from which he believed an unusually large spider to have made a brief appearance before swiftly withdrawing itself. He looked at her again. The good-humoured mouth, previously twisted into an expression of unaccustomed defiance, was now relaxed dejectedly in defeat.

'Guess for yourself,' she said.

'I have,' said Manning. 'Who pays the rent?'

'Dr. Serra.'

'I knew that, too,' said Manning.

'Then why do you ask me? Why are you tormenting me?'

'I was just wondering if you were capable of speaking the truth. That's all.'

'I know how to speak the truth. You don't have to teach me how to speak the truth. I'm telling you the truth now, aren't I?'

157

She dabbed at her lower eyelids which had become unevenly blackened with dissolving mascara.'

'Good. I'm glad of that. Tell me, then, who else contributes to your support?'

'That's a lie. A dirty lie.'

'I hope so, too,' said Manning. 'All I'm going by is the information given in a very confidential report I have here. Fortunately, the general public doesn't have access to facts of this kind. It comes from the police records and, to be perfectly frank with you, I couldn't deplore more than I do this habit that the police have of interesting themselves in the private affairs of ordinary citizens. The report says that although maintained comfortably by Dr. Serra at the aforementioned address, you do not hesitate, and I quote, "when the occasion arises to give yourself to other loves". Deprecating as I do the system, it must be admitted that the report itself, apart from its flowery style, is a model of its kind: seemingly accurate, concise, detailed. It gives a list of names. Shall I read them out?'

'No,' she said. She was beginning to sob, and Manning didn't particularly enjoy the sight. What a shame, he thought. By the look of her I really think she's not a bad girl at all.

'I hardly like to raise the question,' he asked, 'but do you love Dr. Serra?'

'He's a fine man. His wife's a fine woman, too. She's a distinguished woman. They're a lovely couple.'

' — apart from a source of revenue, I mean,' said Manning, wishing, however, to have been able to withdraw this remark as soon as he had made it.

She looked at him miserably, cornered now, defenceless. 'Why are you doing all this to me?'

'To some extent, although not primarily,' said Manning, 'for your own sake. I wanted to know how you felt about Dr. Serra. You wouldn't like these private matters we have been discussing to get to his ears, would you? You see, please don't think I'm trying to exert any pressure, but the fact is that it is all bound to come out if you're placed in a witness box. I mean, evidence of what would be described as your moral character is bound to be brought into it.'

'Why should I be placed in a witness box? What have I done, to be placed in a witness box?'

Manning allowed himself a very faint smile. 'Do you remember Lauro?'

'Lauro?' she said. 'Lauro?'

'Yes, Lauro. I thought, by the way, we had reached a stage now where your memory worked properly and didn't have to be constantly jolted.'

'Yes,' she said, 'I remember Lauro.'

'That's fine,' said Manning. 'I thought you would. And now, tell me, what made you write that statement before Lauro was put away? What were your relations with Pascarella at the time?'

She winced slightly at the name.

'Well,' he said, 'I'm waiting. You should know by now that it's no good trying to cover anything up. In any case, you are no longer with Pascarella, are you?'

'No,' she said. 'The dirty swine. All the same, I can't.'

'You can,' he said. 'It's either that or the other. Take your choice.'

'All right,' she said, 'all right.' She shrugged her shoulders.

'Then it was Pascarella that made you do it?'

A nod.

Manning laid a sheet of paper before her and put a pen in her hand. He went over to the window again to gather his thoughts. Two scunizzi, similar to but certainly not the same as those he had seen before, were coming back up the street. The photographer had gone from the corner, as the passers-by had all reached home by now, where they would be busy with their midday meals or about to start their siestas. The pigeon, or at least a pigeon, had settled on a ledge above the clock face, bending its head quizzically in the direction of the motionless hands which seemed to possess for it some strange fascination. The clouds still lay in twisted ropes along the summits of the peaks.

He came back to the centre of the room, facing her where she now sat at the desk. 'Write this,' he said.

Holding the pen she looked up at him pleadingly, despairingly. 'Please don't let Pascarella know,' she said. 'I don't want him to know. Please, please don't let him know. I couldn't bear it.'

There was a knock at the door and an agent from the Pubblica Sicurezza came in and gave a half salute. He was grinning with satisfaction. 'He's outside,' he said. 'Sorry we are late. He was having a shave. We had to go and find him.'

'Bring him in,' said Manning.

A man with a tout's face came in with a rush, as if pushed violently from behind. An arm came round the door holding a haversack, which was flung into the room after him. Now a third figure appeared.

'Which of you two is the star interrogator the Commissario spoke about?' asked Manning.

'We both do a bit,' said the smaller agent who had come in first, 'but he probably meant my colleague here, Del Giudice. Some of us are made, some of us born.' He laughed.

Del Giudice was a thin, youngish man with pale eyes and rusty hair. He had bad teeth, puny, arthritic hands and the earnestness of a young seminarist. When Manning looked at him he swallowed nervously.

'Going by results,' said the small man with a trace of hero-worship, 'he's our star turn. We go by results, you know.'

'All right,' Manning said, 'you two wait outside in case I want you. Where's the man's kit?'

'It's in the haversack,' said the small agent, whose name was Mosca. He gave the haversack a kick.

'Sorry to bring him like this,' said Del Giudice in a grave voice.

'He's only shaved on one side of his face, but you said not to give him more than fifteen minutes to get his things together, so we took him as he was.'

'That's all right,' said Manning. 'He'll get a shave where he's going to, and a special haircut, too.'

The small agent, Mosca, laughed and winked. Del Giudice's solemn expression remained unchanged.

'Sergente,' said Pascarella in his thick, recognizable tout's voice and now speaking for the first time. 'May I say something?'

'No,' said Manning. 'Go and stand over there where I can see you. No, not there. Facing the window. All right,' he said to the agents, 'I'll call you if I want you.'

The two men went out, Del Giudice turning at the door for a last fervent glance in Pascarella's direction.

'Queer type, Del Giudice,' Manning said to Pascarella, 'a man happy in his work, I should say.'

Pascarella winced. 'Sergente, may I speak now?'

'No, why should you? You may answer my questions, that's all. And get back in the light.'

'Where are you sending me, Sergente?'

'That depends on you. But probably a long way and for a very long time.'

'What about my wife and kids? How are they going to get on?'

'Pascarella, you're a proven liar and a false witness. You should have thought of your family before you signed a statement which you knew to be untrue.'

'Sergente, on the head of my mother I swear —'

'I've got ten minutes to spare,' said Manning, looking at his watch. 'If I haven't got the truth by then I shall give up and let Del Giudice take over. I sent for Del Giudice because he's an experienced interrogator. They say that people usually tell him the truth. I haven't Del Giudice's experience, so I shall just ask you a few plain questions in the hope of getting straightforward answers. If I don't, I shall put it down to my inexperience and then we will see what Del Giudice can do.' What a weasel of a man this was, he thought. The maculation, the lupus of his soul proclaimed itself in every feature.

'In August 1943, in the company of Ugo Lauro, you paid a visit to the Headquarters of the German Command.'

'Whoever said such a thing?' Pascarella struck his chest passionately with a clenched fist.

'You did.'

'No, Sergente, please believe me. No, never. How could I have said that when I didn't go?'

'The trouble with you, Pascarella, is your bad memory. I've got a copy of your statement here and I'll read it to you. It's a pity to take up time like this, because I meant what I said about the ten minutes time limit. However, this is what you said:

> In August 1943 Ugo Lauro came to see me. He told me that two escaped Indian soldiers had taken shelter in his house. He said he was worried because if they were found there he would be shot. I advised him to send them away, but he said that he had heard the Germans paid a reward for the recapture of escaped prisoners. He was very much against the Allies and he told me that if they won the war we would all be finished. I agreed to accompany him to the German Headquarters, and there I heard him denounce the presence of the Indians in his house. Lauro was known to us as an informer of the OVRA.

There you are, that's the statement you signed.'

'Not the last part,' said Pascarella. 'The last part is incorrect. The first part is correct. I agree to the first part.'

'That in August 1943 Lauro came to see you?'

'Yes, that is correct, I swear it. On the head of my mother.'

'About what date in August would it have been?'

'How can I say? It's so long ago.'

'You are sure, though, that it was in August? Would you say at the beginning or at the end of the month?'

'At the beginning, perhaps the first week. No, I'm wrong. It was on the tenth of the month.'

'And how do you manage to fix the date so accurately?'

'How? Why, because the tenth was the festa of my youngest daughter. When Lauro came to the house I was afraid he would frighten the children, who were not yet in bed.'

'Frighten them, why?'

'He was a very big and ugly man. A very dangerous man.'

'How curious,' said Manning. 'Because Lauro didn't come to your house to see you on August 10th, nor did he on any other date during that month.'

'Sergente, believe me. What oaths must I take? On the mourning of my sister who died a virgin — '

' — He didn't come to see you because he couldn't have done. You were in prison at the time, where you remained until September 3rd.'

Pascarella raised his arms wearily and dropped them again as if weighted by chains. 'Eh!' — An indescribable southern sound, accompanied by a slight backward jerk of the head and expressive of resignation.

'Well?'

'They put words into my mouth I didn't say. I signed so many things I don't know what I signed. "Here you are," they tell you, "write this. Sign this." And you know what happens to you if you don't . . . They wouldn't let you live. How can I be expected to feed my kids?'

'Who are "they"?' asked Manning.

'They,' Pascarella said. 'They're always after you. They don't give you a minute's peace.'

'I'll help you to answer my questions,' Manning said. 'You've got five minutes left. What was Marshal Altamura's reason for putting Lauro out of the way?'

'Marshal Altamura?'

'Yes, Marshal Altamura.'

'I don't know, Sergente. Believe me, I don't know. I don't

163

interest myself in these things. Something to do with a dispute between the fathers or the grandfathers, I expect.'

'What did the marshal pay you for the job?'

'Pay me? Pay me? Imagine the marshal paying anyone! Do you think a man will do this kind of thing for money? What will happen to us all if Lauro ever comes back? If the marshal ever wanted anything done, there was no question of payment. The first thing that happened to you if you didn't toe the line was that your wife was arrested as a prostitute.' Pascarella began to sob with facility. 'If that didn't bring you to your senses, they found stolen German equipment in your house. The next thing, if you still hung out, they'd fasten some unsolved murder case on you.'

'And Tiobbe was in the same boat?'

'We were all in the same boat. Not only Tiobbe but all of us. It just happened to be me and Tiobbe that he picked out, but anyone else would have done. It just happened to be us, that's all. And now you'll make us deny all we said, and then we'll have the marshal down on us again. He'll eat us alive.'

'No, he won't,' said Manning. 'I won't answer for Lauro, though.'

'Sergente, may I ask you a favour?' Pascarella's words were half-strangled in sobs.

'Well?'

'Will they be sending me to prison?'

'I don't know. Perhaps.'

'Could I be sent to one of your prisons, then?'

'Why?'

'It's a question of the food. I don't want my strength to go down through the bad diet you get in our prisons.'

By the time he had finished with Tiobbe and had checked the three statements one against the others for discrepancies and had typed out a summary of evidence, together with the accompanying report, the evening was upon him.

This day the heat had been more trying than usual. In the

office it seemed to cling to the battered furniture like some viscous fluid. It pulsated from the yellowing proclamations on the walls and came in waves from the wash-rooms, bringing with it the dank odour of water acting upon metal joints. A puff of dust showered through the window and began to settle. Looking out he caught sight of a swirling wraith, a headless, wind-formed apparition that swayed gracefully up the street away from him, its shape exactly circumscribed by racing scraps of paper.

He locked up the office and climbed the stairs to the roof of the building, where he would sit on the parapet and cool off before going for the evening meal.

The marshal would be at the hotel by now. He was wondering whether to come straight to the point or to keep the results of his investigations to himself. He could not see that there was anything to be gained by not telling the marshal what was in his mind.

This building, with its steel and concrete structure, must have been the highest to survive, he thought. It was as though, poised upon it, he stood in a mighty amphitheatre ringed by unbroken tiers of hills. And in the clear, dry light the details of this colosseum could be discerned with uncanny clarity. He was at a central point from which the roads, straight and purposeful as wheel spokes, thrust forward in all directions into the brownness and into the yellowness of the land.

There were numerous villages which gleamed jewel-like against the dull earth. He saw three dwarfish whirlwinds, slender cornucopias balanced on their points, meandering aimlessly through the fields. And on the roads themselves he could just discern some movement. There were stirring particles of activity — a progression of termites towards the town.

The tide of sunshine had now ebbed from the towns and villages alike. And in the streets, peopled until this hour by rare shapes moving with the caution of fish exploring the crevices of a pool, was heard the tread of the advance guard of returning peasantry; the clump and shuffle of feet; the creaking of wheels;

the low murmurs, silence-spaced, of the older men and women, and the quavering songs of the young girls.

Draining back from the land they came, like venous blood returning to numerous hearts. The peasants of Roccafrosone, noted on undiscoverable grounds for the beauty of their women. The peasants of Sant' Agata, adventurous by tradition, whose jackal-gnawed remains therefore still decorated many distant African battlefields, doubtlessly awaiting comment, by some Herodotus to come, on the relative thickness of their skulls. The peasants of Somma, who spoke such an extraordinary dialect that even their own landlords could understand them only when it came to money matters. The peasants of Tenne, who were given to brooding in their many taverns. And on the other side of the mountains, those of Acera, who were incurably facetious and produced the archetype of clowns, Pulcinella. The peasants of Minervano, who were supposed to be descended from the Saracens and to favour in secret a plurality of wives. The peasants of Montenero, whose ancestors had lived in caves and hovels from time immemorial and who from this were sharp-sighted and undersized. The peasants of Longobardi, who believed in narrow carts and were adept at loading them to enormous heights. And their neighbours from Montesordo, whose carts were wide and low and who hung their belongings all round them in snoods, so that two vehicles could hardly pass on the widest roads. And the peasants of Acquaselva, who still used axles solid with the wheels and who, if spoken to about it, would prove by demonstration that their carts cost less that way and ran as smoothly as any others. And the peasants of Gioiosa, who, conceivably influenced by the name of their village, were light-hearted in every way and attached to no particular agricultural theories.

All these peasants were returning to their beds, while Manning looked over the plains of Malevento, now undulating, rippling with shadow.

'I've been talking to the witnesses in the Lauro case,' said Manning. He said this casually, but before doing so he had placed himself in such a way that he could watch without appearing to do so the effect of this announcement upon the marshal.

The marshal's face showed in three-quarters profile against the window. In this light and from this angle there was something about it of a self-indulgent emperor. The marshal had dined well, and for the last few moment, his eyelids had been narrowing as if in some astute cogitation, while occasionally he was shaken by a slight gaseous spasm located somewhere near the diaphragm.

In the right background, Don Enrico's head, also in profile, sagged gently until one of his chins became entrapped in the sharp edges of his collar. It was then lifted, but immediately began to sag again.

In the left background the anti-Fascists, placed side by side as if deposited against a trifling loan, formed a reredos.

The Café Vesuvio was full of the sound of heavy breathing; the marshal's decisive hiss, the sobbing intake of Don Enrico's breath, which now as sleep overtook him also produced a vigorous fluttering of the lips, the meek snuffling of the anti-Fascists.

' — Pascarella, Tiobbe and the girl,' said Manning.

'Umph,' grunted the marshal comfortably, opening his eyes, however. He was rocked by a hiccough of exceptional violence.

'I got the facts from them.'

'The facts?' The marshal slewed half round in his chair towards Manning, at the same time reaching under his jacket and releasing his top trouser button.

Don Enrico, trapping his chin once again, awoke with a loud groan, relapsed, started to snore.

'You seemed to think I'd done one of your countrymen some sort of injustice. That I'd overstepped the mark in some way. I'm going by your opinion. Well, now I'm going to make up for that by putting an injustice to rights. I hope everybody will be satisfied,' said Manning.

'You're making a mistake,' said the marshal, ostentatiously relaxing in his chair.

'I don't think so.'

'These people,' said the marshal, 'best leave them alone. They're like putty. Worse than that, they're like water. It's incredible to think that anyone can be the way they are. One minute they tell you one thing and the next another. You try putting them in the witness box and see what happens. They're useless. Anything you get from them they'll swear was under duress.'

'It won't be necessary to put them in a witness box. I'll submit the evidence, together with my recommendation. I believe that will be good enough.'

'I hope you are wrong,' said the marshal.

'I know you do.'

'I mean for all our sakes. You're interested in the public safety and security of this area, I believe.'

Don Enrico stirred, grunted unintelligibly, and began to snore in a new key.

'Lauro's better where he is,' went on the marshal, hastily drinking a glass of water.

'Better for you.'

'Better for you too if you knew the facts. As it is, I'm sorry to say so, but you seem to believe anything you're told. I'll have a dozen feuds on my hands if Lauro comes out.'

'Keep you pretty busy.'

'Yes,' said the marshal. 'But don't forget I hold the area together. Single-handed, almost. I have to do it in my own way. All you do is to come along and do your best to upset the balance of nature. Without knowing what you are doing, you interfere. You're like a sleep walker. A man walking about in the dark with his eyes shut and his hands held out in front of him. What it means is I can't hold things together any longer. That's what it means.'

'You're not even officially located here,' said Manning. 'As far as I understood, you're supposed to be helping us out in some

168

way or other. But not satisfied with throwing innocent people into jail on your own account, you trick us into putting them away to suit your ends.'

'You've been misinformed,' said the marshal. 'As a matter of fact, I wouldn't say no to a change of scenery either, but my people won't hear of it. Seems they can't do without me.'

'Well,' said Manning. 'I'm telling you my intentions, that's all.'

'Once again, I tell you, you're upsetting the balance of nature. You want to start something that neither you nor I can stop.'

'I'm told it's a question of a personal vendetta this time,' said Manning.

The marshal clicked his teeth in irritation. 'What nonsense. I don't want to insult you, but how can you believe such things? These are stories you read in children's books. May I give you some idea of what I'm up against? Then I shall ask you to tell me what you'd have done.'

'Go on, then.'

'This man, this great hero Lauro, attacked some Germans in the village of Arzano. Please note that carefully. Not in his own village. He takes good care not to do that. But in the village of Arzano. He doesn't live there. Afterwards he goes away and the Germans come back. Perhaps they didn't tell you that. The Germans find sixteen men in the village and they shoot them all. They also burn all the houses. This means that Lauro has sixteen feuds on his hands. Say fifteen, because one of the men didn't have any relatives. The Germans kill the men, they go away and no one ever sees them again, but Lauro is left with fifteen blood feuds. Arzano is just one of these places. Why did he have to pick out such a place? In this village the bloody shirts of those who were killed will be presented to their eldest sons when they reach manhood. They will carry on the feud. For them this is justice, but it isn't justice with me because Lauro has brothers who'll divide his shirt among themselves as soon as he is killed. For me, justice in this case is that Lauro should cease to bother us, go away somewhere, disappear.'

169

'A story from a children's book,' said Manning. 'But apart from that, you mistake justice for expediency.'

'Expediency and justice,' said the marshal, 'in bad times they're the same thing.'

'Then you admit to the use of extortion in procuring false statements from these people?'

'Extortion?' said the marshal, with no apparent diminution in his good humour. 'The word is completely out of place. It makes me think of one of those old American films we used to see. The gangster stands over his victim, who is tied in a chair. He holds a rubber truncheon. Extortion. As I've already told you, it's impossible to get as far as rubber truncheons in dealing with these people. They tell you so much, the problem is to stop them talking.'

'But with or without rubber truncheons, you were behind it all.'

'Of course not.'

'But you just admitted as much. You calmly admitted that as a matter of expediency it was better for Lauro to disappear.'

'And he did,' said the marshal, smiling reflectively. 'But then there's nothing in that. Nothing more than a mere coincidence. Sometimes I'm lucky in this way, that's all. I think to myself, how much better it would be for all concerned if a certain man were to be removed from the scene, and the next thing that happens is that he is. Sometimes it's quite uncanny. Others have commented on my good fortune in such matters. Coming back to the Lauro question, the main thing as I see it is that Lauro's no longer with us, and that is very good for everyone. The Allied tribunal that deals with such matters are not foolish. They'll have satisfied themselves that the internment of this Lauro was well merited.'

'They had to go by such evidence as they were given,' said Manning. 'It doesn't satisfy me.'

The marshal clapped him on the back. 'Why should we knock our heads against the wall over such things? To live and let live is better.'

XIV

THE routine visit to H.Q., put off twice through lack of transport, could not be postponed indefinitely, so finally, after his third week in Malevento, Manning hitch-hiked into Monteleone.

Although he had not been looking forward to the journey, he experienced a sensation of great relief at the prospect of two days' absence from Malevento.

Monteleone was an unspoiled and undamaged hill town chosen as Section H.Q. by virtue of its central position in the area under their control. The H.Q. had been established in the deserted palace of some minor — and evidently, from the state of its disrepair, impoverished — Italian nobleman.

The F.S.O. looked up from his desk as Manning went in. He was wearing a thin-lipped smile, not, Manning felt, in greeting but as if some mildly agreeable recollection had at that moment passed through his mind. The impersonality of the F.S.O.'s expression was increased by the fact that the light from his desk lamp tended to reflect on his spectacles, which became opaque, the eyes being thus replaced by discs of marble.

The desk was clear but for a folder which Manning recognized as the one in which his report was kept. The F.S.O. opened this and bent over it. Just when Manning thought he was about to refer to the contents, he closed the folder again and slapped down his hand over it. He raised his eyes, which were immediately extinguished by the marble discs.

'Go out again and come in properly.'

Manning was mildly startled because the pleasant expression had in no way been relaxed. He went out and marched in again as stiffly as he could, failing in an attempt, as he came to a halt, to snap together the ordinary walking shoes he was wearing.

The F.S.O. appeared to have taken no interest in this performance but to be absorbed in the reopened report.

'How do you like Malevento?' he suddenly inquired. He was the possessor of a soft, rather agreeable voice. The question was put in a casual and friendly way. He did not look up.

Remembering Wilton's warning, Manning was non-committal. 'It suits me quite well, sir.'

'You wouldn't like a spell at H.Q.?'

'Not particularly, sir.'

Manning sensed disappointment. Any moment now, he thought. He was waiting for the Mancuso affair to come up, having had a request by signals for the fullest details of what had been described as Mancuso's presumed suicide. He could therefore only suppose that the F.S.O. was about to embark upon a lengthy interrogation. His resentment of the man's rather vulgar cat-and-mouse tactics was steadily increasing.

'Mancuso,' said the F.S.O. thoughtfully. 'Ah, yes, Mancuso.'

Manning swallowed an accumulation of saliva.

'Are you convinced of Mancuso's death?'

'Yes, sir.'

'Well, in that case there's nothing further to be said, is there?' asked the F.S.O. good-humouredly. 'The case can be considered satisfactorily closed. I will write a report to that effect.'

Manning waited without comment.

'Good work.'

'Thank you, sir.'

His report was closed and then opened again as if in afterthought.

'What's all this business about Marshal Altamura? What sort of man is he? Does he look like a soldier?'

'I don't know, sir,' said Manning, remembering the rebuff with which the interview had started.

'What do you mean, you don't know?' The F.S.O.'s brow wrinkled in genuine bewilderment. 'The Carabinieri Reali is a militarized force, is it not?'

Manning's conviction that the F.S.O.'s suavity of manner was all part of a rather common affectation was strengthened by observing the latter's tendency to savour his words.

'I have never seen the marshal on parade, sir,' he said.

'Above all things,' said the F.S.O., 'I value a soldierly manner. If you have forgotten what that is I am by no means beyond setting myself the task of teaching you. Should this prove unfruitful in results, I should have no objection to sending you to the nearest I.R.T.D. with a personal note to the Commanding Officer asking him to do his best to smarten you up for me.'

Could not even a training depot — horrible though the thought might be — fail to be an improvement on life in Malevento? Manning wondered.

'Are you dissatisfied with my work, sir?' he asked.

'I am not discussing your work now,' the F.S.O. replied. 'I am dissatisfied with you as a soldier, and please do not bother me in future with unsolicited recommendations relating to the disposition of Italian personnel.'

'Marshal Altamura is behaving badly, sir,' Manning said. 'He tries to give the impression that we support him.'

'But sergeant,' said the F.S.O., his smile now tiring. 'Don't you understand? I couldn't care less. Why should I worry if half the Italians in Italy are put in prison by the other half? As long as they don't bother us, it doesn't matter.'

'May I apply for a transfer from the Section, sir?' asked Manning, taking a sudden and quite unexpected decision.

The F.S.O. did not seem surprised. 'You may — but in these days of shortages of personnel you must be prepared for it to take quite a while to come through.'

'I understand, sir.'

'But while you are here,' said the F.S.O., 'I shall continue to expect a high standard of regimental deportment from you. When you come into my office, do so smartly, and stand up straight. Answer in a soldierly fashion. These are matters affecting morale. Now that the war is over, they become more vitally important than ever before.'

'Do any good with the inscriptions, old man?' Wilton asked.
'Inscriptions?'
'Yes, old man. The tombstones I told you about. Should have thought you'd have had the chance to do something by now.'
'I forgot all about that,' said Manning, smiling faintly. What a fellow he was, Manning thought with sudden envy. It seemed as if nothing could completely extinguish the fires of his youthful enthusiasm.
'Well, never mind,' Wilton said. 'Plenty of time yet.'
'I hope not,' Manning said. 'I've asked for a transfer.'
Peto had drifted up in time to catch this last sentence. 'That means another six months,' he said. At a sign from Wilton the barman poured out another drink. Peto raised the glass. 'Alla vostra.' The bright yellow liquid in the glass disappeared instantly. Manning saw that he had made rapid soldiering progress.
'All the time in the world,' Wilton said. 'It might even take a year. In that case you'd be finished in any event.'
Finished. Was that sinister inflection in his voice intentional? The word tolled in Manning's brain.
'You could commit a minor crime,' said Peto airily. '. . . On second thoughts, no. They seem to overlook anything short of murder these days.'
'Is the Section certain to stay here?' Manning asked.
'Absolutely,' said Wilton. 'It suits the old man having nothing to do. Gives him a chance to concentrate on the sagas.'
'Che fettente!' said Peto, using the most newly acquired piece of Section argot.
'Our hope,' said Wilton, 'lies in the possibility of the Section's disbandment. After all, one suicide, two accidental deaths and a couple of customers for the trick cyclist all in one year is a bit *much*.'

The barman filled their glasses again. Peto shook his head apologetically. 'Sorry this is the best we can do. Run out of everything else. They make this up at a local factory while you wait. Based on an industrial by-product of some kind or other.'

'It does the trick,' Manning said.

The three glasses swept upwards in perfectly balanced arcs, poised at the zenith of their travel to reflect in their curved, amber bases the glitter of the incomplete chandelier. Manning watched Peto's lower lip droop in clownish depression below the rim, while his adam's apple rose and sustained itself with the leisurely dignity of the practised drinker. Peto's eyes met his. They contained the unwavering resolution of a hierophant engaged in some stringent ritual. He had certainly put in some strenuous practice in these last three weeks. His glass tilted slightly and splashes of liquor like drops preceding a thunder shower fell upon the bar's surface. 'Interesting,' said Wilton, 'to know how they manage to get the flavour of metal polish in Italian brandy.'

At that moment there broke into the orderly stream of Manning's thoughts the harsh insistence of a motor horn. It was, however, inextricably confused with another sound of which he had become increasingly aware — the jarring vibration of a telephone bell. Although he had accepted this with resignation as being without external reality, he had rather surprisingly caught himself in unguarded moments looking round in an apparent attempt to locate this unattended instrument. While, in fact, he was concerned with the conscientious evaluation of this phenomenon, looking in half-shy hesitation towards the others who were now drinking sternly, relentlessly, he became aware, vaguely in his rear, of the driver who was to take him back to Malevento and whose face, as Manning turned, loomed suddenly, compassionless and probably even in secret exultation.

Outside, the Italian summer, which centuries of accumulated craft had kept at bay in that darkened room with its tarnished gilt and faded tapestry, now struck at him with the briskness of a well-nourished butcher at work over his block. Out of a subdued and gently humming artificial night they walked into brutal daylight which flowed lava-like round their flanks and laid a smothering anaethetist's mask over their nostrils.

'Been boozing up?' asked the driver in a quiet, refined voice which although coming as it seemed from far off succeeded somehow in penetrating the chinks of those shuddering venetian blinds that had descended over Manning's ears.

Having registered this question, Manning found some difficulty in confecting a satisfactory reply, a mere affirmative seeming for some reason or other to be less than was expected of him.

With the immense care of an ancient man going to stool, he climbed up into the high-perched driver's compartment of the Fordson and sat down. The scalding metal of the bucket seat clenched his haunches with hideous familiarity. The driver pressed the starting button and heat waves rose from the revolving engine and flooded the compartment.

'Why don't you spew out of the window, Sarge?' said the driver in sudden sympathy.

Manning considered this possibility with dignified reserve.

'I find I can't drink in this climate,' went on the driver in a tone of resignation. 'It only aggravates my tendency to melancholia. Ah, that's better.'

Acting as if from some completely external compulsion and with considerable astonishment Manning had put into practice the driver's suggestion. In reasonable preparation for a further reaction the driver leant across him and wound the window down to its limit. 'Would you like me to stop the car?' he asked solicitously.

'By no means,' said Manning. 'On the contrary, let's go faster and get some wind into the cabin. Don't think I'm drunk, by the way. I never felt better.'

Indeed, at the moment this was true, although he had to admit to an obscure difficulty in forming certain words which, on the other hand, when finally run to earth he seemed compelled to enunciate with disproportionate emphasis.

They were plunging down over the progression of wasted slopes that would carry them to the valley, curving in miraculous fashion between the trunks of pines whose bosoms seemed to gasp in faint surprise as they passed. Down the road they corkscrewed, dropping with the characteristic but much accelerated flight of a startled lammergeyer. Carrion crows voiced unheeded their solemn warnings. At the turns he had brief visions of a multitude of white farmhouses, strewn sparsely over the plains below like the eggs of some noxious vespine insect from which voracious grubs would shortly emerge. Against the walls of these farmhouses, which lay close to the road, broken wheels leaned in bitter symbolism, and by each door crouched a beldam who might have been placed there to mature for death as part of the household routine when in the morning the early melons were taken out and stacked in the sun.

The rack of old age, he cried inwardly. The torture chamber that all must enter.

The driver, now a charioteer, nostrils distended, wrenched at the wheel with finely shaped hands. They ploughed through a hamlet, the houses divided neatly on either side as if from a clean coulter-stroke. Elderly peasants on their way to the tavern, cloaked with the sombre majesty of Burgundian nobles, paused to regard them gravely. He had a vision of a dog in mid-air, a splendidly shaped animal, poised for a hundredth of a second upside down, legs extended heraldically to paw the air, body curved in an incredibly rhythmic posture.

They passed a solitary girl who pivoted slowly, with the perfect control of a ballerina. In the prolonged moment of passing he saw her eyes widen and her face light from within, with the dawning joy of a child that comes unexpectedly upon a flower. Her hair stirred with the wind that rushed divided from them, and she smiled and veiled herself mysteriously.

What beauty, he thought. He felt a sudden internal warmth, a rush of gratitude at the smile of a girl he would never see again. This he would remember. He would cherish in his memory for ever. Of such things, torn immediately from the sight, from the clasp, is pure happiness fashioned. Stop. Return. — Too late, she would have vanished. He was relieved that their swooping progress had carried him far from her — that he could not stay, turn back to unmask the secret blemish in that perfection.

Somewhere in the sky above him a bell boomed gravely, but with inexplicable nearness.

'Why do you drive so fast?' he asked the driver, finding himself compelled to plan this simple sentence stage by stage before giving it utterance.

'It soothes my nerves,' the driver said.

Listening with proper sympathy Manning discovered himself to be clutching a bottle which he had evidently brought with him quite unknown to himself at the behest of some benign prompting of the subconscious. He offered the bottle to the driver, who refused with a courteous smile. Not a bad fellow at all, Manning thought. He was sure he could do worse than confide in him the matter of the strange behaviour of the peasants in the streets of Malevento, this problem having suddenly reasserted itself with irritating insistence.

Just at that moment, however, another curious matter occupied him, calling, so it seemed, for prior elucidation. The landscape which spun from them, pivoting on their wheels with the vertiginous flux of a whirlpool, had suddenly assumed an intolerable symmetry, a geometrical division into balanced squares and triangles, as unbearable in its repetitious motive as the binding of an oriental volume. In whatever direction he looked, receding lines of telegraph poles neatly bisected the view. At exact intervals — the time in which he could count twenty slowly — a perfectly quadrangular farmhouse was whisked into his vision and whisked away again, and these farmhouses had been indecently bereft of their broken wheels, their acknowledgment of the supreme force of destiny. Nor were there to be seen before them black, submissive crones attempting to warm from their veins the coldness of the approaching night of non-existence. Even the regimented tree-tops, as evenly spaced as the serrations of a Moorish battlement, released exact contingents of birds which at their approach winged away in exasperating formation.

The driver seemed to interpret his alarm. 'A State farm project,' he explained, twisting furiously at the wheel to avoid a sow, attended on each flank by an identical number of young. Ceasing to mutter poetry, the driver launched into a brief statistical survey.

Much relieved, Manning raised the bottle again, only to find that although the cork was firmly in place it had become inexplicably empty. He was about to mention this in a casual and inoffensive manner to the driver when he was struck by another curious feature of the journey. It consisted in the prevalence of unsuitably dressed pedestrians who picked their way along the road verge in absurdly formal lounge suits, which under their layer of dust were obviously fabricated from some dark and sober material. The first of these forlorn dandies had given him quite a turn, as there was something about his outline and his carriage that irresistably recalled the marshal. The succeeding urban apparitions had, in fact, become even more like the marshal, which in a way was reassuring, but then at last there had arisen desperately from a pillar of dust like a devil from a smoking pit a face that *was* the marshal's, and that without any possibility of doubt.

'What's wrong with me?' he implored, suddenly clinging to the driver's arm.

'You're tight,' said the driver, employing, however, a vulgar army expression in a voice which seemed to Manning to be one of incredible refinement. The driver was now recovering with some difficulty from the dry skid provoked by the sudden wrenching of his arm.

'No,' said Manning, 'not tight. Although I'm prepared to concede I might be ill.'

The driver removed his eye from the road for a fraction of a second to observe him. 'If you mean you're bats,' he said, 'it's not much use applying to me. You want to spew again?'

'Where are we?' asked Manning, studying the landscape in sudden panic.

'Just coming into Malevento. We came back a different way. Rougher. Scenery more elemental.'

'Stop!' cried Manning. It had become a matter of great urgency for him to confront the marshal, who by now would have rescued himself from the sea of dust in which they had left him, striking out bravely, a mile or so back.

With this resolution firmly implanted in his mind he found his feet on the earth again, while the Fordson swooped round him and roared softly away, absorbed immediately, swallowed up in the twin volcanic eruptions that arose from its rear wheels.

And now he was here, marooned in this way. And where was Malevento, towards which the marshal would now be hastening by secret paths? Before him humped gently a burnished meadow studded with puny flowers, a plot of land well suited for a potter's field, seamed with dry water-courses from which arose to his ears the rusty susurration of fronds – the sound of the wind stirring those tall, silver-feathered stalks that live on in such places upon the memory or in the hope of water.

Ah, Malevento. City of evil wind. He saw it now, set like a repellent mirage above the mighty and corruscating desert of the soul that stretched out before him. Through its charred streets, pictured in an inescapable vision, fluttered constantly a genus of day-flying moths, settling disconsolately upon the broken features of its statuary, clinging in hopeless thirst to the green-rimmed spouts of its waterless fountains. Above this town death swung its censer.

And in Malevento assuredly there awaited him the burghers with averted faces, Don Enrico gesticulating and spitting at his back, Alberto standing ready to refill his glass with flame-searing liquor. The Sindaco, screaming in his father's ear: 'We've got him, Papa. We've got him.' And the old man ruminating with

180

the leer of an obscene cockatoo over the corpses under the spinach. The coffin-maker, of course, studying his proportions with a calculating eye. And the marchesina, now a succubus, a female fiend with turkey-shaped extremities, hurrying towards him at this very moment to press poisonous kisses on his lips. The marshal, too, would be there, enigmatic but menacing. And finally, reinforcing the ranks of all these strange enemies, the saints themselves, who had materialized for the occasion and marched in grim procession from their catacombs to Malevento, where they awaited him with portentous maledictions.

From the almost tangible reality of this vision he began to run, while from above, below, from the sky enclosed in its metallic and reverberant horizon, from the hills encircled with marshes and carrying their crushing burdens of clouds, pealed out suddenly a skull-shattering clarion. He closed his eyes; black lightning flashed and crackled against the pinkness of the lids. The sun struck at him with its scimitar. He fled, zigzagging like a prisoner exposed to the ley de fugos, flapping his arms mournfully, searching for some oblivion concealed in the secret folds of that earth. This asylum he found in the shape of a decrepit farmhouse.

Farmhouse? — Hovel or croft rather, yet in the meanness of those urine-stained walls there remained in a ten-millionth part dilution something of Rome, something of Athens, something of Knossos; an elusive and nonchalant correctness of proportion, a divine afflatus still breathing weakly through a hundred generations.

In the forcing house — the fertile cellar-darkness — of such rural barracks, humanity spawned unchecked. Here the family grew into a weak and vulnerable tribe. Here also death reaped his snatch-crops. Trees appropriate to the graveyard, of the kind having sombre and mossy foliage, covered the house with a shadowy ambuscade of jaguars.

The garden was encrusted — desolate labour of vanished children — with bleached tritons, the high-wound turbans of monstrous escargots, parched and flaking conches; their unicorn protuberances smoothed by the scrubbing of sand on tropical beaches.

An important movement caught and directed his eye to where ants which had raided in the domestic darkness were streaming back across the threshold laden with a booty of decaying scraps. As he bent to observe this activity more closely, an old man pounced upon him like a tarantula darting from a crevice — a frantic puppet, his face still dazed from the anaesthesia of some fearful adversity. 'Figlio mio,' he whined. 'Sonny.' He pawed feverishly at Manning's cheeks, standing on tip-toe, pulling at the lapels of his uniform in an attempt to raise himself up, to bring Manning's face within the range of those clouded eyes. From the black interior of the house emerged two more sombre figures, who placing themselves with the dour condolence of Job's companions on either side of the old man, took an arm apiece and began to lead him away. 'But don't you see?' screeched the old man in sudden desperation, looking wildly from one of his companions to the other. 'It's my son, Giannino. Why are you taking me away from him?' 'It's not Giannino,' said one of the men roughly, 'don't be foolish.' 'How do you know?' appealed the old man, struggling violently. 'You don't know Giannino. Let me go.' His cries and protests were silenced by the hollow slamming of the door.

At least, Manning was saying to himself, I've found one of them who doesn't cover his face. At least there's one.

But just then the door opened and one of the men came out again and approached him, smiling sadly. 'Please excuse the old fellow. He's off his rocker. Half-blind into the bargain.' He peered closely at Manning, his smile suffering sudden and premature death.

'Just imagine mistaking you for his son!' He made an apologetic grimace.

XV

A N D so he found himself lying on his bed again. It was
night, the hours of daylight having suddenly swirled and
vanished, disappeared without warning as if down the
waste-hole of a bath. All that had occurred during the day was
now condensed into a few impressions, brush strokes drawn by a
talented Japanese on a background of vapour from which
sketchily emerged a jagged mountain top, a wind-racked tree
and a pathetic human form.

The wild tintinnabulation in his ears had ceased decisively as if
with a single gong stroke, and now there had supervened a silence
oppressed only by the whispered scheming of insects and by the
waxing and waning of the mosquitoes' minute buzz-saw. The
water pipes, deprived of their contents, emitted at intervals a
remote and mournful sound.

He found himself anxiously awaiting its repetition, for by it he
was measuring out a throbbing which had started obscurely
behind his eyebrows, but which was now spreading outwards and
backwards, gradually involving in this way the temples and
threatening his ears. Arbitrarily he had decided that there could
be only twelve more of such expiring gurgles from the pipes
before either the pain would go or he would fall asleep again.

From where he lay, he was looking directly into the mirror
which he had previously arranged so as to reflect the sky. In the
bright surface of the glass there hung, by some trick of reflection,
the image of five almost full moons, each one slightly overlap-
ping the next. It recalled some game of skill, conducted in a fair-
booth, which had involved dropping such discs upon a shape
which had to be completely covered by them — a feat which
the dark-faced showman had accomplished with absolute
insouciance. The existence of these five reflections was by no
means disturbing to him in itself. He had noticed it on the

preceding night but one, and had accepted it as a phenomenon possessing an obviously simple explanation. He also recalled from his previous observations — casual as they had been — that these reflections varied in brilliance and that the most brilliant image, which would undoubtedly correspond to the true one, was the second from the right, whereas the faintest lay at the extreme left. These facts he confirmed once more, feeling very slightly relieved that no variation in this order of brightness had taken place. The faint image on the left was extremely faint, and as wraiths of practically transparent cloud drifted across the moon in the sky, this reflection disappeared altogether.

What was significant about this particular night was that there was undeniably something about these reflections that was troubling him. They had an inexplicable connection — one, however, which he accepted without question — with that pulsating pain behind the eyes. As he waved his head from side to side these five moons separated widely and then approached one another again, but no amount of changing his position could entice them entirely to coalesce. This was a source of increasing irritation, almost of dismay, because he knew that, once the moons could be persuaded to fuse, the pains in his head would stop. No assumption, indeed, had ever seemed to him to be more self-evident.

And now a voice somewhere below in the courtyard began to sing a song, a current Neapolitan favourite which Manning half recognized but of which the singer could only remember two lines that he sang over and over again. The tune possessed a vulgar but pleasing lilt. It was of the kind that insinuated itself unnoticed into the mind, and was thereafter expelled only with difficulty. In this existed the trap. Because after the first two lines, which were easy to possess, to remember, the melody took an unfamiliar turn, went off into an elusive half-oriental mood, following no normal, accepted pattern for its development. It was here that the difficulty occurred, both for Manning and for the singer:

> Turmiente doce è ammore ca me tene ncatenato
> e chistu core nun s'è mai lagnato . . .

Again the song began and Manning waited with every nerve
in his body for its triumph over this African diversion. But in
vain. The rich and throaty voice hesitated, limped off on a
wrong note, trailed away into a gently exploratory humming,
then started afresh.

It was obviously a matter of vital importance that the singer
should finally surmount this barrier, which was connected in
some way with his failure to induce coincidence of the moons
and therefore – taking the matter to its next logical stage – to
hurl back the raging pain that was beating its way into his brain.
He saw quite clearly that the only way in which all these objectives might be achieved would be by his wholehearted
co-operation with the singer. Therefore, when once again the
voice started he rocked himself into a new position, observing
with satisfaction that the moons responded by rushing together,
hanging for a moment, a pile of golden coins in space. But one,
alas, that he could still count.

At this moment the singer reached the end of the second line
and started on the third:

– ca sta sciupanno . . .

It was all over, he thought in triumph. The danger point had
passed. Straining every muscle, however, he suddenly overbalanced, pitched right out of the bed and fell on the floor.

He awoke in utter darkness, shivering and with a torturing
thirst. Somewhere uncertainly located in the night he could hear
a man with an old, assured voice talking to a crony, but all that
drifted up from the jumbled mutter of their conversation was the
word 'buono . . . buono . . . buono . . .' repeated at intervals and
in comment, no doubt, upon some completely unsatisfactory
situation. Through the window came a breeze that flicked icily
on the cold, sweat-soaked skin of his chest. The thunder behind
the brows had receded, died down in a distant rumbling, but all

his joints ached as if he had been beaten with a cudgel from head to foot.

Once more he reached the washroom, and now the spiders, those hairy ones disdaining webs which hurled themselves down the walls to gorge upon senescent flies and those which caressed the bodies of entrapped moths with limbs of incomparable delicacy — these and doubtless many other varieties were but invisible presences. A passing rat pressed itself intimately for a fraction of a second against his naked foot.

The position of the washbowl and the foul water it contained was suggested by the faintest possible phosphorescence. The drinking mug had disappeared, and choosing between the possibility of typhoid and the probability of death from malaria accelerated by dehydration, he could think of no alternative but to plunge his face into the water and to drink deeply. A corklike object bobbed against his nose and on being recovered stirred unmistakably in his finger-tips — a cockroach of monstrous proportions which, hurled from him, struck the wall with a faint crunching sound.

A great weakness fluttered the muscles of his legs, and it seemed that the warm and stagnant liquid he had just drunk so copiously had been transmuted in a trice into ice-cold sweat which, starting from every pore, began to drip from nose, ears, hair, fingers, even running down his eyelids and filling his eyes.

He reeled back into the other room and collapsed upon the soaking bed. He lay there on the uneasy edge of delirium while slowly and stealthily down in the street the noises heralding the dawn began. A cart rattled past somewhere in the darkness below him with axle creaking and wheels crunching on the stones as it slewed sideways over the uneven surfaces. The horse trumpeted asthmatically through its nostrils. Then came the clop-clopping of boots marching confidently down the metallic road, only to be muffled as their wearers began to stumble painfully over the soft piles of rubble and to make their way through half-filled craters.

These risers in the night gave each other dazed morning greetings and cursed in good natured, sleepy voices — avoiding blasphemy — as they stubbed their toes against fallen masonry. A bell, one of the mediocre variety always chosen for this purpose, began to ring monotonously, almost with irritation, a summons to the first devotions of the day.

But why no cocks? he thought. Without cocks there could be no dawn. And then the solution of this mystery occurred to him.

Of course, they had eaten all the cocks. And this same solution might well be applied to the otherwise inexplicable freedom of the night from the caterwauling of cats and from the howling of dogs.

Certainly they had been consumed. They had been involved inextricably in some spaghetti flavouring compounded with sinister artistry by the Sindaco, while his old father stood by, smacking his chops in toothless delight. The marshal, of course, would have previously claimed the choice morsels, either by muttered threats or merely by bringing pressure to bear. Certain less coveted parts would have passed with more difficulty and with some compression down Don Enrico's padded throat. To the marchesina's lot, privilege and perquisite would have fallen those dubious tit-bits well represented in poultry by the parson's nose, while the anti-Fascists would have been left to dispute among themselves the right to make soup with the miserable bones.

Yes, by God, he said to himself, they've eaten them all.

Of course they had. Every living thing conceivably adapted to human consumption had been foully devoured. Not only the cats and dogs — with the exception of a certain hairless one that prowled ceaselessly in the purlieus of his office, its mange-inflamed skin the colour of boiled bacon — but even the young storks had been ravished from their nests and the fat-covered vertebrae of their necks gnawed with savage delight. Even the rare fish in the aquarium. Even the fish. Had they not slyly angled for them and then devoured them whole like sardines, their voracious teeth crunching with impartiality through the marvellous luminous systems of grenadier fish, through the embryo lungs of climbing perches, through the goitrous pouches of chiasmodons, through the vestigial eyes of hagfish, through the electrical generating systems of baby rays, through the membranous appendages hanging from the snouts of elephant fish? Through suctorial mouths, mucous canals, adipose eyelids? Through gills infected with parasitic worms? Through ventral suckers, tubercles, barbels and feelers? Through reproductive and excretory organs, oviducts and ani? And after the feast, had not hands been politely raised to cover innumerable mouths, while the bristly remains of erstwhile diaphanous fins had been hooked from the interstices of the teeth?

In this way had vanished, had been involved in a vile metabolism, the gorgeous denizens of the deep, as well as the most dignified representatives of winged creation.

But what was unthinkable and quite unpardonable in the circumstances was the loss sustained to humanity by the extermination of all the cocks, in the absence of which, of course, the dawn could not come about, could not vanquish this inexhaustible night.

Clearly, no. In some confused way he half saw through the absurdity of this syllogism before it suddenly transformed itself, amoeba-like, into an ever-increasing number of extravagant shapes.

Why, for instance, could they not have been persuaded to go a stage further and to hunt down the cicadas, to lure them into cunningly contrived wicker traps, to organize in a festive spirit a drive, a Bartholomew's night, against these terrible insects, to be followed by an immense frying, according to individual taste, either in oil or in breadcrumbs?

When he opened his eyes again they were flooded with aching daylight. He was disappointed, cheated, because beyond the window, instead of the cool, grey dawn for which he had yearned, a pestiferous panther skin covered the sky from which the light rolled down and lapped over him in vibrating waves.

Shortly he became aware of a presence in the room, a form hovering obscurely somewhere over on the far side, away from the window; a form from which there came no sound but only, perhaps, a slight emanation like an electrical discharge.

Rolling his head — in the interior of which he immediately experienced a sensation as if padded weights had shifted heavily — he saw the marshal, who wore an expression of great concern and who on observing this sign of life began to tip-toe towards him, stopping while still a good six feet away. When he spoke his voice assumed a faintly sacerdotal intonation which, Manning felt, he normally reserved for use at death beds.

'My dear friend,' said the marshal, 'you're sick. I was worried when you didn't appear for breakfast.'

'Would you mind bringing me some water?' Manning asked him.

The marshal retreated mournfully towards the washroom, and presently re-emerged, horrified. 'But my dear friend,' he implored in a clerical near-falsetto, 'you can't possibly drink that. Can you wait a moment? Allow me to run up to the hotel and bring you a supply of mineral water.'

'Tap-water will do,' said Manning. 'You'll see some sterilizing tablets lying about somewhere.'

The marshal found the tablets and returned with a mug of water. Handing this to Manning he almost skipped back to his previous position.

'I'm not infectious,' said Manning. 'This is malaria.'

The marshal shook his head doubtfully. 'How do you know? I don't want to alarm you, but to me you have all the appearance of a sufferer from typhus. There's something indefinable about you that practically advertises it. How do you feel?'

'I'm cold,' said Manning, 'and I have a pain in the head.'

'Yes,' said the marshal, pursing his lips judiciously. 'But preceded, of course, by a profuse sweat. Don't tell me. I can see by the state of the bed.' He leaned over and retrieved the empty mug, shuddering faintly at the chromatic sediment in its bottom.

'Nausea and sickness?' he asked mellifluously. 'Retention of the urine, perhaps, or — ' he sniffed with delicacy — 'loss of control over both bowels and bladder?'

'I've got malaria,' said Manning with what would have been stubbornness had it not been for an increasing indifference that had possessed him. He hardly cared one way or the other. If the marshal continued to insist, he felt that in the end he would agree to typhus.

'It's easy to confuse at first,' said the marshal with sympathy. 'The first symptoms are similar. After that the real trouble starts. Take a look at your chest and abdomen and see whether you have a measly eruption. Are you dull and listless? Of course you are. Do you ramble at night? Give no thought to the head — it never lasts — it's what follows it that really matters. Constant delirium, sometimes requiring restraint. Then the characteristic deepening of colour, the appearance of sordes on the teeth and, of course, a blackened and leathery tongue.

'After that,' went on the marshal dreamily, 'floccitation — the tendency of the patient to pluck at the bed clothes, difficulty of respiration accompanied, I'm afraid, by groaning. All the while the heart so weak, practically inaudible. Urine scanty and highly coloured. Then finally, alas, profound coma occasionally preceded by convulsions. I have known cases of coma vigil, in which the sufferer lies quite unconscious, eyes open and fixed, the pupils contracted to pin points — perhaps this is more merciful, taking it all round. Death usually supervenes at the end of the second week, and decomposition is rapid.'

'You've certainly studied it,' said Manning weakly.

'Most of my acquaintances were carried off in that way,' said the marshal. 'I couldn't help becoming familiar with the details, some of which are sufficiently horrible to impress themselves upon the mind. I haven't mentioned abscesses affecting the pudenda, suppurative inflammation, gangrene, imbecility. At its worst, typhus can be practically indistinguishable from the plague.'

'Sorry to disappoint you,' said Manning, rallying with a desperate effort of the will, 'this is malaria. I've had it before.'

'How earnestly I hope you are right,' said the marshal. 'But tell me one thing: is there some intolerance of light and a singing in the ears?'

'There was,' said Manning, 'but it's going off now.'

'It doesn't mean a thing,' said the marshal. 'The rapid alternation of symptoms is quite bewildering. Let me look at your chest and stomach.'

Manning bared his skin and the marshal risked coming a foot nearer to him to peer at it.

'There's certainly no rash,' he admitted.

Pulling up the damp blankets again Manning shivered violently at their contact. 'I've had malaria half a dozen times before. I know what to expect.'

'If it's malaria,' said the marshal, 'you shouldn't stay here, even if you don't want to go to hospital. You need looking after. A few days rest.'

Manning eyed him dully without replying. He felt utterly listless, worn out. He had two desires only, and these left no room for any other. First, a constant supply of drinking water. Second, a cold cloth to lay on his forehead. After that the only other possible desideratum would be a dry bed.

He noticed incuriously that his antipathy to the marshal had been dulled to a vanishing point by the fever's opiate. The instinctive mistrust which he had felt since the first day of their meeting had also died down. It was just too unimportant. In fact, everything was unimportant. Everything but that pain behind the eyes.

'I will go for the doctor,' declared the marshal. 'He shall pass his verdict. Above all, don't let him persuade you to go into the hospital here — even if only while awaiting the arrival of your own people. Patients are accommodated two in each bed, and you would be certain to pick up at least one other variety of sickness.'

'I shall be up in two days,' Manning assured him feebly. 'All I want is some quinine or some paludrine, and a supply of decent water.'

'I have a suggestion to make,' said the marshal. 'I'll arrange with a family to take care of you. Decent people of my acquaintance. They'll give you a room in their house. We're not talking of anything being done for nothing. They'll be glad of a little extra money. I hope we're not too rash in assuming that it isn't the typhus.'

The marshal's solution seemed unavoidable. Either that or the exhaustion of the unthinkable journey to some remote military hospital, to be reached after days, perhaps, of lying shivering with ague on a stretcher in a train. Or, on the other hand, a nightmare trek in the back of the Fordson, the driver hounded by his familiar furies crashing and bumping over hundreds of miles of the worst roads in Italy. Certainly there would be strings of some kind, as yet not perceived, attached to the marshal's offer, since it was clearly impossible to associate the marshal in any circumstances with a disinterested motive. Such conduct would have been against the marshal's code. But he just could not bring himself to care. The will-numbing reality of the fever carried all scruples, fears, hesitations before it. Other considerations became secondary and trivial when set beside his pain-racked head and his immense, bloodless weariness.

XVI

THE decent people of the marshal's acquaintance proved to be a brother and sister. With their old mother they occupied a house in the northern suburb of the town.

The brother was sharp-faced, active, energetic, with darting eyes and nervous, strumming fingers; a pale man, even under the sun, of uncertain occupation. Through economic difficulties in his youth he had been preserved from the futility of a professional career. Potentially an accountant, a chancellor, a grey eminence, a man by nature enchanted with figures and calculations and their attendant adventures, Matteo was a member of that legion of southern schemers who were usually unsuccessful in their intrigues by reason of the sheer weight of numbers of the others of their own kind in competition with them. This type of man it was who speculated with meagre reward in small parcels of boot-menders' sprigs, or who made occasional semi-repaying journeys to distant cities, buying and selling there such commodities as babies' dummies, fish hooks or shirt buttons. The ancestors of such men had despoiled the shattered chariots and the abandoned baggage trains of Pyrrhus. Only a year or two previously a great host of them had gone intrepidly, filtering their way in the rear of the advancing armoured spearheads, elbowed aside by embattled partisans, thrust off the roads by wildly driven columns of supply vehicles, actually sniped at, decimated by uncleared pockets of resistance, but breaking their way indomitably, for all that, into beleaguered and falling cities, to be the first to buy the goods in the shops at uninflated prices. Clutching their suitcases they went, their garments padded grotesquely with notes of high denomination and leaving no corporeal recess or cavity unexploited for the purpose of carrying other more valuable, more concentrated media of exchange. In endless columns they advanced, these men in slick town clothes, affable, voluble, gesticulating, undaunted by hardship and unshaken by peril in their quest for the trader's holy grail; the cheap market in which to buy, the dear market in which to sell.

Matteo carried in his head all the inordinate price variations obtaining throughout the different regions of Italy. The mere knowledge, however, of some of these extravagant discrepancies caused him intense mental torture. Hence his nervousness and the increasing difficulty with his digestion. Imagine the agonizing realization that in Milan silk could be found at a tenth of the price he could get for it in Naples, while he could buy as much olive oil as he liked for a hundred lire a litre in Foggia and get six hundred for it in Rome. But how to effect these profitable exchanges in the absence of transport — itself the very factor which produced such alluring price discrepancies — was the difficulty that balked all but the wiliest and most desperate of his colleagues of their fair margin.

So Matteo paced the room in frustration, rolled his eyes, clicked his teeth, formulated schemes and yet more schemes. He was hag-ridden by the grim thought that if he were to count up his total profit since the Armistice, when free enterprise had come into its own, it was doubtful if he would have made as much as the average peasant who sold his produce at fat, black market prices, without any problems of distribution to worry him.

The sister, Lina, was nothing less than a Boeotian goddess, a presence in a rusty black dress, the archaic simplicity of which only drew attention the more inevitably to certain fatal characteristics she possessed. This dress followed the hollows as well as the protuberances of her outline with an almost excessive passivity.

Lina's black hair parted in the centre and rushed like a turbulent river towards the temples, falling then, with a tendency to cover the outer corners of her eyes, in a cataract of thick, rope-like coils over the outline of her breasts. Her eyebrows were strongly arched and thick, her nose rather long and slender, the tip of it being inclined to tremble as if in sensitive appraisement of an odour of cooking. Her mouth was not wide, but had very full lips. Her skin was dead white, her stalwart and stockingless legs slightly pimply. She had the flanks of a beautiful horse. At a rather later date Manning was to be half fascinated and half repelled to notice as she bent over him the existence of fine black down in the ravinous cleft of her bosom.

This village Proserpina was of a physical type not uncommon in the south, which the marshal, Manning remembered, had characterized with melancholy appetite as being notorious tearers of sheets. Her manner, he observed, had about it something of unstudied indifference, even sullenness, the eyes habitually downcast. She did not smile, and contented herself with regarding him occasionally, he suspected, with swift, sidelong glances as she flounced past in her laceless and flat-heeled shoes.

When he first tried a halting and not very successful compliment, it seemed to go unnoticed, although perhaps there was the merest flicker of deprecation in the turned-down corners of her mouth. Neither did she speak a great deal, and when she did it was in an indifferent, grumbling tone, accompanied at almost every sentence with a shrug of the shoulders.

It was extraordinary to Manning that this girl could be the sister and presumably the female counterpart of the nervous and mercurial Matteo.

The third person in this southern trinity was the old mother, whose blood relationship with the other two, and more particularly with Lina, was equally if not more hard to accept. She had the leathern face of an aged squaw — completely masculine — with sparse, lank hair. It was indeed incredible that the robust and brooding beauty of Lina could ever come to be transformed into this likeness of a sexless mummy. They shrink, too, Manning thought, noticing how tiny the old woman was. They even shrink. Simian rather than human she was, with a lipless mouth sewn together with coarse threads. Those lips of Lina's, capable of forming only two expressions — that of yielding love or that of the smouldering but assuredly feigned antagonism that preceded it — how could they waste away until one day they would part only in a grimace of bewilderment, revealing for a moment a frightful vision of the teeth of a skull, then to be recompressed in bitter and wooden resignation? How could this be so? How could she petrify as surely as Lot's wife, even if the grim process took a generation to reach its horrific completion?

He looked at the old woman again — a fearful and compulsive look. She was as if enclosed in crackling mica. Wherever the skin could not wrinkle — for example, where it was stretched over the collarbone by the weight of the ancient, dragging dugs — it was as if the mica were disintegrating in layers, as if a sharp tap with the knuckles would be sufficient to cause it to flake away and shower to the ground.

This was the family in which Manning had been driven to take refuge. It was to be, he promised himself, a strictly temporary expedient. Within three or four days, he knew, the attack would have passed and he would be able to move back into the office.

So for two days he lay between the greying sheets of a huge four-poster bed, while the fever waxed and waned. He was attended chiefly by the old mother, who sought to tempt him, but without success, with strange messes of food. She showed her obvious disappointment when he rejected something she had set before him with special pride: a plate of macaroni garnished with skewered sparrows. 'You don't like them?' she squeaked in astonishment. 'Yes, of course, as soon as the fever goes,' Manning reassured her. 'I'll get my appetite back then.' 'But don't you understand?' said the old woman despairingly. 'You can't expect to come by a windfall like this every day!' She caressed with the tip of a finger that was like an oak twig the tiny triangle of a sparrow's breastbone. 'What a pity! When they are out of season, too.'

Lina's occasional visits were concerned with replenishing the water supply. She entered the bedroom in a shrinking, hesitant manner. When he asked her for a wet cloth to lay on his forehead, she performed the office for him, allowing the cool tips of her fingers to touch his temples, and then immediately averting her eyes, which were screened by a palisade of lashes.

On the occasion of one of these visits, Manning stirred himself to an attempt at conversation, praising the magnificence of the bed on which he lay. Quite casually he wondered as he said this whether one or many bodies had preceded him there since those sombre sheets had first been white.

'Oh, so the gentleman likes the bed, does he?'

He noticed the playful emphasis on the word gentleman, although there was no relaxation in Lina's rather stern expression.

' — Well, so he should. It's the best bed in the town.'

'Splendid,' he agreed, 'quite an heirloom.'

'Yes,' she said, warming slightly. 'It has a wonderful history, too. We are very proud of it. In my great-grandfather's time the last of the brigands were surrounded in this house. The police couldn't get them out. Every time they tried to break in someone was shot. In the end they called the priest to act as a go-between. He got the police to agree that if the brigands surrendered there would be no further bloodshed. Well, as the police captain had decided to kill all the brigands, the only way he could find of doing so without breaking his word was to have them smothered gently, one at a time, in this bed.'

'They were laid comfortably on the mattress,' suggested Manning, 'and another mattress held considerately in position over their faces?'

'No,' said Lina. 'They used pillows. They had very large pillows in those days, which we don't use any more. It is supposed to have been a very long job. They were a long time over each man because the priest was very strict about no violence being used.'

'And it was after that that your ancestor bought the house?'

'Yes, of course. Imagine how envious all the neighbours were.'

When Manning got up for the first time he spent an evening sitting with the family in the long, narrow living-room — so narrow, indeed, as to be almost a passage.

In this room the furniture was curiously arranged so that a number of moulting armchairs formed a row down one side and facing them, with only a very small space between were a row of ordinary chairs. The other pieces of furniture included a sideboard bearing two glass-enclosed creations of flowers made from seashells, and a mirror in a luxuriant baroque frame, the glass of which had been so closely painted over with flowers as to leave practically no reflecting surface. There was a small table bearing a vase of elegant proportions. It contained fleshy and pink-veined lilies round which crawled coronals of seemingly in-toxicated flies. The room smelled as if it had recently been swept with vigour and the dust had not quite settled again.

On two of the ordinary straight-backed chairs but at opposite ends of the room sat the women, the mother silent and motion-less, enduring life's ordeal by fire, gazing weakly into space as if bemused by the vision of a drab eternity. Lina sewed, also in silence. Matteo, in an armchair at Manning's side pursued chimaera of commercial fantasy, launched spectral argosies, cornered vast markets and netted staggering gains. 'If only it were possible to get a little lorry, a little insignificant truck of some kind, a camioncino, and drive it up to the Austrian frontier.' He whistled and dismissed with a swirling motion of the hand a gaudy vision that had hung, half materialized, just before his nose.

'And what would you do when you got there?'

'Do? — Madonna mia!' Bright-winged tanagers of speculation flashed in the dark forest of his brain. 'Think of the tyres coming out of Austria and Germany. You could pick them up at your own price. Nothing you can't buy. Lorries, Jeeps, anything you like. All for next to nothing. Make a fortune in one trip. All you need is some sort of cover. Just a chit to get you through and back.' Matteo blasphemed mildly, and his sister looked up in sharp disapproval. The mother continued to appraise without enthusiasm the spectacle of eternity.

Manning brought up the matter of paying for his lodging, and Matteo waved his hand in genial protest. 'We'll talk about it some other time.'

'I'd like to talk about it now.'

'Tomorrow, then.'

'Today.'

'We're not short of money. I want to be your friend — to serve you. I mean that with all my heart.'

'Yes, I know,' said Manning. 'And thank you. But all the same . . .'

'Well, then, if you insist what am I to do? Pay me anything you like — say two hundred lire a week.'

This was ridiculous, the lira at that time being officially four hundred to the pound, although in reality worth far less.

'It's not enough,' said Manning, 'I'll give you a thousand.'

Matteo looked pained. 'Why should we talk about money? As if there are no better things in life. We are poor but happy — gay. . . .'

At this moment Lina looked up again and made some comment in dialect. Matteo snapped back at her like an infuriated terrier, turning blandly to continue the argument with Manning: '. . . happiness — joy — harmony — the beautiful things of life. These are the things that count. Money — no.' He waved his index finger with severity.

Manning produced a thousand lire note, folded it and tried to put it into Matteo's hand, while Matteo pushed it away with gentle fastidiousness. The note thus oscillated gracefully for several seconds between the two of them. '. . . the bigger things,' Matteo was saying, 'the more important things . . . bonds of affection. I quite understand that you should want to feel independent. Just give me a packet of cigarettes once in a while and a bar of soap for Lina.'

'Listen,' his sister broke in. 'I want to ask the gentleman

something.' As she raised her head her eyes were temporarily eclipsed by the thick locks of hair. 'Please tell me,' she said to Manning, sweeping back her tresses. 'I read in a magazine that here in Italy girls of good family — living, of course, in such awful places as Venice — actually think nothing of exposing their skins to the sun. Naturally, such dreadful customs will never spread so far south as Naples, far less here. But do they do the same sort of thing in England?'

'Yes,' said Manning, 'even the English have fallen so low.'

'Oh, even the English.'

'When there's any sun to expose the skin to,' said Manning.

'I don't speak only of the shamelessness of it — in these days we have learned to expect anything. But don't these girls understand what will happen to them.'

'And what will happen?'

'They will dry up completely, like monkeys. They will look like leather water bottles. Surely you have noticed the peasants. Absolute witches. Fancy anyone ever going out in the sun unless she were obliged to do so, let alone exposing her — oh — limbs to it.'

'Don't you go out in the sun at all, signorina?'

'I never go out unless it is absolutely unavoidable. The well-brought-up girl doesn't. Even in the courtyard here I keep my face covered as much as possible and see to it that the sun doesn't touch my skin.'

In the crepuscular light of the narrow chamber Lina's face shone palely. 'Why should I go out?' she said. 'The less any woman's seen in the street, the better for her and for her husband. She should await him in the house. Be in attendance upon him. Be there at all times.' Her voice vibrated with sudden sensual intensity and her face was contorted in some emotion that seemed for a moment like grief but which was not.

Matteo told him afterwards: 'Her husband's away. We don't mention him, and naturally it's not pleasant for a girl of her disposition. A frightful deprivation. Bad for the health, if you understand me. A girl like that can easily fall into consumption.'

Manning was sympathetic. He recalled the expression that occasionally invested Lina's features with the anguish of one of those fleshy female martyrs of the Neapolitan school; now realizing with some disillusionment, however, that its origin was not of the soul.

'Put yourself in her place,' said Matteo. 'The climate just doesn't allow it. For a single girl it's a different matter. What you don't know about you don't miss.'

'I shall be starting work tomorrow,' Manning mentioned.

'Work?' said Matteo. 'Always work. You Anglo-Saxons kill yourselves with work. Well, I suppose I can't talk; I'm the same myself; can't keep away from it. I'm unhappy if I feel I'm not pulling my weight. It gives me a bad conscience. In the end I can't sleep. Well, I suppose it had to be. Means we'll be seeing you in the evenings from now on.'

'Yes,' said Manning, 'in the evenings.' Saying as he did so just what he had been determined — until that moment — not to say. There was no doubt about it. The final return to the office would have to be postponed. It was only reasonable. Give himself a week or two. Say even the accepted sixteen days the Army allowed after a malaria attack, to get his strength up. Do his work all the better for it. Of course. After that he would go back and face the mosquitoes again, a giant refreshed.

'But come up for a siesta,' urged Matteo. 'After all, what's the use of trying to work before four o'clock? There's never any-one about wherever you go. They're all in bed. Down to it with their wives. Madonna mia! They don't even just lie down on the bed. They undress and put on their nightshirts. It's the curse of Italy, the siesta. Don't let them talk to you about the Spaniards, or the drainage, or Mussolini, or over-immigration. It's the siesta that's finishing us off. It gives the women a second chance at you. But then, what's to be done if everyone else is doing the same thing? Look at me. When I'm away from home trying to locate business contacts, between twelve and four you might just as well give up. Bow to the inevitable. It saves making yourself bad blood. Better to go off and have a nap somewhere in a tavern. Personally I prefer God's fresh air. Don't take me too literally. I don't mean right out in the open — exposed — you know, but a really nice snooze in a car parked in a side street with the radio turned on soft. Heaven.'

'What kind of programme do you go in for?'

'Music. Sacred or operatic for preference. All the afternoon programmes in Italy are really intended to produce a good siesta. I float away like a cherub on a cloud.'

XVII

Nᴇxᴛ morning Matteo cornered him.

'Will you do me a favour?'

Of course, this had been bound to happen. The only remarkable thing was that such a request had been so long in forthcoming.

'What sort of a favour?' He tried hard to keep the ungraciousness out of his tone.

'Nothing important. I want to go to Foggia.'

Manning felt reprieved. It was not, then, so serious as he had feared.

'Well, what's stopping you?'

'Only a pass.'

'I thought that was just a formality in these days. Don't they give them out at the Municipio?'

'Yes. It means slipping someone a thousand lire if you don't want to be kept waiting.'

'I'll get you one for nothing.' Manning was really relieved. He could hardly believe he was getting off so cheaply. Tomorrow he would move out. Yes, tomorrow. Well, if not tomorrow, Monday at the latest and start the week well. He had seen the red light.

'I need the pass right away.'

Uh huh. He wasn't out of the wood yet.

'Today is a public holiday,' Matteo said, 'the Municipio is shut. Tomorrow is Sunday.'

'Well, what am I supposed to be able to do about it?'

'You can write me out a pass.'

'Be all the same if I did. I'm not authorized to issue them.'

'A pass with your stamp on it is all I want,' Matteo said. 'It doesn't want to be fancy in any way. Just a slip of paper with your stamp underneath, saying it is all right for me to go to Foggia. That's all I want.'

'They won't take any notice of it,' Manning said.

'Don't worry about that,' said Matteo. 'You leave that part to me. They'll pay more attention to it than a regular pass from the Municipio.'

'Who sees the pass?' Manning asked.

'No one. That is, not usually. Sometimes bus conductors ask for them, but in this case a friend is giving me a lift in his car.'

'Why don't you chance it, then?'

'I like to be on the safe side. I feel more confident with the law behind me.'

'Wait till Monday.'

'I can't.'

'I'll get you a pass for nothing on Monday.'

'Monday's too late. I've got a big deal on. If I have to wait until Monday for a pass it means I can't travel until Tuesday morning. I hope you'll be able to help me out, Don Roberto.'

'It doesn't seem to make sense to me,' Manning said. 'I don't issue passes. What sort of a deal is it?'

'I've got a chance to place a parcel of injections.'

'A parcel of what?'

'Injections. Reconstituent ones. We're getting deliveries from the north at last. First deliveries since manufacture was restarted.'

'Would you mind telling me what reconstituent injections are?'

'Certainly not. They use them with a needle. Pulls you together when you've been overdoing it. You know what I mean. Very popular with women down here.'

'Oh,' said Manning.

'The better class women. They fetch a big price, especially in a market that has been starved for so long. The trouble is I have to get everything tied up by Monday night, or the deal's off.'

'How are you carrying the goods?'

'I'm not carrying them. It's a kind of multilateral barter arrangement. No cash involved. At least, not at this stage. I'm arranging to exchange the goods, when I get them, for fertilizer.'

'When you get them? Haven't you got them yet?'

'Well, not exactly. The main thing is, I've got a week's option on them. I know the fertilizer is waiting for me at Foggia. So I go down there and conclude the deal.'

'And your man in the north will take the fertilizer?'

'Of course not. What would an industrialist want with fertilizer? Probably never heard of it. In any case how could I shift it? It's as big as a mountain. I've got no transport. That's where the owner's risk is covered. He knows that nobody wants to take it away for months, so he can afford to wait a little for his payment.'

'Ah — you sell it.'

'No, I've already got an exchange option on cloth in Bari.'

'Then you will sell the cloth?'

'Well, no. A wine merchant from Palermo will take the cloth. Delivery of the wine will be taken by my agent in Milan. Fortunately, the wine merchant has his own auto-treni.'

'And there your agent will sell the wine?'

'Yes.'

'And buy the reconstituent injections?'

'That is so.'

'Which you will then pass to the possessor of the fertilizer?'

'Yes, yes. At least, in part. The rest, of course, will be my profit. I expect to come out of this with a large stock of injections. Enough to enable me to start up business on my own account. I shall have enough to revitalize the womanhood of southern Italy.'

'The better class womanhood.'

'Of course.'

'But all this majestic campaign hinges upon one small thing,' said Manning.

'Please?'

'I refer to the provision of a pass.'

'Ah yes, of course, I was forgetting that. That is so. Other-

205

wise, all is in order. Everything is set for the word go. The time-tables are worked out to a nicety. It all dovetails.'

'Potentially, Matteo, you are a public benefactor.'

'Perhaps. I hope so.'

'But with all this organization, why on earth didn't you go to the Municipio for a pass yesterday?'

'Yesterday the deal trembled in the balance. It is only this moment that I have received word of acceptance. It was the fertilizer merchant who was the weak link in the chain. In commerce of this kind quick decisions must be made. If the Foggia man had turned down my offer, it would have meant a journey to Potenza instead.'

'For fertilizer?'

'No. A small deposit of kaolin there has come into the market. This could have been bartered for barbed wire, which would have been equally interesting to the cloth merchant at Bari.'

Manning accepted his defeat. 'You're leaving tomorrow. When do you expect to return?'

'Tomorrow night. We're leaving at dawn.'

'Then you want a pass for one day only?'

'Yes, that will do.'

Manning tore a sheet out of his notebook and wrote:

> CIANFONE, Matteo, fu Rinaldo, is authorized to make one journey to Foggia on 1.7.45, returning to Malevento on the same day.

He stamped this and gave it to Matteo. Now he would build up his defences and thus protect himself from any further, more serious, embarrassments.

'I want to pay for my lodgings now,' he said. He hoped Matteo would respond to the comparative brusqueness of tone he had assumed.

'Don't talk like that,' Matteo said. His expression was reproachful. 'Lina and I expect you to stay with us while you are in Italy. Don Roberto, please understand this — you are more

206

than a brother to us. We want you to consider this your home.'

It was starting all over again. A puerile combat he just couldn't be bothered with. He felt in his pocket and got hold of a couple of thousand lire notes. But he just couldn't be bothered. He couldn't find the energy to continue to play this routine farce. He pushed the notes back and determined just to leave quietly and to post the money to Matteo after he left.

'This is your home,' said Matteo, lingering upon the word with a richly sentimental, almost tearful inflection. Throwing out his hands he embraced in an hospitable gesture the double row of chairs, the glass encased shell flowers, the fleshy lilies, now flaccid and moribund but still fly-enticing. This gesture was intended to provide the signal for a conventional move by Manning which would in turn permit Matteo to plunge more deeply into the jungle of emotional clichés. Manning, however, was resolutely refusing to abide by the rules of the game.

Matteo became anxious.

'Don Roberto, I can never repay you. You want some wine from Foggia?' Manning shook his head, trying to smile.

'Cloth, perhaps. A nice suit length of cloth?'

'No thanks. I'm also fixed up for kaolin, barbed wire and fertilizer.' Why be ungracious? he thought. You had to repay them in some way. Think yourself lucky it's no worse. After all, he had been trapped into giving a pass which was really of no importance. He might as well be pleasant about it. Smiling a trifle wearily, he slapped Matteo on the shoulder. 'Save me an injection or two when you get them.'

'Thank you, Don Roberto. For you a whole box of injections and a syringe in an engraved presentation case to go with them.'

It was night. Heat lay upon his limbs like a foul-smelling quilt. The south wind had overtaken the town, not blowing in gusts but coming through it and over it in a stealthy current; stirring the acacia leaves but not strongly enough to raise the dust; sucking away the life from blooms cultivated on balconies.

He took off his shirt and lay on the bed in his shorts, trying to read but unable to concentrate because of the jumble of stale thoughts which had settled at the back of his mind and which, although no longer constantly asserting themselves — no longer clearly defined — were always there: a heavy sediment he was unable to dissipate.

He read a page of the book without retaining a single sentence. He read the page again and put the book down. The dim light was straining his eyes. He wound his watch. It was already almost fully wound. The time was ten-forty. He picked the book up again.

Glancing down, he saw the skin of his solar plexus folded in deep parallel creases by the angle at which he was sitting. These creases were full of sweat. His eye escaped from the page, broke away and went wandering round the room: a chest of drawers, lop-sided through the collapse of one leg; a washstand, with pitcher and basin adorned with hideous, cabbage-like flowers; a couch, disembowelled by a decade of love or a century of formal visits; a small cupboard containing many assorted chamber pots (in such things, he had observed, Italian houses — and probably with justification — never economized); a sideboard converted into a kind of shrine, with a gaudy madonna of china flanked by extinct candlesticks. Then, after that, the chest of drawers again, washstand, couch, cupboard full of jerries, domestic altar. And then again, before he could drag himself back to the book, once more round the walls, irritatingly divided into panels, just as they had been in Pompeii, but instead of frescos huge faded photographs of women proudly displaying their Edwardian fashions, and soldiers in baggy uniforms, with plumed helmets and fiercely flashing eyes.

'Don Roberto,' he heard Lina's voice calling softly outside the door. He reached for the towel hanging on the back of the chair and draped it over his shoulders.

'Don Roberto, I've brought you a drink. — Con permesso.'

She came in, carrying a tray, and put it on the bedside table.

From the amber liquid in the bottle came a dusty glitter like motes gleaming in a sunbeam. Lina poured out a glass, and the metallic fragments held in evenly spaced suspension swirled and danced.

'Liquore d'oro,' said Lina. 'The gold strengthens the heart. It's a drop we saved since before the war.'

'A celebration?' Manning asked.

'This is the anniversary of my first communion.'

'Will you drink, too?'

'Oh no, Don Roberto. I never drink. It's not correct for women to drink.'

'I won't drink without you.'

'All right, then, I'll taste it from your glass.' She raised the glass to her lips. When she lowered it, a few flecks of gold leaf adhered to them.

In this unrevealing light the face was overtopped by a cloudy and opaque mass. Her hair had been built up into an elaborate confection, billowing rolls coaxed into position one upon the other and held in place, no doubt, by cunningly disposed wires and clips. She had become a swarthy Pompadour.

And in this light her eyes were flat and eclipsed. The eyes of an idol. The rusty black dress had been renovated by the gloom, although a faint sheen still marked the rounded protuberances of the form which seemed to strain beneath it.

Since she had come in he had been conscious of a faint but increasing tension in himself. The response, as it were, to an electrification of the atmosphere; as though the wind had suddenly changed, veering round to the west and bringing with it thunder clouds which now raced over the rooftops.

From her body came a faint emanation of olive oil, of fragrant molecules shaken from incredibly fecund hair roots and now floating like disturbed bees over her blueish scalp.

'Don Roberto,' she said, 'don't go away.'

He studied her face with curiosity and with concern. Her voice had quite changed. It was now no longer Lina's voice but a voice of a certain special order which for purposes of rough classification could be bracketed with that of Anna Consomato. It was very soft and very persuasive and it was beautiful, too, but it was also a powerful weapon, and there was no doubt about that.

This new voice of Lina's inspired several emotions in Manning. At the moment they were surging up within him, undefined. They were in conflict, and soon the victor would emerge. The voice went on again. It was pitched several tones higher than the one kept for everyday use.

'Don Roberto, why do you want to leave us?'

Why shouldn't I? An inner warning died still-born. He registered with alarm and then resignation that as a first step to the unforeseeable end he was prepared to treat this matter as one for dalliance. His internal qualms had stilled like a hen stroked into passive acquiescence by the hand of an amateur mesmerist. If she wanted him to stay, he would stay. He knew that perfectly well, although he might pretend to hold out for five minutes more.

'I didn't think you had much time for me.'

'Yes, I like you, Don Roberto. When my brother's not here I'm a different person. I'm like a bird out of a cage. He's very severe with me.' The gold-flecked lips were parted appealingly, displaying tiny but perfect teeth between which flickered the elusive lizard of a tongue-tip. 'Here alone — what kind of a life is that for a girl? All day long I am alone, except for Mamma, who doesn't speak. I'm dying for someone to speak to.'

The face was nearer now and the black dress sagged feloniously at the neck. Manning felt a constriction of the throat and gulped slightly. In spite of the sultriness of the night a cool jet of air played suddenly on his neck, his spine, the small of his back, his flanks.

'You can come here at midday. We don't eat very well, but you can come to see me.'

The voice was now quite frankly that of a conspirator. It lingered caressingly in a flowery mead of slurred vowels. With infallible instinct she had assumed his compliance.

'You could come and see me.'

Yes. Without taking a step. Hardly, in fact, having said a single word, he was plunged deeply and willingly into this conspiracy. He felt a growing exultance and noticed that his hands were trembling slightly.

'Tonight Matteo won't come back. I'm happy.'

'He'll come back.'

'No. They will not travel by night. The roads are dangerous. Not tonight. There, I've filled your glass. Drink again.'

'It's rather sweet,' he said. He raised the glass. She reached out and took him by the wrist. 'Let me taste it again.' She guided his hand with the glass to her mouth. Her eyes watched his over the brim. There were flecks of light in their flat blackness. Her cheekbones bore a bloom of coarse face powder, and a tiny pulse leapt and trembled in her temple. The lower eyelids flickered as the gold leaf swirled in the glass. He felt darting shocks enter him at the three points where her fingers touched his wrist.

The surface of that Niagara of black hair had resisted his hand and could only be penetrated finger by finger. The sullen beauty of Lina's face, now held close to his, had been invaded by an unbelievable fierceness ... eyes wide, nostrils wide, lips drawn back tightly. And then suddenly she had thrown off her passive role, joining with him in a wild and compelling collaboration; a turmoil of thrusting limbs. It was as if it were she who was possessing him. In this conflict there was a defeated reluctance, and the knowledge of danger, but it was too late to turn back.

He awoke uneasily, summoned from sleep by the nagging of an internal clarion which deposited him hastily and with no drowsy period of acclimatization on the shore of an unglamorous reality.

It was shortly after dawn, and the objects of the room were lapped in a greasy light. His uneasiness deepened into a half apprehended nausea.

There was a movement somewhere, and his eyes focused across the rumpled, wintry ocean of bedclothing on the form of Lina, an ungainly statue going through the brief ritual of her toilet.

She looked round and saw him and smiled puffily. Her face seemed to be slightly inflated. Or perhaps it was the angle from which he saw her.

He caught sight of an alarming reflection in the washstand mirror, an unwillingly glimpsed postcard produced with pornographic intent by a sidling tout. She continued with her toilet, and their eyes met again in the mirror.

Manning knew that her very indifference to his regard involved the assumption of an established and immutable relationship. In it there dwelt some kind of obscure proprietary right.

Lina's hips emerged with emphasis, cadaverously white and cruelly divested of attraction below her short vest. In her movements she was adopting postures of unfailing awkwardness. It was as if a tipsy artist's model had set herself to go through an awful parody of her poses. She bent over, becoming absurdly top heavy in her appearance. It looked as if she were in danger of being overbalanced by the weight of her heavy breasts. Last night's odour of perfumed unguents had staled and beneath it drifted a shifty and rancid exhalation.

He turned his head away.

Now he remembered quite inevitably the occasion when he had been out strolling with the marshal and Don Ubaldo, and a girl with amazing sexual characteristics had come towards them. Along she had come, enveloped in an aura of coquettish indifference, with every male that she passed turning his head; some going on with their heads turned over their shoulders but still continuing, reluctantly; others stopping altogether in their tracks, rooted to the spot. The marshal, too, had been affected, spun round irresistibly, a man caught up in the eddy of a tornado. This experience had afterwards wrested from him some remark of groaning approbation, produced as if under torture. Don Ubaldo, who prided himself on his asceticism in this as in all other matters, reached up and plucked a briar-like flower growing from the wall above their heads.

'Smell it,' he had commanded, holding the flower to Manning's nose. Manning smelled the flower. 'It's sweet.' So it was — an elusive sweetness, at first sharp and positive and then fading swiftly. It was impossible to describe.

'Smell it again.'

He had inhaled once more. Now the sweetness had quite faded and in its place had risen a sour odour, a bitterness of sap, of a virile and self-sufficient life-juice that disdained further concealment. Don Ubaldo had watched his face and smiled.

Yes, that had been Don Ubaldo's parable, but the part which Manning had not thought fit to investigate at the time was whether this secondary bitterness, too, was of evanescent quality; whether, in fact, if one returned to the flower after a few moments, the original sweetness would have revived, however brief its abiding. Well, he had had the excitement, the triumph and the satisfaction which presumably could now be re-experienced only on a lesser scale, and it had been like making, for an insignificant down payment, the acquisition of some extravagant, quite unserviceable and even embarrassing possession — a fantastic whim far beyond the reach of his pocket to satisfy. For this he must now begin to pay in the easy instalments of bad conscience and ennui.

Lina had come to the bedside, and at her approach he felt a slight constriction of the pit of the stomach. Her lips, which were bloodless and slightly cracked, were clenched over a safety pin; her hair, cascading wildly over her face, gave her a distraught expression. There were deep purple shadows under her eyes, in the whites of which fine red capillaries had flowered. The top lip was a little bruised on one side, and noting this Manning shuddered inwardly.

'I must go, darling,' she said. 'I must leave you. At any moment that devil Matteo will be back.'

He nodded. 'Yes,' he said with flooding relief. To be alone and to sleep peacefully. They were the two things he most wanted from life at that moment.

She was looking at him, obviously hurt, and shaking her head in disappointment. 'Don't you want to love me?'

He groaned slightly. 'Yes — but Matteo.' Instalment number two of the debt, he thought miserably.

'Never mind about Matteo,' she said. 'Why should we care about Matteo? I love you.'

Her face assumed the expression of fierce concentration with which he was already discouragingly familiar.

'Go on,' she said, '. . . please.'

He took her by the shoulders with what affection he could muster, noticing irresistibly the frayed top of the greying vest. He felt her breasts flatten under the contact. They were hot, damp and rubbery, and shortly there would form between them a localized and squelching vacuum. The room now wore a sullen flush of dawn. Desperately his eyes sought a way of escape beyond the cage enclosed by the blunted mahogany of the bed posts, across the storm-driven sea of bed clothing and displaced pillows. But already hairs had closed his nostrils and were entering his mouth. He was choking as surely as the brigands had choked in that very bed. Now the powerful limbs began to flail. He closed his eyes and lay there limply, and suddenly she pushed herself away from him and got up.

'A fine lover,' she said. 'What's the matter with you?'

'I was thinking of Matteo,' he said.

'Don't you love me any more?' she insisted.

'Yes, I do,' he forced himself to say. Another instalment of the payment, he thought.

And yet, when she had gone, he knew quite well that by the night it would have returned. Some of it, at least, if not all. It would have returned with a filling up of that emptiness, that hollowness deep down within him. By the night, gracelessness would be changed once again into grace. That which was now repellently animal might become attractively pantherish. What revolted at dawn could be precisely what enchanted at midnight.

XVIII

H E heard the car draw up outside. He had been shaving, and only at that moment he noticed the box of face powder standing on top of the chest of drawers. When he picked it up he found that the bottom had split and the powder showered out. He jerked at one of the drawers violently, only succeeding in tearing the knob off. The next drawer came open easily and he stuffed the box into it out of sight, at the same time noticing a couple of hairclips which he swept off the drawers to the floor.

There was a tap at the door, and before he had time to get to it the handle turned and the marshal's head came through the opening. The marshal was looking excited. He grasped Manning's hand and seemed to pull himself into the room, collapsing heavily into a chair. He slapped his knee and clicked his tongue in exasperation. Lina was hovering in the doorway.

'It's rotten luck,' said the marshal. 'Who would have thought such a thing could have happened?'

Manning didn't say anything. The marshal was occupied in wagging his head disconsolately, his eyes half closed. Manning risked another nervous glance round the room.

'An incredible piece of bad luck,' the marshal said.

'Something's happened to Matteo, I suppose,' Manning said.

'Yes. He's in the can at Guarda. There's a new marshal there. He's promotion crazy.'

'Well, what's all the fuss about? He's in the can at Guarda. By all the excitement I thought you were going to say he was dead.'

'He's a friend,' the marshal said. 'You want to give him a hand, don't you?'

'No. Not particularly. Not if I can help it.'

'I should have thought you would. If for no other reason, to help this little girl here.' The marshal chose this moment to sniff the atmosphere dreamily. Manning had noticed with dismay that in his last sentence something of an offensive assumption had crept into his tone.

'I've been on the phone about it,' the marshal said. 'It's practically a technical matter. A sudden local enforcement of out-dated anti-Black Market regulations. They carry on like this for a few days and then they drop off to sleep again. Makes it awkward, though. Good thing we can get him out all right.'

'Glad to hear it.'

'No trouble at all, in fact. Just means going down there and having a word with the marshal. Explaining he's a friend. Easy as that.'

'When are you going to do it?'

'Not me. You.'

'What do you mean, me? If you want to get him out, do it yourself. What's the difficulty?'

'For you, absolutely none,' said the marshal. 'As an ally, everything you say goes here. You walk straight into the Carabinieri Station and ask for Marshal Coccozza. Explain to him that they've got a friend of yours by mistake — somebody working for you, if you like — and do they mind if you take him away? There's nothing more to it than that.'

'Then why don't you do it?'

'I've just explained. You are an ally, you've got prestige. They'll do anything for you. You ought to know that by now. With us it's different. Professional jealousy comes into it. I daren't poke my nose into another marshal's territory.'

'You can't and I won't, so our friend Matteo stops where he is.'

Lina had him now by the arms. 'Don Roberto, you won't leave my brother there, will you?'

Manning tried to free himself, but without violence it would have been impossible.

' — After what I've sacrificed for you. After what happened.' The tears were beginning to flow.

With exaggerated understanding the marshal separated them.

Holding Lina off with a gesture that exhorted patience, he took Manning into a corner, a corner where Manning noticed what appeared to be an article of feminine clothing, thrown at that moment into inescapable relief by a single shaft of sunlight.

'The thing's easy,' said the marshal. 'Why make a fuss about it? One doesn't stop to think of such trifles where a friend is concerned.'

'I had no intention of giving him a pass in the first place. I knew something like this would happen.'

'You gave him a pass?' said the marshal. 'In that case, don't forget to get it back at the same time. In fact, unless you're entitled to issue passes, what you tell me makes it all the more necessary to go down there and straighten things out.'

'I want to think about it,' Manning said. 'I don't want to do anything in a hurry.'

'Don't delay, my dear fellow. Delay in such cases is fatal. Let's go down there now and snatch him away before they get organized. Go in as if you owned the place. Throw your weight about a bit. It impresses them. You don't want to be too humble with people like that.'

'Don Roberto,' said a voice, dripping with honey, 'you won't let me down.'

The marshal waved at Lina imperiously. 'Be quiet. Don Roberto knows what to do without your help. She's a nice girl,' he said to Manning. 'Mustn't let her get out of hand, though. You come to me if she gives any trouble. I've known her since she was a little girl.'

'What the hell are you talking about?'

The marshal merely laid a soothing hand on his arm.

'Look,' said Manning to Lina. 'I'll go down and try to bail your brother out. But I shan't be back tonight. I'll send up for my things.'

'He doesn't mean it,' said the marshal. 'He doesn't mean that. He flies off the handle sometimes, like all of us do. He's all right.'

217

As they got into the car Manning said: 'I want you to understand something. I'm not all right. From now onwards please consider me useless for all purposes. Rule me out. I'm no longer interested. I want to be left in peace.'

The marshal, holding the steering wheel with one hand, had extracted with the other the religious medal he wore on a chain round his neck, with which he fumbled before replacing it. 'How lucky,' he said, 'that Matteo was picked up so near home. We'll be there in half an hour.'

The Carabinieri Station at Guarda was a trim, red brick building having an entrance on each side of the main gateway.

Manning was shown into the waiting-room on the right. There was a notice on the wall which said that carabinieri battalions had always distinguished themselves in the forefront of any action in which they had been engaged. Such notices were displayed in all Carabinieri Stations. There was also a dramatic picture showing a pink-cheeked and spruce young carabiniere leaping, dagger in hand, among a group of fierce Abyssinians clustered about a machine gun. He was obviously about to exterminate them.

The carabiniere who had received Manning came back and showed him into Marshal Coccozza's presence. The marshal was just buttoning up his jacket. He was a man past middle years, shortish, heavy, nearly bald, and with permanently narrowed eyelids. He struck Manning as being the type of a Civil Servant rather than a policeman, and there was something Teutonic about him — an ageing and undiscovered Himmler.

Now he remembered the associations that the name Coccozza had started. Of course, Coccozza was the new man who was making such a stir in the area. Energetic and efficient, he was supposed to be, and pretty ruthless, too. The stirrer up of untold troubles. Arresting right and left, racket busting, unearthing scandals of all kinds: this tired looking, elderly man, who would not last long, of course. So they said. He was treading on too many toes. Already, mysteriously, his transport had been withdrawn and two of his men transferred, leaving him with only two to carry on. Manning remembered that he had admired Coccozza from his reputation. Now ironically he found himself on the other side of the fence.

Marshal Coccozza got up and shook hands. He motioned Manning to a chair. Manning noticed that he moved rather slowly.

Coccozza sat down and laid his two big hands, palms downward, on the table. He was like a lion couchant. On the wall at the back of his head was a portrait of Vittorio Emanuele and at its side a darker square of colour in the faded pink of the wall where a picture of Mussolini had hung until recently.

Coccozza peered at Manning inquiringly. His eyelids were pink, and what could be seen of the eyes rather glassy. Manning imagined that he had just taken off his spectacles and put them away in his drawer. His stare was discomfiting, and Manning hoped that Coccozza was seeing him through a myopic haze. His uniform was stained down the front and frayed at the sleeves, but all the same there was something about him that made Manning able to believe his reputation well justified.

'Marshal,' said Manning, I've come to pick up a prisoner of yours.' Getting out his notebook he went through a bit of play acting, running his finger down a pretended list of names. 'Let's see, now. Ah, yes. Cianfone, Matteo, fu Rinaldo.'

Coccozza made no reply. He continued to appraise Manning with a kind of vague cordiality through those narrow, pale, glassy eyes. He's not taken in, Manning thought. He wants me to go on talking. Hopes I'll give myself away a bit.

'Cianfone has been working for us.' He put the notebook down on the desk and drew a line through an imaginary name. He shut the notebook and put it away. 'Busy?' he asked.

Coccozza nodded slowly and with deliberation. The unwavering scrutiny continued, and Manning checked the birth of a smile which he knew would have been a very nervous one.

'Yes,' Coccozza said. 'There's plenty to do. We are always busy. The country's full of dirty scoundrels.' He snapped out the last word with something like passion. Manning looked up, surprised. The vague geniality had faded out. Coccozza's eyes were even narrower.

'So you want to take Cianfone?'

'Yes, he's employed by us at present on a very important job. Confidential, I'm afraid. So we can't spare him. If you can give a note of the offence I will see that it is dealt with.'

'I should prefer to hold him for a few more hours. I've some investigations to make.'

'Sorry,' said Manning, steeling himself. 'I can't wait. I'm a very busy man. Have to insist on taking him now.'

Marshal Coccozza shrugged his shoulders and rang a small hand bell on the table. The carabiniere appeared in the doorway.

'Get Cianfone.'

He opened the drawer of his desk, produced a sheet of paper, smoothed it out and began to write, slowly and laboriously, in infantile copper plate. He looked up several times. Manning thought, he's making sure of my appearance. His uneasiness was deepening with every minute.

Coccozza finished writing. He re-read what he had written, his lips slowly forming the words. He isn't so blind, either, Manning thought. He made one or two careful alterations and then blotted the paper, which he passed across the desk.

'What's this?' Manning asked.

'A receipt for Cianfone.'

Of course it was. And now an urgent problem arose. Was he to sign his correct name? Because he was sure that Coccozza was going to report the matter. If, on the other hand, he risked signing a false name, he would have put himself irretrievably in the wrong if he were ever found out. He also felt certain that if called upon to do so, Coccozza would be able to furnish a very accurate description of him. What a mess to be in! Apart from the few minutes when he had been occupied in writing the receipt, Coccozza had never ceased to watch him, and now that faint but menacing geniality had returned.

Manning hastily signed, scrawling his name in such a way that he hoped it would be practically undecipherable. Coccozza took the paper back, examined the signature most minutely, folded the paper and put it in his drawer.

Manning got up and he got up, too. They shook hands and Coccozza smiled, but without speaking. As Manning walked to the door, where Matteo was waiting, he called out 'Arrivederci,' but the other appeared not to have heard, as there was no reply.

On the return journey Matteo was crestfallen and silent. The marshal discoursed cheerfully on any topic that came into his head.

Manning remembered the details of Coccozza's office. He tried to recall the man's exact words and the various changes of demeanour that had accompanied them. He remembered the way Coccozza had studied his face and his uniform. In his imagination the interview was now beginning to increase in significance. There were certain details which he had registered without setting any particular importance upon them, but which now bulked menacingly.

'Did you get the pass?' the marshal asked abruptly.

'No,' said Manning, 'I forgot.'

'Do you want to go back?'

'No. Better leave things as they are. If I go back it will only make things look worse.'

'Whatever you think best,' said the marshal.

He slept in the house again that night, but there were no signs of Lina. In the morning he caught only a glimpse of her in the kitchen for a moment. He was a little surprised, and perhaps also a little deflated to find that she made no effort to come near him.

Matteo wanted to apologize.

'Believe me, Don Roberto, it was nothing to do with me. The owner of the car would insist on carrying contraband. What could I do about it?'

'Nothing,' said Manning.

'But don't you see, Don Roberto, I wasn't even to know what he had got in the car.'

'No,' said Manning.

'You see, Don Roberto — '

'Forget about it.'

'I'm sorry to let you down, Don Roberto.'

'For God's sake forget that it ever happened. And now, while we're about it, let me settle up what I owe you.'

'You don't owe me anything, Don Roberto. It's the other way round. I am eternally in your debt after the way you helped me. Believe me, Don Roberto, I can't tell you how sorry I am that this should happen.'

There he went again. They were just like orientals, Levantines. They flowed all over you, submerged your resistance with a kind of sticky exudation. This would go on endlessly, if unchecked. Matteo would continue to spread out his callus over the jagged edges. Things would quieten down again, and then in a few days he'd be coming along as meekly as if nothing had happened and asking for another pass. There was nothing for him to do but get out quickly.

The same evening the signal arrived. He had been expecting it and was resigned to it, and even before he opened it he knew what it contained.

> Carabinieri H.Q. Naples complain release by you prisoner Cianfone, Matteo, from CC.RR. Station, Guarda. State reasons for action taken.

XIX

MANNING'S reabsorption into the social life of Malevento was marked by what seemed to him a change of heart on the part of its citizenry. The number of defamatory letters had decreased. A note from the marchesina awaiting him at the office bore quite simply the words: 'Come to me.' At the Hotel Vesuvio the marshal welcomed him boisterously. He sprawled with exuberance over the breakfast table, savouring a last mouthful of raw bacon, casting occasional stern glances in the direction of a dim group that moved in and out of the potted palms like vulnerable game in a savannah. Alberto appeared with a bottle of brandy bearing a cynical imitation of a French label on which a number of words were misspelled. 'Three stars,' he said with a charming smile. 'Very special — absolutely contraband. We got it specially for you, Don Roberto.' There awaited him, too, an unexpected tribute from Lina. It consisted of a cake in the shape of a heart, with some red, gelatinous substance intended to represent blood flowing from it.

Don Enrico occupied his usual chair, seeming indeed not to have stirred since Manning had last seen him. He had returned to the use of one spittoon.

The schoolmaster, Don Ubaldo, entered with Filosa, the coffin-maker. Both of them came over and greeted him in the most friendly manner before joining Don Enrico. In response to Manning's inquiry about his business, Filosa was resigned. 'Well, I'm right out of stock now. Cleaned right out. Even to the extra small ones. All gone. The business is still there — I should say it's holding up well — but what can you do about it? If you can't meet the demand, you can't meet it, that's all. Might as well settle down and take things easy.'

After the meal Don Enrico invited Manning and the marshal

to his table and offered them toscana cigars, courteously lighting each in his own mouth before handing it to the recipient.

They were complimenting the schoolmaster on the acquisition of a new suit. Of a thin and brittle-looking material, it appeared to be made of some skilfully treated bark rather than cloth. Don Ubaldo gave a demonstration, holding the sleeve between thumb and finger. 'It's National weave, issued to low grade civil servants and paid for in instalments out of income. My last resource. I have worn my way right through my furniture. My socks came out of the sofa cover, my underclothing from the curtains, and my shirts from the bed sheets. National weave is a faithful imitation of the best imported cloth. But, naturally enough, you have to be careful not to stretch it. In fact, not to sit down in it, if possible. It's inadvisable to expose it near an open flame. And, above all, you have to keep the moths away. There's nothing sustaining in national weave for a moth. Consequently, if one were left to itself with it for a few days you'd find nothing but the buttons.'

'Now, this is the genuine article,' said Don Enrico, inviting the attention of the table to the jacket he was wearing, which was of a thick, closely woven black material bearing the subdued patina of a couple of decades' wear. 'They don't make stuff like this any more. It will last all the time I'll need it, and after that there'll still be enough life left in it to pass it on to some youngster.'

'According to my old father,' said the schoolmaster admiringly, 'you were always a dresser; always a great one for the ladies and for smart clothes. Your name came up only the other day when I was down paying the old chap a visit. "Is Don Enrico Cozzolino still alive?" he asked me. "Yes," I told him, "Don Enrico is still going strong. He's a big capitalist now and he doesn't get about much these days," I said. "Doesn't have to. But you can always find him in the Café Vesuvio. No matter what time of the day you go there," I told him, "you'll always find Don Enrico." "Ah," said the old man, "I don't wonder at Don Enrico doing well. For one, I don't grudge him his good fortune. In fact, I predicted it," he said. "He deserves every bit of it. A darling of the gods, if ever there was one. I prophesied it all for him," he said. "Enrico will fly away from us all. He will take wings and fly. He's not an ordinary man like us." He remembered like yesterday the way you danced, the way you took all the girls off. "You should have seen him at the festa of Monte Vergine," he told me. "He danced all night, he didn't notice fatigue like we did. That's why he had to have so many partners." You were a wood-cutter, the old man said, in those days. He claimed that after you had done a day's work you used to chop trees down with a few strokes of the axe, just for the fun of it or to make an impression with the girls. Quick with the knife, he hinted you were, too. He could tell a tale or two, according to his story of what happened to anyone who wanted to pick a quarrel with you. "They don't breed that kind of man any more," the old chap said.'

'Did he say that?' asked Don Enrico.

'Yes, he said that, and more. He said . . .'

But Don Enrico no longer heard him. Instead he saw himself again a boy, in a brief, sad, golden, beautiful, devastating vision, a vision that clouded over the melancholy, pink-rimmed eyes with their drooping lids. A vision also that gripped with choking fingers at his windpipe.

A thick, blueish vein suddenly swelled up on each side of his nose and began to pulsate. Petrified, Don Enrico sat there, mercilessly bereft in that moment of the opium administered to him by the years in progressively increasing doses, his biceps flowing unresistingly over the arms of his chair, his strong bones clogged with fat, seeing suddenly with the stark clarity of a night landscape painted by lightning the boy of fifty years ago, seeing him as a quite separate being, unrelated in any way to the man of today. A pagan angel, yes, a bright form from whom time's abhorrent layers had scaled, from whom the monstrous chains of the flesh had been struck away. He saw himself standing there, truly god-like. Standing there triumphant at the summit of

Monte Vergine which, barefooted as he was, he had reached effortlessly at the head of the pilgrimage. He held out his hand to a splendid girl and drew her up after him. A girl like a fine and precious replica of the image of the Virgin herself, who bore in her ears ornaments representing the sun and who wore over her hair a muslin veil embroidered with white lilies. What eyes! Half closed they were barred by lashes. The torturing perfume of her hair, the scythe-like swishing of twenty layers of petticoats as she walked . . . *Bright angel, where art thou now?* Ah, the flowers that bloomed mysteriously, that blazed in the sombre background of our country! He cried his wordless thoughts almost aloud.

And now he saw himself throw away, hurl from him, skimming through the air, the tall conical hat with its ribbons (worn in defiance of the new sober fashions from the north), and they danced, his black hair flailing his temples, in the midst of the other newly arrived and dancing couples; girls that moved with a grace only known to fauns gliding in the thickness of woods, and men whose every vice was cleanly and fairly expunged by two magnificent virtues: generosity and fearlessness. Boys and girls, then, that displayed the mystery of God in their gesture. Thus they danced, first to the wailing of bagpipes, the decorous pecorara, and then — leaping high into the air, high, high, leaping and whirling — the tarantella, dance of exorcism and joy. Leaping and whirling he danced, object of envy and of sighs, a figure to inspire vendettas.

After the dancing, they bought, for the love of the Virgin, the votive offerings, the arms, hearts, hands, breasts and eyes of wax; and for the girls they bought suns and moons of gold, rings, pendants and brooches. Throughout the night hours they danced, chaperoned only by the Virgin — and there also under the beech trees . . . yes, under the beech trees . . . he could smell them now, the new dampness of the leaves before dawn . . . there under the beech trees . . . the illusion was so strong that he put out his hand as if to touch that darkly seen, alluring presence. . . .

226

The clangour of the till, like Cinderella's midnight chime, recalled him from the unutterable beauty of this vision. He was trembling violently, rigid with a sudden fear as his eye focused in horror on the rolling slope of his belly. Was there no escape? Could it not be that he was the victim of a dream, a nightmare that had prolonged itself through a half-century of cruel illusion? And, if so, would not the Almighty now take compassion on him and recall him to his waking self? Unknowingly with the psalmist he cried: Save me, O Lord, for the waters are come in to my soul. I sink in deep mire where there is no standing.

The till bell rang again and he heaved himself out of his chair and staggered towards the sound. On the way back to his seat he hesitated, as if something, some partial solution had occurred to him. He beckoned to Alberto.

'I'm not feeling too well. Bring me a bottle of mineral water.'

'Salesiana?' asked Alberto.

'What's it good for?'

'Colitis of the mucous membrane, gastro-enteritis, nervous disorders.'

He shook his head. 'Let me see . . . I forget now. Villa Maggiore. What about Villa Maggiore?'

'The kidneys, spleen, the urinary tract in general. What do you want it for?'

He wanted to say, the soul. 'Is that all you've got?' he asked.

'There's a new one just come in,' said Alberto, 'Salza Termidora.'

Don Enrico nodded apathetically. When the bottle came he placed it before him, and slowly drawing his fingers along the lines read the label with some difficulty:

1. The waters of Salza Termidora are naturally medicinal waters.

2. Owing to the composition of the earth, the constant temperature and the waters' mineral content, they are stable and may be transported and used far from the source of

227

origin without any alteration in composition; an advantage known to be absent in the case of many other brands.

Yes, yes, he said to himself testily, but what next? What does it do?

Don Ubaldo leaned over and examined the new bottle helpfully. 'I don't care much for the label,' he said.

Don Enrico's slight exasperation increased, welcomed subconsciously, perhaps, as a counter-irritant, an antibody to the sharp despair over which at last a numbness was falling. 'Who cares about the label?' he demanded. 'It's the chemical analysis that counts. Just listen to this. It's not worth drinking. No lithium, not even a silicate — the measure of our so-called civilization. It gives you some idea of the plight we are in. Not a decent bottle of mineral water to be had anywhere.'

'What's the recommendation?' asked Don Ubaldo, meekly but with hope.

Don Enrico studied the label again. 'The recommendation — let's see. Ah yes, here it is. "For the pancreas . . ." Good God. ". . . general weakness, sexual debility, and above all for chronic inflammation of the womb and consequently sterility." '

He clamped the bottle down in disgust.

Manning had been listening with only half his attention, and now his hand closed over the signal in his pocket. He beckoned to the marshal and went over to an isolated table.

The marshal joined him.

Manning took out the signal and translated it for the marshal's benefit. 'Well, what are you going to do about that?' he asked.

'It's a pity you didn't get the pass back,' said the marshal. 'However, don't worry. I have a plan. It's quite simple. You must tell your officer that Cianfone was employed on an important investigation for you.'

'Very clever,' said Manning. 'And what am I going to do about reporting the results of the investigation?'

228

'That's easy, too. There will be a real investigation. A genuine one. One in which Cianfone can easily be involved. I'll arrange it all for you.'

'What sort of an investigation?'

'You are interested in the reported formation of a Neo-Fascist Party, aren't you? Well, then, our Cianfone has been approached to become a member. He was sent by you — to whom he revealed the matter — to Foggia for more information of the Group H.Q. there.'

'But all this will fall through,' said Manning. 'It will come to nothing. Then it will be shown up for just what it is. A cover-up for Cianfone. They'll assume straight away that I was working some black market arrangement with him.'

'It won't fall through,' said the marshal. 'It won't fall through because we'll get results. We shall have something tangible to offer your officer. Let's consider the possibilities involved. Say, for instance, that as a result of information given by Cianfone we were able to carry out arrests of persons coming from Foggia with false papers and carrying concealed arms. We could afford to sit back with complaisance — to strike our chests with our hands. This would be a feather in your cap, would it not?'

'It would,' said Manning, 'if it weren't out of the question.

'You are a defeatist,' said the marshal. 'Tomorrow you'll see. Marshal Altamura keeps his promises.'

'But how does this happen to come to light only now and so conveniently? Why should these dangerous characters decide to leave Foggia for Malevento just at this moment? Doesn't the coincidence strike you as being a bit far-fetched?'

'I have a little confession to make,' said the marshal. 'I, too, have been interested in this new movement — on behalf of our own organization, of course. In addition to his business trip, Cianfone actually obtained information for me regarding the matter I've just mentioned. Even if this difficulty had not arisen just now as it did, I was about to inform you of what I propose to do.'

'And what do you propose to do?'

'Tomorrow night we shall set a trap for them. Our men will be passing through on their way to Naples. We shall establish a road block outside the town. We shall catch our birds. You'll see.'

'And where will the road block be?'

'Ah,' said the marshal, 'we shall wait in ambush just where they don't expect us. To avoid the town they will take a secondary route which skirts it. The surface is very bad indeed and the bridges are all down. We shall lie in wait at one of the bridges where the traffic is obliged to slow down to walking pace. In this way no one will escape us. You'll be surprised at our haul. You can safely reply to that message from your officer.'

'Good,' said Manning. 'There's only one thing that puzzles me now. If you were interested in Cianfone's going to Foggia, why didn't you issue a pass yourself?'

'I could have done so, in just the same way as I could have had him released yesterday if the worst had come to the worst. But for you it's so much easier than it is for me. A great impression is always made by an ally. Less explanation is required. The thing is done quickly and without argument. For this reason I felt justified in allowing you to come to my assistance.'

XX

Cacti, posed like Javanese dancers, threw down their indigo shadows across the road.

Two carabinieri squatted behind a Breda machine-gun with the silent boredom of Indian peones. The third carabiniere had gone off up the road, escorted by a pale shadow projected by the lamp he carried.

The detectives who had been called in for the bandit hunt were back again. Their straw hats had been discarded and, perhaps as a distinguishing uniform of the night, they wore white raincoats flung loosely over their shoulders, the empty sleeves hanging down. Their faces, occasionally turned towards the moon, showed up as those of highly evolved rodents; hilarious flying foxes about to embark upon a nocturnal visitation.

Three hours of silence, frayed only by the crepitations of gleaming-eyed animals; the dogs in the neighbouring farms which barked with their muzzles turned towards them; the flight of owls traced by their diminishing lamentations.

A light winked on the dark brow of a hill and disappeared, and the marshal, his face sombrely revealed in no more than a few impressionist strokes, stiffened with anticipation. A dim fire-fly crawled fitfully down the horizon, was extinguished and relit; a fortuitous spark trembling in suspension about the silhouetted spines of a cactus.

After many seconds — minutes, even, it seemed — this light appeared not to have moved — to have become no brighter — although undoubtedly representing a rumbling, exhaust-belching monster trailing towards them its rope of Diesel fumes through the night's torpor of arbutus and cistus; a worn out and juddering contraption that stubbornly blustered its way over this terrible road.

The marshal spoke fussily to the carabinieri with the Breda, receiving a pessimistic reply. 'It's a washout, marshal. It never fires more than a few rounds before jamming up.' The light now fluttered down slightly, was lost as if finally extinguished in a pit, and then after a few minutes appeared again, now level with them, coming towards them, swelling visibly, dividing like the separation of exploded suns, at last near enough to be seen jerking under the series of shocks administered by the road surface.

Now they could hear the grumbling of the exhaust, the body rattles, the snatching whine of the transmission. Although the shape of the vehicle was yet undefined behind the spread of the headlights, the moon glinted palely on the windscreen.

The carabiniere swung the red lamp. They heard the driver race the engine and change down. The exhaust note muted, became a hollow, sucking snarl; a petulant backfire in the silencer fanned sparks on to the road.

The marshal, with Manning following him, ran forward to the driver's cabin. The detectives came out of their huddle, like rugby players, the sleeves of their raincoats flying as they advanced. As the marshal flung open the door of the cabin, the driver raised himself slightly and put his hand under himself as if to recover an egg just deposited there. The marshal, bringing up his hand in which a Beretta pistol had suddenly appeared, not swinging the Beretta to use the butt, but using it rather as one might a knuckle-duster, cracked him on the temple. The driver toppled sideways, stiff as a tailor's dummy, his feet coming up off the controls, and the marshal put his hand in and extracted from the seat what appeared to be a horse pistol.

Some of the detectives swarmed past them, clambering into the driver's cabin, treading freely, it seemed, on each other's backs and heads, while others paused to examine the marshal's find, whistling with delight at the immensity of the pistol's bore.

From the back of the lorry was being torn another prisoner, a young man who from the magnificence of the military uniform he wore seemed to be a general, but whose strange adiposity had aroused the marshal's suspicions. Thrusting his hand in the opening of the splendid tunic, the marshal produced an unending succession of bundles of thousand-lire notes, which seemed thereafter to disappear as if into some capacious but invisible bag. The victim thus despoiled, the detectives bore him away with the purposeful air of tribesmen at the climax — involving a largely symbolical act of anthropophagy — of some important ceremony.

Another star which had detached itself from the skyline and unobserved by them had curled down the rim of the night-entranced landscape, suddenly showered its beams upon them from close range.

Lorry number one was hastily driven on to the side of the road. The carabiniere set the red lamp in pendulum motion, but there was no responsive calming of the exhaust note as the vehicle came charging on, bouncing and shattering itself over the pot-holes, its huge square snout looming, the moonlight reflecting dully off its metal angles. The headlights faded out, and the carabiniere with the lamp and the lounging group of detectives scattered in rout. The marshal signalled to the Breda, which coughed hoarsely, racking at its vitals. A frosty decoration appeared high up on the windscreen. With an irritated flapping of his hand the marshal signalled for the fire to be lowered.

With the first shot the roar of the engine had died away, and now the tyres tore at the road surface as the bus — as it now appeared to be — plunged forward with locked wheels, while an invisible riveting machine punched a line of holes across the bonnet and sparks flew from the metal of the chassis.

Ricocheting bullets chirped briefly in several directions. The bus slid forward another few yards, then grunted asthmatically to a standstill, depositing at this moment on the road a gush of oil, as if emptying itself in ultimate and despairing defecation.

The driver clambered down and came unsteadily towards the marshal, who slapped him smartly across the mouth. The blow seemed to cause the driver no surprise. He fumbled to bring a bunch of papers from his inside pocket.

'I've got my licence and my permit,' he said.

'What were you doing off your route?' the marshal asked, jolting him with another routine smack. The driver was unable to reply to this question, and the marshal smacked at him briskly but without emotion.

'Who paid you?' The marshal paused for a moment and frowned at his grazed knuckles.

The man mumbled something and the marshal pushed him away into the arms of the detectives, who received him with the nervous tenderness of priests entrusted with an important sacrifice.

Now they entered the bus, lit by a faint viridescent glow provided by the failing battery.

The marshal's eye darted hither and thither over the rows of wax-works faces of the passengers; faces of the newly drowned floating murkily just below the surface, dim confessional faces, faces in which fear was heavy and lethargic, still half drugged by sleep. Here were peasants crowded without ease among their bundles and smelling of hens' droppings; commercial travellers dabbing themselves with eau-de-Cologne; a priest peering disconsolately and without concentration at a missal; two soldiers on leave; girls muffled in clothing as if for an Arctic voyage, all were ghoulish in the fast waning light.

The extent of the travellers' possessions could be gauged by the degree of uneasiness they evinced as the detectives approached to search them and their belongings with the gestures of importunate lovers.

Manning and the marshal were hard at work checking papers. The marshal had already found the man betrayed by the driver. He was led away, arms extended with some difficulty in the bus in the attitude of one accepting martyrdom.

Manning came to two girls at the back of the bus. They were travelling together, going to Rome, and their papers were not in order. When he pointed this out, one of them, sitting next to the window, was rather insolent, snatching the identity card out of his hand and putting it back in her bag. By this incident in

234

particular she impressed herself upon his memory. From a second glance he also noticed that she bore a distinct resemblance to Lina. He was beginning to realize that there were a great many girls like that — girls with a quantity of black hair, white oval faces, straight noses and rather resentful eyes. They looked at you and immediately looked away again, with a studied, almost insulting unconcern. At all events, this girl was like Lina, and the one who sat beside her and was probably her sister was like Lina too, except that her face was spoiled by a number of small skin eruptions.

Her papers were out of order as well; the identity card was practically illegible and whoever the photograph was of it was not of her. The original had probably fallen off, and she had just stuck on another of some relative or girl friend. The impression of the rubber stamp had obviously been tampered with. She had no pass to travel from Foggia. When he asked her a question she did not even trouble to reply, but just shrugged her shoulders. He had to ask her again quite sharply.

He would have been quite entitled to hold the pair of them, realizing at the same time that if he were to start doing that kind of thing with all the people whose papers were out of order there would be just no end to it. The extraordinary thing would have been to find someone whose papers were in order in every way, and then, of course, it would probably have been a dangerous political suspect, because it was precisely these people who put themselves to trouble in such details. All the same, Manning thought, types like these girls, who obviously did not bother about breaking the law, should at least trouble to be polite about it when the matter was brought to their notice. He turned his back on the pair and walked away without a word.

At that moment there was a new flurry of excitement produced by the arrival of another car; and the false Chevalier, who had been strutting up and down the bus, pouting and cracking his finger joints in increasing boredom, now whirred away like an excited partridge.

Manning followed him to inspect the new arrival. It was a rich prize — an auto-treno; a Diesel lorry complete with trailer and loaded with all manner of contraband. Some of the detectives were already swarming over the sacks, probing, sniffing, essaying. It was as if monstrous and gluttonous maggots had suddenly hatched out among the load. Others stood by, their voices hushed, as if in the presence of a holy mystery, by the magnitude of the windfall.

Manning was looking for the marshal to inquire about the prisoner taken on the bus. Undoubtedly he would be a dangerous Neo-Fascist, and there was no time like the present for a preliminary interrogation. It was a good thing to fling a few searching questions at a man before he had time to concoct his story; while, in fact, he was still shaken and jittery with his arrest. The marshal was nowhere to be found, and he went back to the bus.

The passengers, who had been told that there was no chance of a relief arriving in under seven or eight hours, were now huddled up and trying to sleep. He was going out again when a female shape loomed up. There was enough light for him to be able to recognize the blotchy face.

'Where's my friend?'

'I've no idea. How should I know?'

'She got off the bus.'

'Why? Who told her to?'

'I suppose she has a right to relieve herself if she wants to?'

'I suppose so. Well, what about it?'

'She's been gone half an hour.'

'Probably went for a walk. I'll give you permission to go and look for her if you like.'

'No thanks. Not me. I know where I'm well off.'

'Well off?' Manning said. 'What are you talking about?'

'You people are all the same,' she said. 'I know the kind of thing you get up to.'

He was back by the roadside when the marshal flitted noiselessly from behind a darkly silhouetted tree trunk, an unconvincing materialization at a séance of shadows.

'A successful night,' he said to Manning thoughtfully. 'We can consider all our objectives attained. The person in uniform is very important, and undoubtedly a Neo-Fascist. The money was probably for distribution to outlying cells. The second prisoner is more interesting still. Probably an organizer. Gives no account of his previous movements. Papers look as if they are faked. Imagine that: he paid the driver five thousand lire to avoid Malevento.'

'A good start,' said Manning. 'As the night goes on we should get a few more.'

The marshal was doubtful. He studied his watch. 'Three ten,' he said. 'We might as well call it a night. Never anything much after three.'

The detectives had finished their inspection of the auto-treno's load, and now, the sleeves of their raincoats drooping listlessly, they circled about it like temporarily sated winged insects.

'All this stuff,' said the marshal, 'is seized. It goes to the public granary for distribution at fixed prices. For a few days there will be coffee, sugar and oil.'

They were driving homewards through a landscape graven on dim silver. 'The prisoners,' said the marshal, 'will be kept in the cells for tonight at the Carabinieri Station. The driver of the first lorry is of no consequence. A charge of illegal possession of firearms, that's all.'

The road suddenly hung before them unsupported over a dark void. They turned off, crawling uneasily down a crumbling bank, to cross the river bed whose waters forked thinly like viper's tongues among the boulders. Above them hung the shattered masonry of the bridge. They climbed the opposite bank in a series of engine-racing rushes.

'That's the fourth tonight,' said the marshal, referring to the demolished bridge.

'When will the interrogation be done?' asked Manning.

'Tomorrow morning,' said the marshal, yawning painfully. 'We'll make it at the Carabinieri Station immediately after breakfast. I'll be there to help you, of course, but it is understood that you are to get the credit for tonight's successes.'

But next morning, when they met at the hotel, the marshal was despondent, almost heartbroken.

'My dear friend, I hardly know how to break the news to you. A most unfortunate thing has happened. I was told only a few moments ago. The car carrying the prisoners last night went over one of the bridges. Fortunately the driver woke up in time to turn the car over the parapet, and the drop was only a small one, but all three prisoners succeeded in escaping.'

Manning was stunned. He groped for words.

'The car overturned,' said the marshal. 'How they could have got away I can't imagine. They were handcuffed. They can't go far.'

Manning managed a sarcastic laugh. 'I suppose full descriptions have been passed to all the Carabinieri Stations?'

'Yes, that's right,' said the marshal. 'It's already been attended to. I'm not at all without optimism about the chances of a recapture.'

Manning laughed again.

'They're handcuffed,' said the marshal. 'Imagine that. It's a great handicap. I don't give up hope.'

'I'm thinking about the report I have to send off today,' said Manning. 'I'd like to see the officer's face when he gets it. "Sir, Acting upon information supplied by Cianfone, Matteo, referred to in previous report, a road block was set up outside Malevento and three suspects were arrested. All three made their escape shortly after." I can imagine his face.'

'But you wouldn't word it like that,' the marshal said. 'You'd wrap the thing up discreetly, describing the circumstances. Naturally, you'd bring in the part about the car going over the bridge and the long but unsuccessful chase across country which was only given up when the mountains were reached. You'd stress the possibility of an early recapture.'

'Yes,' said Manning, 'but as far as the officer reading it is concerned, it won't make a scrap of difference which way it's worded. The facts are there and they're going to look pitiful however they're camouflaged.'

'Hold up your report for a day or two,' the marshal said. 'Something may turn up. I'm confident, in fact, that it will. Let's give it two days and then have another road block.'

Don Enrico came up at this moment and, surprisingly, extended his hand. 'I want to thank you for thinking of us, Don Roberto.' In extreme mystification Manning shook hands with Don Enrico, who then turned and paced gravely back to his usual chair. Alberto, too, was grateful about something Manning could not understand.

The marshal explained later. 'Whenever we make a big haul of contraband, we always find a few half-full sacks, broken crates or leaking barrels of oil. These aren't worth taking to the granary, and they've come to be regarded as the perquisites of those who seize them in the first place. It encourages zeal. I knew you would approve of my passing your share as well as mine to Don Enrico, who, after all, treats us very well.'

'I suppose the officials at the granary get their cut, too,' said Manning.

'After we've delivered the contraband we lose interest in it,' said the marshal, 'consequently I haven't the faintest idea, although I hope that no irregularities take place.'

Calculating that the granary would be shut by five o'clock, at half-past four he called there and Manning saw the director.

'I wonder if you would have any objection to letting me see your copy of the receipt issued for the seized contraband delivered here today?'

As far as he could see the director's mystification was genuine. 'There's been no contraband brought here.'

'Are you quite sure?'

'Quite,' said the director. 'The granary is empty, I'm sorry to say. It's weeks since anything came in.'

At the Hotel Vesuvio Don Enrico and Don Ubaldo were solemnly discussing the evils of the times when Manning joined them.

'The tale of violence and bloodshed continues,' said Don Ubaldo, shaking his head over his evening newspaper. 'Here is a report of another body discovered on the Viterbo road.'

'Does it give the full details?' asked Don Enrico.

'The bullet,' said Don Ubaldo with academic relish, 'is stated here to have penetrated the left mammary region and after passing through the pericardium, liver and stomach — incidentally bursting the spleen — it left the body through the tenth intercostal space. There were head injuries also.'

'That's what you call reporting,' said Don Enrico. 'The *Giornale*'s account tomorrow will be another example of journalistic vagueness at its worst. There's no doubt about it, you do better with the *Corriere*.'

'Thank God the *Corriere* is steeped in the unhurried traditions of the past,' said Don Ubaldo.

'There was another case the other day at Carlona,' said Don Enrico, 'which involved the slaughter of a carabiniere by three contrabandists. The *Giornale* just left it at that. The notice occupied exactly three lines. This modern craze for streamlining and speed is all very well, but were we supposed to guess the significant fact that the carabiniere lost the fingers of his right hand while trying vainly to ward off the knife thrusts of his inhuman adversaries?'

There was a moment of silence while Don Ubaldo turned the sheets.

'Here's an interesting stop-press item,' he said: ' "Girl alleges rape by unidentified police officer," ' he read on. ' "Maria Siniscalco, native of Foggia, in a complaint laid before the

Questore of Malevento today stated that while travelling on the Foggia-Rome bus, which was stopped last night at a contraband checking point near Viterbo, she was the victim of a criminal assault on the part of one of the officers who had been engaged in searching the bus. Siniscalco was able to give only a partial description of her assailant. She stated, however, that a member of the Allied forces was included in the party conducting the search. It is therefore hoped that the Allied Authorities will identify this man, who in turn it is expected will be able to throw further light on the alleged incident." '

'The full account in tomorrow's paper should be interesting,' said Don Enrico.

Don Ubaldo dismissed the possibility with a wave of the hand. 'They won't even mention it,' he said. 'There's no news value in such items. They are too commonplace. There have been four almost identical cases in the last month; and, in any case, the *Giornale* dealt with the whole situation in an editorial last week.'

'What situation is that?'

'Why, the situation that as things are a girl can't travel alone, either by road or rail, without running the risk of being attacked.'

'In my opinion,' said Don Enrico, 'and I give it after mature reflection, a girl who travels on a bus at night unaccompanied by her family, cannot be raped. The thing's a contradiction in terms. I'll go so far as to say that in my young days, if we'd ever come across a girl in such a situation — which, of course, would have been impossible — we should have felt that an overture of some kind was expected of us. Rape! That's a hard word. How on earth do they expect you to distinguish between a little routine and playful resistance and genuine disinclination?'

'Have all these cases reported taken place on the Viterbo road?' asked Manning.

Don Ubaldo shook his head. 'No,' he said. 'Whenever the contraband control people have a check up, the traffic stops using the road. They find another route. If this goes on much longer there won't be any more main road traffic. They'll be running the bus services across the fields.'

'Why should we quarrel?' asked the marshal. He had remained as unruffled as ever under Manning's onslaught, appearing at that moment to be concerned only about the unsatisfactory shave he had just received. He caressed the contours of his incipient jowl with discontent.

'Marshal,' said Manning, still very slightly surprised at his own vehemence, 'I'm going to have another shot at getting you transferred. You know I did so once before. But this time I'll give them a few new reasons for my request.'

Manning had just swallowed a small tumblerful of brandy, which had come out of a new bottle — a liquor whose manufacturer had disdained to dissemble beneath any badly spelled French description. 'Dagger Brand,' said the mustard-coloured label with sinister bravado. This swashbuckling ichor had now entered his veins, in which bright, aggressive flowers unfolded their petals.

The marshal varied his smile a trifle. It was now placatory. 'I pin my faith on the combined inefficiency of our two systems. Either of them, taken by itself, is a powerful enough obstacle to getting things done. In combination they are invincible. What I mean is that your people won't take action under six months, and ours take eighteen months to two years to make up their minds to do anything. We've plenty of time together yet.'

'Go to hell.'

'I can't believe it's you who are speaking like that,' said the marshal. 'Why be unfriendly? We get on well enough together. We've a great deal in common.'

'You're supposed to be here to co-operate with us,' said Manning. 'From what I see you are only interested in looting and rape.'

'I won't take you up on those points just now,' said the marshal, 'chiefly because I can't believe you really mean what you say. You're not yourself, if you'll excuse my saying so.' He picked up the Dagger Brand, sniffed it and shook his head.

'You got away with enough loot last night to keep you in comfort for the rest of your life.'

'How you can drink that stuff I can't imagine,' said the marshal. 'Your internal organs must be metal-lined. Just look at that.' The marshal was observing with fascination a chemical reaction taking place on the table top, where a splash of Dagger Brand had fallen. The wet surface of the marble was coated with tiny white bubbles. Looking up from this he held out his hand, and Manning found a slip of green paper held under his nose. On this were printed the words: 'Ammasso Pubblico — Ricevuta.' Below that was a scrawl of writing in indelible pencil. 'The granary receipt,' said the marshal. 'I was hoping that between gentlemen one's word would have been sufficient.' The marshal's tone was reproachful. 'We've been busy all day. It's only a short time ago that we were able to deliver the load.'

Manning was trying to make out the excessively rhythmical alien handwriting. It reminded him of the oscillations recorded by a seismograph. 'Doesn't this say a total of five quintals?' he asked the marshal.

The marshal took the paper and studied it with concentration. 'Yes, that's right.'

'There was at least five tons on that auto-treno,' said Manning.

Pursing his lips, the marshal emitted a geyser of shocked protest. 'My dear friend, did you examine the load? How can you say that? There were at least thirty sacks of charcoal.'

'Can I see the charcoal?'

'Whenever you wish. Do you think I'd tell you that there was charcoal if it were not true?' The marshal was genuinely pained now. He shook his head sorrowfully.

' — And the driver of the auto-treno?'

'That, alas, no. He has already gone back to Foggia. There was no charge against him.'

243

'You've got it all tied up very neatly,' Manning said. 'What are you going to do about the girl?'

'Do you mean the girl that went to the Questore?'

'Yes.'

'Why should I have anything to do with it?'

'It all links up,' said Manning. 'I couldn't find you last night. You were missing for quite a while. And so was the girl. I expect she saw enough of you to be able to pick you out in an identification parade.'

'I'm really surprised that you should credit me with such silly ideas,' said the marshal. 'These charges of rape are an everyday occurrence. Usually they're brought by unscrupulous persons against men of established position. We've our own way of dealing with such people. If they can't be brought to see reason by argument, we have to use other methods. A counter-attack in the form of a charge of clandestine prostitution, for instance. It's a very hackneyed method, of course, but it always works.'

'What about the man they found shot?'

'I haven't read the case myself,' the marshal said. 'I must get a paper. What times we live in!'

'Was he the one who was carrying the money last night? I mean the uniformed one?'

'I should be upset if I thought you meant that,' the marshal said. 'I do.'

'You aren't hinting at foul play on my part? What a cruel suggestion to make. My dear friend, I won't believe you're taking advantage of me just because you know I can't produce the man to clear myself of such a dreadful suspicion.'

'I shall demand to see the corpse.'

'A good idea,' said the marshal. 'I should do that. Wait a minute though. Didn't they tell me the poor fellow's unrecognizable? That leaves us no better off than we were before.'

'I know of one thing that will upset your plan,' said Manning.

'Tell me,' said the marshal with polite interest.

'When they release Lauro. You'll be the first person he'll want

244

to see. From what I hear he's a bad man to have as an enemy. If I were you I should arrange to be posted well away from this area before it happens.'

'It's funny you should have mentioned that,' said the marshal, 'because only yesterday I had news of Lauro. Your people have already been in touch with my superiors about it. I must admit that I was amazed that the thing had gone so far. It shows that some remarkable improvements have been made in matters of liaison. Naturally, I received full support from the powers that be. In fact, it was most gratifying to know I was so well thought of. They made a strong recommendation that Lauro should stay where he is.'

'He won't stay there much longer now that the war's over.'

'After he comes out,' said the marshal gently, 'he'll be re-arrested by the Italian authorities. If the thing's done as well as I hope, it will be merely a case of our police taking him over from yours at the gates of the internment camp.'

'On what grounds?'

'I hardly like to tell you this, but the fact is I haven't decided yet. If we were not more or less in the same line of business and therefore interested in each other's technical problems, I shouldn't be too keen to make such an admission. Between you and me, though, I think it will probably be criminal libel against the Royal Carabinieri in the person of myself, an offence of this kind being punishable in Italy with a stiff sentence. We Italians are sympathetic with those whose honour is attacked.'

'Bastard,' said Manning.

'Cornuto is more effective,' said the marshal. 'Bastardo-cornuto, better still. You don't mind my telling you?'

'Your sister — '

'And that's going too far. I can't imagine who teaches you these dirty expressions.' The marshal rubbed the wet table top with the tip of his finger, inspecting with interest the whitened patch of stone where the liquid had fallen on it. 'I always thought you Anglo-Saxons were phlegmatic. We live and learn.'

He looked up again at Manning with sympathy. 'I repeat what I said before. Why should we quarrel? It's better for us to co-operate than to fall out. Even if we admit that I'm usually successful in dealing with opposition, I don't close my eyes to the fact that as a combination we could work wonders. Tomorrow night, for instance, I propose to organize another road block. If you join me, we shall get some more prisoners to satisfy your officer. We could, of course, benefit from the arrangement from other points of view which I need not trouble to specify.'

'I'm not interested in listening to any proposition from you. Our association is finished.'

Fatigued though the marshal's smile was, it had still survived. He reminded Manning of an ageing wolf, which having preyed exclusively in pastures stocked with tethered goats, had become slightly adipose, though still immensely predatory. He consulted his wrist watch, from which a yellow light glinted jauntily. Manning recognized this as the remarkable instrument he had last seen in the possession of Zi' Stefano.

'Time for a few minutes relaxation,' said the marshal, settling down in his chair. He raised his hand in a breezy farewell greeting as Manning went to the door.

XXI

Two envelopes awaited him on the office floor, the dispatch rider having called in his absence and pushed them under the door. They were the long buff envelopes which he had become accustomed to associate with triviality. One was marked 'Confidential' and the other 'Secret'. For a moment he thought of leaving them both until the morning. He found himself still clutching the bottle of Dagger Brand. He put it down on the desk, picked it up again, and putting the neck to his lips took a short pull. There was the usual flavour of pollution which emerged slyly only a second or two after he had swallowed. He shuddered. He put the bottle down and picked up one of the envelopes, tearing a corner off it and then inserting his finger and ripping the envelope open. He pulled out the folded sheet and read it twice before its significance hit him.

> You are informed that in response to your application for a transfer you have been posted W.E.F. 5.7.45 to 109B Section. Transport will be available to collect you 3.7.45 at 09.00 hours.

— which meant the driver getting up before the crack, he thought. And this inconsequent thought was all that came to him for a moment — his first reaction to the most momentous piece of news he had had since reaching Italy. He was stunned by the suddenness of the thing. It was like tidings of a very near relative's death. But somewhere above a cloud-banked horizon in his brain a ruddy, glowing sun was rising, dispelling the mists of the natural wariness with which he was inclined to assess such windfalls of fortune. For now the hideous tangle of events, instead of slowly unravelling themselves, had suddenly been cut through. At one stroke he was free. How many hours had he? — Thirty-six. Out of which, by taking into consideration an ample siesta, twenty-four could comfortably be slept away. He gripped the bottle purposefully.

Now the envelope marked 'Secret' was open. For security reasons the message was contained in a second, inner envelope. He slit this open. It contained the usual duplicated circular announcing the escape of a P.O.W. or internee. It was headed by a list of six recipients of such circulars, three British, two American and one Italian. Manning supposed that in each case this circular would be quietly filed, exactly as he was about to treat it, without so much as a glance.

Attached to it, however, there was a small typewritten sheet on which it occurred to him there had been added certain details of the case to which it had been specially desired to draw his notice. From this a single phrase detached itself and caught his eye.

'. . . it is thought likely he may make . . .'

Why 'thought likely' and then 'may'? he wondered. Under the influence of Dagger Brand this particular sample of military jargon had become aggressive. Bellicosely he returned to the beginning of the sentence.

> Lauro escaped from his escort while being transferred from Cieti to Mandorla. As the point at which he made his getaway was nearest on the route to his home at Malevento, it is thought likely that he may make for this.

As Manning read he felt the cup of his happiness fill to the overflowing. It had been almost too neatly arranged by fortune. Rather too much like the plot of one of the old silent movies. In a few hours he would be away, with the exquisite satisfaction of knowing that the marshal would be left with Lauro on his hands. It would be worth while to keep in touch with someone in the neighbourhood and learn the outcome of it all.

And now, he thought, there was not a moment to lose. He must get back to the hotel before the marshal had finished his after-dinner nap, and break the news to him in person before he had time to receive it from the carabinieri. The nearest point on the Cieti-Mandorla road would be about thirty-five miles away, he calculated, so Lauro might be expected at any time.

A moment later he was running up the street in the gathering twilight, his feet, buoyed up by the brandy, silently treading the air.

To his tremendous relief the marshal was exactly where he had left him, dependably sprawled in his chair, his head lolling to one side on his shoulder, his face bearing upon it the imprint of utter peace.

In this moment it struck Manning again that the marshal, even in sleep, had about him the half-conscious watchfulness, the capacity for galvanized action, of one of the greater reptiles. His bulging eyelids were those of a cayman. No breath seemed to come from his lips. A fly alighted on his cheek and the skin twitched vehemently.

'Marshal,' said Manning, bending over to whisper in his ear, consciously dramatizing the affair and feeling within him a rising tide of pure delight. 'Bad news.'

The marshal's eyes opened wonderingly, at the same time appearing to recede slightly in their sockets. His head still rested on his shoulder, his eyes now focused on his surroundings. He winced.

The café had been filling up for the evening, and the marshal's waking vision ranged over a distant semi-circle of figures, all of whom were regarding him benignly. They formed a double rank, as if arranged for a photographic group; below, such dwarfed fantasies of Gothic stone carvers as Vittorio and Orfeo; and, standing behind, the scrawny Fascists and the equally scrawny anti-Fascists. And all these celebrants, as they appeared to be, raised glasses in the direction of Manning and the marshal, whom they were about to toast as benefactors.

'Bad news,' said Manning, fighting to keep a straight face but betrayed by the muscles that writhingly escaped his control, producing despite himself an agonized, almost insane, grin. 'Lauro escaped this morning. He's on his way here.'

There was an eruption. With a reptilian twist and a bound the marshal was on his feet. 'He got away? Are you sure?'

'Sure,' said Manning. 'Bad news, marshal.'

'Bad news for me. Worse for you,' said the marshal. He flung his arms out, and the rank of skinny boyars fell back, clutching their glasses.

'Get your gun,' the marshal said.

'My gun, why?'

'To defend yourself. You don't want to have your throat cut like a calf.'

'This has nothing to do with me,' said Manning. 'I've finished here. I've resigned.'

They were out in the street now, and the marshal was standing close to the café window, counting by the light coming through it the number of bullets he held in his hand: 'At what time did he escape?'

'This morning early.'

'He'll be here tonight. We must be ready for him.'

'I want you to let me know how you get on,' said Manning. 'I'm off on the third.'

'It's how *you* get on that you should worry about,' said the marshal. 'No man wants to die before his time.'

'What about another drink before turning in?' said Manning. 'Unless you're staying up to receive visitors, of course.'

'We need clear heads,' said the marshal, 'we both of us need clear heads. I need one and you need one.'

'Not tonight,' said Manning. 'I'm celebrating. As a matter of fact I'm going to ask Alberto to put me up at the hotel. Probably won't get home under my own steam. If you won't have a drink, I'll see you in the morning.'

The marshal gripped his arm fiercely. 'My friend, do you realize your mortal enemy is at large. A man who will tear you to pieces like a tiger?'

'Lauro's a good friend of mine,' said Manning. 'When he knows the facts he'll be grateful to me.'

'He does know the facts,' said the marshal. 'That's just the thing. He does know the facts. It's probably for that reason he took the trouble to escape. Someone has told him in prison of his wife's betrayal. These things soon become known.'

'His wife?'

'Yes . . . Lina.'

'But her husband . . .'

' — was away. Of course. But you were not curious, my friend. If you'd have asked her she would have told you.'

Suddenly the crooked pieces of this jigsaw puzzle swirled and rearranged themselves in Manning's mind. Now they fitted together as neatly as the sutures of a skull. He accepted this monstrous *fait accompli*, with dazed resignation.

The marshal was watching him warily, expecting, perhaps, a violent reaction. There was a silence which the marshal broke.

'Our interests in this matter are now identical.'

Manning shook his head. 'No, they're not. I've finished with all this. One more day and I shall never see the place again. I'll take a chance as to what happens in the meanwhile.'

The marshal attempted to take his arm confidentially, but Manning shook himself free.

'What you don't seem to understand,' said the marshal, 'is that even if you do manage to get away yourself Lina will be killed. Lauro will cut her in pieces. Such crimes are common here. He'll think nothing of killing her. What has she done to deserve that?'

'She tricked Lauro and she tricked me,' Manning said.

'It takes two to make that kind of trickery,' said the marshal. 'I mean, the kind she did with Lauro. You knew she had a husband and she'd have told you who he was if you'd have asked her. It suited you not to know.'

'I'll come with you,' said Manning, 'but only for Lina's sake. I hope Lauro succeeds in killing you.'

This would be instalment four of his payment, he thought. A

very heavy instalment, this, but possibly the one with which he might liquidate the debt.

'We'll go first to your office and get your gun,' said the marshal. 'We have a desperate man to deal with.'

That evening rain had fallen, rare and unexpected at this time of the year. Suddenly the congested sky opened up and the rain had flooded down, filling ruts and potholes with bright, yellow, opaque liquid like the yolk of eggs; forming deep smooth beds of mud in the angles between roadside and bank; leaving millions of clear, shining pebbles to protrude from the surface of the roads.

Now it was night, but the moon, newly risen, was half-obscured by drifting clouds.

Manning and the marshal were patrolling the roads in the marshal's car. A carabiniere had been placed on the bridge where the three highways from the south, east and west converged. As a further precaution a carabiniere or an agent of the Pubblica Sicurezza had been stationed at a point about two miles along each of these roads, and also along that leading to the north. It was not thought likely that Lauro would come this way, as the point on the Cieti-Mandorla road where he had escaped was almost due south from Malevento. The marshal had posted the most reluctant of the Pubblica Sicurezza agents on the north road. Nobody felt pleased about this extra duty, but whereas the carabinieri did not dare to grumble, the Pubblica Sicurezza agents made their discontent quite clear in their surly attitude.

The marshal's theory was that Lauro would hide until nightfall, and would then approach the town along the road that went to Potenza. Probably getting a lift until within a mile or two of the town, he might then be expected to leave the road and cut across the fields. The carabinieri and the Pubblica Sicurezza agents had been instructed to stop and inspect all the traffic coming into the town. It was now well past midnight and there were very few signs of activity.

They reached the point along the Potenza road where the carabiniere Giuseppe had been left concealed in some bushes. They had to cruise backwards and forwards several times before Giuseppe could be found. The marshal was not altogether happy. He suspected the man of taking a nap.

Manning's hangover was already under way. His only hope of postponing it was by another drink. He took the bottle out of the locker in the dashboard and lifted it to his lips, noticing with alarm the angle to which it had to be tilted. The liquor flowed over his numbed palate. Its revolting flavour had quite disappeared, leaving only a neutral peppery fieriness. The half-formed crystals of depression in his brain redissolved.

'That was a dirty trick of yours,' he said to the marshal.

'I had to protect myself,' the marshal said.

'You bloody scoundrel.'

'We'll be friends,' said the marshal. 'Everything will turn out all right.'

'Your dead souls.'

'Don't say that. It shows you've been mixing with people of no breeding.'

'I'm doing that now,' said Manning.

' — And give me that bottle. You'll want all your wits about you before the night's out.'

The carabiniere at the bridge had been chosen for his dependability. As the traffic coming in from all the southern highways had to pass this spot, there were a number of pedestrians and carts. The carabiniere was subjecting everyone to a most rigorous scrutiny. He began with name, father's and mother's names, occupation, present address; and from these particulars, notebook in hand, he developed a regular and laborious interrogation. However unlikely the subject might be, all were being put through the same mill. He was in the centre of a little group when Manning and the marshal came up.

The marshal snorted with impatience. 'For God's sake, be reasonable, man.' After a brief glance he shooed away the peasant couple with an old father, and the obvious commercial traveller, who had been the subjects of the carabiniere's examination.

Crossing the town to reach the Monteleone highway on the north, they found the Pubblica Sicurezza agent Del Giudice. He was sitting on a milestone, smoking, his hands in his pockets. The normal solemnity of his manner had degenerated into sulkiness. 'If you feel like sending someone up here to keep me company,' he said, 'I'll hang on. Otherwise I'm clearing off.'

'We'll see what the Commissario has to say about you, my fine fellow,' the marshal told him. 'As soon as the detectives turn up I'll take that chap off,' he said to Manning. 'They should be here any minute now.'

The agent Mosca, who had been left on the Naples road, was not to be found anywhere. 'Here's a terrible example of the lack of co-operation between the two outfits,' said the marshal. 'I can't rely on these Pubblica Sicurezza chaps at all.'

The third Pubblica Sicurezza man had been left on the Viterbo road, and they were just going to give up the search for him, when they found him lying on a bench outside an isolated tavern. He was drunk, and when the marshal tried to get him to his feet the man just swore at him.

'The situation's bad,' the marshal said. 'It means taking a carabiniere off guard at the house and putting him on here. One of us should stay at the house.'

The marshal had turned the car round, and now the bridge was in view again. The carabiniere there was standing in the middle of the road, arms outstretched. 'He's here, marshal.'

'Here? What do you mean, you fool? Where?'

'I was questioning a couple on the bridge, but they turned out to be a man and his wife who missed the bus at Vetri. . . .'

'Yes, yes. Go on, idiot. Where is he?'

' — I was questioning the man and his wife — a respectable couple — and I saw someone coming up the Viterbo road —'

'That drunken swine,' said the marshal. ' — Yes, go on. Spit it out now, for God's sake.'

' — he came up to within a few yards of me and then he must have seen me talking to the pair of them because he turned round and cleared off. When I shouted after him he ran for it.'

'Why didn't you chase him, you fool?'

'You told me not to leave my post here, marshal.'

'Dirty Madonna!' cried the marshal, moved to rare blasphemy. 'What have I done to deserve it? You see the kind of half-wit they give me to hold the place together with? Which is the nearest ford?' he asked the carabiniere.

'You can get across at the cemetery if you don't mind getting your feet wet.'

The marshal let the clutch in and they jerked forward, going over the bridge into the town and then turning quickly right again past the single blackened wall of the cathedral, down through a narrow sky-vaulted cloister of ruin, then right once more, bumping over the flattened heaps of debris, down towards the river. Cypresses flanked the churchyard gates, fitfully revealed as cowled forms enshrouded in their cloaks.

They got down from the car. Manning thought of Lauro as a hooded monkish figure tall and emaciated. He pictured him now as clearly as if seen in the flesh. He has gone down by the sedge path, he thought, where the river widens out to become a swamp. He has crossed the ford where the stones of the ancient bridge still stand. Now he has climbed the opposite bank, the steeper bank on the very slopes of which the cemetery wall had been built. And now he would have vaulted the cemetery wall and would be coming towards them, the collar of his jacket held up to obscure his face, and a long knife in his right hand. Manning gripped the tommy-gun, and at that moment the moon came out, fully revealing a great sloping field strewn in confusion with white stones. The graves had been tightly packed, and the catastrophe which had overwhelmed Malevento, not having differentiated between living and dead, had produced a chaos of stone-lined craters and stone-studded mounds. The wealthy of Malevento had favoured marble representations of their dead, and of these there were many broken fragments of arms, legs, torsos and heads jumbled together with crosses, scrolls, funerary urns and angels with sad, severe faces, crusader swords and half-folded wings. The night had drawn up from this place the sour smell of elders. As they went forward snail shells crunched beneath their feet.

Below the cemetery the river, dimly seen when the moon shone, was as still as a black pool. From this angle the gravestones seemed to continue right down to the water's edge.

They had almost reached the ultimate wall. Here had been recovered and piled up many of those statues which had not been completely smashed and which one day might therefore be replaced. Here also was a boundary of a few ancient cypresses with thick, gnarled trunks. Immediately behind them ran the wall, now cutting off the dark view of the river. They would take a few more paces, Manning thought, and then they would turn either to the right or to the left and go round the perimeter of the cemetery. He hoped that the marshal wouldn't suggest their splitting up. He was conscious of the noise made by their footsteps, and just as they had trodden crashingly among some marble fragments the marshal suddenly took him by the arm, dropping down behind an erect headstone and pulling Manning after him. This headstone only partially covered them. The marshal pointed into the penumbra ahead and Manning thought he saw a movement. A cloud passed over the moon; and trees, statues and wall were absorbed in a common obscurity.

The cloud raced away, dragging its train of silvery vapour, and the objects about them were again separate in the light. By the wall they could see nothing. 'When the moon goes in,' said the marshal, 'let's make for the tree.' It was about fifteen yards from them. The marshal drew his pistol and Manning cocked the gun. In the last seconds before darkness descended, his eyes were arrested by the words on the headstone against which they crouched: '. . . our dear son . . . a hero's death . . .' An aeroplane winged stiffly across the marble, but the sculptor, familiar with the complex wings of doves, had shown himself unhandy and at a loss when confronted with the strange simplicities of the mechanical world.

It was dark again and they moved quickly from behind the headstone, making for the tree. The tiny cloud, however, was already passing. The scene lightened and before they had taken half a dozen steps they saw a dimly defined form standing in the open between them and the wall.

'Lauro!' cried the marshal. 'In the name of the law, surrender.' He pushed Manning back with his hand and backed away himself.

A moment of darkness again, and the form was gone.

'Lauro,' the marshal called again. 'Lauro.'

The moon came out. There was a more than life-sized angel with bowed head and drooping wings, and beneath the shadow of these wings something moved. Flame spurted from the marshal's pistol. Two shots, divided by a stunning silence.

Petrified by uncertainty, Manning felt something like a tourniquet tighten above his knees. In front of them the refuge of the tree awaited, and behind the partial shelter of the headstone. On the left was the marshal, his hand still outstretched as if in accusation. Darkness again. The marshal whispered hoarsely, his voice seeming as close as if his mouth were against Manning's ear: 'If he weren't armed he'd give up.'

It was light, brilliantly light. The marshal's hand went up, pointing to the angel whose marble arm, Manning noticed, was also raised but no more than in a gesture of sorrowful resignation to the divine purpose. The space enclosed by the drooping wings was empty.

Now it was neither fully light nor dark. The moon was veiled in thin clouds, and it was as if a portion of the trunk of this nearest tree detached itself and moved towards them, coming forward slowly, silently.

Looking for the marshal, Manning saw him shaking his gun like a rat and then throwing it down and backing away. The marshal's coat was off, and wrapped over his left arm. His right arm was bent before him, a rent in the clouds showing a blade held in his hand, a tiny, insignificant weapon, no more than a clasp knife. There was a glitter also from the hands of the advancing stranger.

Manning raised the gun, feeling that the catch was at the single rounds position. He could no longer reason clearly and he found that the rapidity and depth of his breathing made it difficult to hold the gun still. Vaguely he pointed the barrel down and pressed the trigger once. The gun flinched in his hands, illuminating the tombstones with weak lightning. The man came on towards him, now in the full moonlight, his eyes staring, mouth open. Manning pressed the trigger again, and again, and again. Each time the gun convulsed responsively and all the time he knew that no bullet could halt that relentless advance. And yet there they were, face to face, Lauro's eyes wide, and the wide open mouth from which no sound came, and then quite suddenly the eyes which had been level with his were below his and he was looking down into the eyes and into the face, and Lauro was going down, straight down, slowly, as if he were being drawn soundlessly down into a pit. Down he sank, down to earth, finally face down, without ever raising his hands.

The marshal leaned over him and turned him over on his back. 'He's handcuffed,' he said. He looked up and smiled. 'Think of that. He was handcuffed all the time.' He laughed in Manning's face.